Hidden Treasure

Chinkapin Series Book 1

Margaret Rodeheaver

Pares Forma Press

MACON, GEORGIA

Will Way Books / Pares Forma Press
Margaret Rodeheaver
212 Will Way
Byron, GA 31008
www.MargaretRodeheaver.com

Publisher's Note: This is a work of fiction. Names, characters, places, and incidents are a product of the author's imagination or are used fictitiously. Locales and public names are sometimes used for atmospheric purposes. Any resemblance to actual people, living or dead, or to businesses, companies, events, institutions, or locales is completely coincidental.

Book Layout ©2017 BookDesignTemplates.com
Book Cover Design by 100 Covers

Ordering Information:
Quantity sales. Special discounts are available on quantity purchases by corporations, associations, and others. For details, contact the publisher at the address above.

Hidden Treasure/ Margaret Rodeheaver. -- 1st ed.
Print ISBN 978-1-7327837-4-4
Large Print ISBN 978-1-7332880-4-0
EBook ISBN 978-1-7327837-5-1

*To the customers and volunteers
at the Treasure Chest
and thrift shops like it around the world*

Contents

Chapter 1..1

Chapter 2..19

Chapter 3..27

Chapter 4..37

Chapter 5..41

Chapter 6..47

Chapter 7..57

Chapter 8..67

Chapter 9..75

Chapter 10. 91

Chapter 11. 99

Chapter 12. 103

Chapter 13. 117

Chapter 14. 123

Chapter 15. 137

Chapter 16. 151

Chapter 17.. 159

Chapter 18.. 171

Chapter 19.. 181

Chapter 20.. 189

Chapter 21.. 201

Chapter 22.. 219

Chapter 23.. 231

Chapter 24.. 247

Chapter 25.. 255

Chapter 26.. 261

Chapter 27.. 275

Chapter 28.. 287

Chapter 29.. 307

Chapter 30.. 319

Chapter 31.. 331

Chapter 32.. 339

Chapter 33.. 349

Chapter 34.. 359

Chapter 35. 371

Chapter 1.

Laurie Lanton drove through the shady neighborhood of gracious homes and larger-than-average yards, feeling envious. She thought of the house she had lived in before her divorce, but put it out of her mind as she pulled into Mary's driveway.

"I'm running late," Mary called out, stating the obvious as she pulled her front door shut behind her. She hopped in the car stuffing keys into her purse and digging for her sunglasses. "Want to stop at the Coffee Pot? I'll buy you a latte."

"You just said the magic words, girlfriend." Laurie indicated the slight baby bump at Mary's waist. "Click the seatbelt around that belly of yours, and let's go."

The Coffee Pot was across the square from the courthouse in the center of the town of Chinkapin, Georgia. Or what was the center, before the freeway was built a few miles to the west. Laurie turned her rusting Chevy Malibu onto Main Street and parked near the café.

New in town, Laurie had been in the Coffee Pot just once before. She paused again to admire the vintage décor and coffee-themed artwork. Formica-topped tables and chrome-and-vinyl chairs fit the 1940's music wafting from the speakers. She closed her eyes, inhaling the aroma of freshly ground coffee beans.

After she and Mary placed their orders, Laurie noticed a small stage at the back of the café. "I hear you have an open mic on Friday nights," she asked the cashier. "How does that work?"

The girl paused as she made change, and pointed to a poster near the door. "Just show up around 7 p.m. and put your name on the list. Musicians perform in the order they sign up." She pushed the cash drawer closed with her hip and handed Mary her change. "Everyone does two numbers, and if they get enough applause they can do a third. Are you a singer or a musician?"

Laurie laughed. "Not much of either, actually. Someone I know told me about it."

Mary looked questioningly at her. "Chase," Laurie explained. "That new guy in the choir. He mentioned it when I met him Sunday."

"Oh." Mary raised her eyebrows. She accepted her coffee from the barista and moved toward the door. "Better grab a couple of napkins."

Back in the car, Laurie got a whiff of Mary's coffee concoction. "That smells interesting. What did you get?"

"This one is ... let's see. Cocoanut, raspberry, and chocolate."

"Is there any coffee in there?" Laurie teased. "Actually that sounds pretty good." Overall her friend was eating well during her pregnancy. But Mary did indulge in a few strange food cravings once in a while.

"I'm keeping notes. Some of my combinations might end up becoming brownies one of these days." Then Mary turned businesslike. "Have you submitted your application for the job I told you about?"

"Yes, 'Mother.' In fact, I already interviewed. I'll know something by the end of the week."

Mary always looked out for her. When Laurie sobbed to Mary over the phone, telling the story of her husband's infidelities, Mary took charge, just as she had done when they were in college together. She said if Laurie was going to have to rebuild her life, she might as well do it in a warmer climate. As usual, Laurie didn't argue. She moved to Georgia, where Mary and her husband Pete had relocated for Pete's job.

"Just trying to help out," Mary said, looking pleased with herself. "That job had your name written all over it."

"*My* name? It's mostly a clerical position," Laurie said, turning onto Redding Road.

"Yes, but it's with a newspaper. And you want to be a writer, remember? You'll find a way to turn it into your dream job. I've got faith in you."

"Thanks?" Laurie said doubtfully. She did think she had a good shot at the job, but didn't expect it to be as wonderful as Mary thought. The good thing about it was it was part time. It would supplement Laurie's savings while allowing her to pursue other freelance writing opportunities, and maybe even her dream of being a novelist.

As usual, Mary was still talking. "Keep your eyes on the prize. Success is the best revenge. It's never too late, and all that reinvention stuff. You'll show that dirtbag."

"I'm not worried about DB," Laurie said. But the thought of her ex dampened her mood. He was always so dismissive of her "little writing hobby" as he called it. A little revenge, a.k.a. success, would be pretty sweet. "By the way," she said. "I mentioned during the job interview that I was a member of St. Mark's, and the editor didn't know where it was!"

Mary laughed. "Did you tell him?"

"Yes, I did!" she answered. They said it together: "across from the Tasty Chick!"

As soon as Laurie moved to Chinkapin she had joined St. Mark's Episcopal Church, where Mary was a member. Mary had even convinced her to join the choir.

But it struck Laurie as odd when people around the small town didn't know where the church was. It had been in the same spot for 60 years! She quickly took to calling it "St. Mark's Across from the Tasty Chick."

Everyone in town seemed to know where the Tasty Chick was. After all, it did have the best chicken tenders this side of Eatonton (wherever that was.) "St. Mark's Across-from-the-Tasty-Chick" didn't have the ring of, say, St. Andrew's by-the-Sea, but it did help people find the church.

The other thing that put St. Mark's on the map was the Treasure Chest.

St. Mark's and the Treasure Chest stood side by side on two shady acres just north of downtown Chinkapin on the old Redding Road. The Treasure Chest was a thrift shop operated as a ministry of the church. It was staffed by volunteers, and all the items sold were donated by the community.

People never knew what they might find at the Treasure Chest, but they got it for a bargain price. After covering expenses and a donation to the church, the proceeds went to various charities around town. Folks at the local food bank, the community arts center, and the animal shelter all knew *exactly* where St. Mark's and the Treasure Chest were, without having to be told they were across from the Tasty Chick.

"I saw the status you posted the other day," Mary said.

"Did you? Good." Laurie tossed her head. She had posted a status on the Treasure Chest Facebook page, letting customers know that by Tuesday all-new spring and summer clothing would be out for sale. "I may not have my life together, but at least I can do some publicity for the Treasure Chest. I won't let all that practice writing advertising copy at the *Sun Herald* go to waste."

It was almost 10:30 when they arrived at the Treasure Chest and dropped their purses and coffee cups in the staff office. Then they went to find Carol, the volunteers' committee head, to ask where they were needed. Carol and Alice, another volunteer, were already in the women's clothes section packing unsold winter clothing into large cardboard boxes.

"What happens to the stuff we box up?" Laurie asked.

"My husband Don will take it to the mission in Redding," Alice explained. "Either that, or the fellow from the Methodist church will pick up the boxes for their Appalachian ministry. Nothing here goes to waste." Alice was one of the original group that had established the thrift shop, and was very proud of the good it did in the community and beyond.

"Are we saving anything?" Mary asked.

"Clothes that aren't too wintery. And of course we'll keep some of the better brands," Alice told her.

Mary looked at Laurie and shrugged. Laurie shook her head with a frown. She didn't shop much, and didn't always know which brands were sought after or worth holding onto. She looked again at Alice's chic-casual outfit and blond hair.

Carol seemed to read their minds. "We can do this room, if the two of you want to tidy up the furniture room. It needs sweeping and dusting something awful."

"Sure," Laurie said. "Maybe I'll find something to spruce up my apartment." *Something small*, she thought. Her current living quarters were a furnished one-bedroom apartment not far from the freeway. It was "cozy and economical," according to the apartment-finder website she'd used. She admired the creativity of the people who wrote real estate ads.

The furniture room in the Treasure Chest was even smaller than Laurie's apartment. The building had once been a doctor's office, and was divided into lots of small rooms. The former waiting room was now full of ladies' clothes. Kitchen items filled one of the paneled consulting rooms, and the other displayed books and décor. Exam rooms housed men's clothing, children's clothing, and linens. Another served as a dressing room. There were also a small staff kitchen, an office, and rooms at the back for sorting and tagging donated items.

Laurie entered the furniture room and took in the assortment of lamps, chairs, luggage, and end tables, plus a few random sporting goods. "Everything but the kitchen sink," she said aloud.

"The bathroom sink is still here, though." Mary pointed to the porcelain basin half hidden under a table covered with lampshades and globes. "I don't think we're ever going to sell it."

Laurie picked up a lamp and idly flipped the switch. "I had one just like this in the old house," she said. Was it in storage, or had her brother hauled it to Goodwill? She couldn't remember what had become of everything she and DB had, back when they were happily married.

David Benjamin Monroe, aka "DB," or more often these days "Dirtbag," hadn't wanted anything from the house. Laurie supposed it was because of the ever-stylish, soon-to-be next Mrs. Monroe. Naturally, she wouldn't want anything to remind her of her predecessor. Laurie was glad she had switched back to her maiden name.

Mary poked under the table with an old aluminum crutch. "I'm surprised Evelyn hasn't thrown away this sink. She throws things out left and right, and Anne is almost as bad, especially when the two of them get together." Mary rattled on, gossiping about various other volunteers at the shop while Laurie tidied the lamps and shades. "And clothes! Evelyn seems to think any clothes more than three years old should go straight to the mission. Most of the clothes in my closet are twice that. We can't all be in vogue all the time. It's not so hard when you're tall and skinny like her. You could drop her through a straw. When you're 'curvy' like me, and can't find anything that fits..." Mary trailed off with a sigh.

"You're the one who wanted to get pregnant," Laurie reminded her with a stab of envy. She had always wanted children too. Now she was glad it hadn't happened with DB. That certainly would have complicated things. "And you do too have new clothes. All those maternity clothes you bought!"

"Oh, hah-hah," Mary replied. "I sure was glad I found a lot of them here! This place has saved me a fortune."

"And you were always curvy in a good way, not *curvy*, curvy. Once the baby is born you'll be fine again. If I know you, you'll have me out running around the block getting fit along with you."

Laurie headed to the staff kitchen for some damp paper towels, still thinking about getting fit. That was something she had told herself she would do once she moved south. In this part of Georgia there would be no snow to speak of to keep her indoors, and truth be told she did need to shed the few "stress" pounds she had put on during her break-up. Otherwise, she considered herself to be in decent shape, all things considered. Those things being that she would prefer to be sitting in a chair reading, or pounding away on her laptop, rather than out pounding the pavement.

On her way to the staff kitchen Laurie met Anne and Evelyn in the hall stacking pictures and frames. "Need help moving these?"

"These are going to the dumpster. They're just taking up space," Evelyn said. A two-inch stack of bangles clattered on her wrist as she tucked some stray hairs behind her ear.

Anne added "Some of them have been here forever. All the pictures and frames were half price last month, and these right here didn't sell."

"Hmmm." Laurie bent to flip through the stack. "I can see why. Some of the frames are nice, though. Has anyone called the arts center to see if they can use them?" Laurie had recently discovered the Chinkapin Arts Center, located in the old armory, while driving around exploring her new hometown.

"Be my guest," Anne said. "It would be better than just pitching them."

"I'll get a box and pack up the nicer ones." On her way to fetch a cardboard box, Laurie passed the toy display, located on shelves in a wide hallway in the center of the building. "Hey, someone has really cleaned this up! It looks great!"

Joan poked her head out of the children's clothing room off the hallway, and pushed her glasses up her nose. She wore her graying hair in a no-nonsense, short cut, and looked like the former school teacher she was. Laurie reached over and brushed cobwebs off her shoulder. "Evelyn did that earlier this morning," Joan said. In a lower voice she added "I think she threw out half the stuff that was there."

Laurie didn't comment. There were factions among the volunteers, and as the new person on the block, she did not want to take sides.

"It does look nice, though," Joan admitted finally, and ducked back into the children's room.

"I'm going to take a picture," Laurie said aloud. She went to the office and got her smart phone. After moving a few of the stuffed toys closer to the games and puzzles, she framed the image with the camera app, and snapped a photo.

Next she logged into the Treasure Chest's Facebook page, and typed the following: *Looking for spring break fun? The Treasure Chest has great deals on toys, puzzles, and games.* She added the photo and tapped *post*.

"Okay, picture frames," Laurie reminded herself. She fetched a cardboard box from the stack in the back of the shop. Anne helped her fill it with the nicer frames and pictures, and Laurie loaded it into the trunk of her car.

Finally she returned to the furniture room where Mary was wrestling with half a dozen fishing rods. "Sorry! I got side-tracked," Laurie said. She wiped down the display table, rearranging lamps and shades as she went.

"I've done about all I can with these," Mary said. "You want to get the little vacuum, and we'll call this room done?"

Laurie went to the office for the vacuum, but didn't find it in its usual corner. "Who's got the vacuum?" she called, leaning back through the doorway.

Several volunteers stood with heads together over the jewelry display case beside the check-out counter. The women all looked at her.

"Never mind the vacuum. Have you seen the gold ring?" Joan asked.

"The one that was right in the middle of the display case?" Laurie asked, eyebrows raised.

"That would be the one," Joan answered. "We don't get many solid gold rings. When did anyone see it last? Anne, didn't you work Saturday?" Joan turned to face her.

"I did. With Evelyn," Anne said. "We did a lot of sorting and tagging, to get ready to put the new clothes out, but we worked there in the office where we could watch the counter."

Evelyn agreed. "And we weren't that busy. I mean, we sold lots of clothes because of the sale, but there weren't that many customers in here."

"Mostly our regulars, and a few from the church" Anne added. "In fact, Chase was here buying a couple of shirts. I remember he asked if the ring had sold yet. Lord, I hate to have to tell him it disappeared, after he donated it to the shop."

"He donated it?" Laurie asked, more curious now about the ring.

Joan nodded.

"Maybe he took it," Evelyn suggested. The others murmured disbelief. "There's just something about him. I don't trust him." She wrinkled her nose and turned away.

"Is anything else missing? Maybe we just haven't noticed," Anne said. She looked carefully in the display case, but nothing else seemed out of place.

"You know, it would be easy to reach over, slide the case open, and take something out," Evelyn said. "I've been saying that, but no one listens." She looked out of the corner of her eye at Carol.

"But surely we would see that from the office," Anne said.

"Well, but we were back and forth to the work room," Evelyn reminded her. "And I helped a customer back in the linens room. She never did buy anything, after I unfolded and refolded every comforter we had back there. You know, that's what they do sometimes, these *people*. They work in pairs, and one of them gets you distracted, while the other is stealing everything they can get their hands on." She shook her head. "I just think it wouldn't have been that hard to take the ring."

Joan gave her a long look, then turned to the others. "Well, we obviously have to make the case more secure." She and Anne examined the display case, while Laurie went in search of the vacuum, pondering.

Laurie had met Chase only recently, but Evelyn's accusation didn't sit right with her. And it wasn't just because Chase was in the church choir where Laurie and Mary also sang.

Laurie found the vacuum and returned with it to the furniture room where she filled Mary in on what had happened. "I wonder why Evelyn accused Chase of taking the ring," Laurie said.

"Who knows?" Mary shrugged, rubbing her lower back. "Sounds like she just doesn't like the guy."

"Anne said he donated the ring." Laurie thought someone had said he was divorced, and wondered if the ring had belonged to his ex.

She tried to remember what she knew about Chase. He didn't have any remarkable features that stood out in her mind. Just a pair of soulful, rather sad eyes in an angular face. He had seemed friendly enough, though. He was about average height, maybe her age or a little older. "He's got a nice voice," she said aloud. "How old would you say he is? Maybe late twenties, early thirties?"

"Thereabouts," Mary said. She didn't seem to want to talk about him. Finally she turned to Laurie and blurted, "I think there's something in his past, some substance abuse problem which cost him everything he had, including his wife. I haven't wanted to ask any questions, but I overheard part of a conversation he had with Mother Barbara. I think she's letting him use the church as a home base." Her face had a pained look as she added, "I think he's homeless."

"Wow!" Laurie stared for a moment open mouthed. "And I thought I had problems."

"Laurie..." Mary hesitated a moment before giving her advice as usual. "Just stay away from that guy. You really don't need to be thinking about men right now anyway. You just divorced DB, and you said you wanted to stay single for a while. You try to please people too much. And you always pick the wrong guys. I hate to see you jumping into anything."

"Oh for cripes sake! I just asked about the guy, and you have me walking down the aisle!" She pointed a finger at Mary. "And don't forget, *you* were the one who introduced me to DB."

Laurie flipped the switch, turning on the noisy vacuum to prevent any more conversation, and scrubbed roughly at the carpet.

Her friend was right. Laurie did tend to meet all the wrong kinds of men; that part was true. That was why, when Mary and Pete had introduced her to preppy, ambitious DB, Laurie had thought he was so perfect. If only she'd asked more questions. That was one thing DB had hated, claiming she was grilling him, or interrogating him. Well, if she'd asked a few more questions about where he was all those evenings, she might have got out of the marriage sooner. As it was, it was six years down the drain.

Lately it rankled Laurie that people were always telling her what to do, what not to do, what to think, and who to spend time with. For years it was her ex, and before that, it was Mary, her best friend. And now she was falling into the same routine, letting other people run her life for her.

Laurie *had* vowed to stay away from men for a while. But when she was ready, she intended to do her own matchmaking. She had no reason to disbelieve what Mary said about Chase. But she told herself she would get to the bottom of the theft, just to show Mary she was wrong for a change. And to prove Chase innocent.

Chapter 2.

Sunday morning Laurie dashed up the stairs to the choir loft at the back of St. Mark's Episcopal Church just as the small choir finished their vocal warm-ups. She wore one of the tops she had snagged at the Treasure Chest the previous day, a red, boat-neck shirt with three-quarter sleeves and silvery studs around the neckline. Red and sliver always looked good on her, and she liked to look attractive, even if she would have to cover her outfit with choir robes soon.

Mary cleared the seat next to her in the alto section, and Laurie plopped onto the chair. "Cute top," Mary said, smiling. She knew where it had come from. "Did you buy those pants yesterday too?"

"No. These are my old, black stand-bys. They go with everything."

Steve the organist struck up the first hymn. "Wait. What are we singing?" Laurie asked.

"376," Bob said behind her. Laurie turned to thank him, and to sneak a look at Chase. He was simply dressed in a pair of jeans and a plain oxford cloth button down shirt, tucked in at the waist. He had an angular face, and a rather square chin. If she'd seen him out somewhere she might not have given him a second glance. He looked up, and she gave a half-smile and turned away.

Mary was still flipping through her hymnal looking for the right page, but started singing "Joyful, joyful we adore thee, God of glory, Lord of love." She seemed to know everything by heart, without even having to see the music.

The choir sang the first verse in unison, and then broke into parts. Laurie followed along as best she could. She couldn't read music, but did have a fairly good ear. At least she recognized the melody, the "Ode to Joy" theme from Beethoven's ninth symphony.

Halfway through the second verse she stopped singing and just listened. With the sopranos in the front row and all the men in the row behind her, she was in a good spot to hear the harmonies. Bob and Alan sang tenor, and John and Chase carried the bass part. It was amazing how good the small choir sounded.

After rehearsing the rest of the morning's music they donned their choir robes. They formed two lines behind the cross in the narthex at the back of the church as Steve started playing the processional hymn. Singing, they walked up the center of the nave. They split into two columns at the communion rail, and took the side aisles around the church, finally climbing into the loft. Laurie took the steps one at a time, trying not to trip on her long robe. She was always a little out of breath until the end of the hymn.

Mother Barbara read the opening sentences as Laurie looked past the row of sopranos and down at the parishioners below. Despite swearing off men, one of her reasons for joining St. Mark's was to meet people. So far everyone was friendly, but for a divorcee hoping to find eligible bachelors it was disappointing. Overall, it was an older congregation, and there just weren't very many young bachelors to choose from.

Laurie shifted casually in her chair and glanced at the men behind her. Aside from the teen who ran the sound system, Chase was the only single (and, presumably, straight) male in the choir loft. She tried to recall exactly what Mary had said about him, but determined she would get to know him on her own.

Chase noticed Laurie looking at him. He smiled, and she did a quick about-face, focusing her attention on the scripture readings and Mother Barbara's sermon.

The sermon was shorter than usual because of a baptism listed in the bulletin. "Pay attention," Mary whispered. "You'll be a godmother soon." Mary wiggled into the front row of the loft, nudging one of the sopranos out of the way, and watched over the railing.

Laurie hadn't witnessed a baptism at St. Mark's yet. She could hardly see the baby, swaddled as it was in a long white blanket. Parents and godparents stood with the infant at the front of the church. They presented the child for baptism, and answered a series of questions designed to make sure they intended to raise the child in the faith. Then everyone in the congregation renewed their own baptismal covenant. *This is a beautiful service*, Laurie thought.

Finally the group walked down the aisle and gathered around the baptismal font, which was at the back of the church and almost directly under the choir loft. Laurie could no longer see what was going on, so she listened, and followed along in her prayer book. Mother Barbara solemnly intoned, "We thank you, Almighty God, for the gift of water." She paused, and Laurie heard the sound of trickling water as the priest poured it into the basin.

From behind Laurie came an almost inaudible response: "Because you need it to make coffee." She slapped a hand over her mouth stifling a laugh, and looked over her shoulder. The men were snickering too - all except Chase, who shrugged, smiling. Laurie gave him a thumbs up. She couldn't live without her coffee.

The baptism over, the congregation welcomed the newly baptized. Then Mother Barbara said, "The peace of the Lord be always with you."

"And also with you," the congregation responded. People milled around the church greeting one another, hugging or shaking hands. In the small loft, choir members shook hands or hugged, chatted, and pulled out the sheet music for their anthem.

"I take it you're a coffee drinker," Laurie commented to Chase.

He shifted his feet and pointed to the travel mug beneath his chair. "My favorite beverage. Thank God they decided it's good for you. I'd hate to have to give coffee up too."

Laurie wondered what he meant by that, but Mother Barbara had started a few announcements, and then the choir sang their offertory anthem.

The service continued with the Holy Communion, and Laurie gradually sank deeper into the mystery of the sacrament. She felt renewed by the closing prayer and the blessing.

The service ended with a joyful rendition of hymn 376. The volume in the nave quickly rose as people chatted together, greeted Mother Barbara, or moved toward the parish hall for coffee hour. As the organist impro-

vised on Beethoven's "Ode to Joy," Chase suddenly started singing in German in his clear, warm baritone.

"He's in good voice today," Laurie murmured to
Mary, watching Chase singing as he shed his choir robe.

"He could use a good haircut," Mary said.

In a brief practice session the choir rehearsed the
next week's anthem, and then were dismissed from the
loft. Usually their rehearsals lasted a bit longer, and by
the time they got to the parish hall the coffee was long
gone and any snacks were reduced to crumbs. Today
Laurie helped herself to coffee and half of a cinnamon
roll.

She took a seat in the parish hall next to Bob, who
was telling Mary and Pete about a production he was involved in at the little theater in Redding. Chase joined
them at the table with his refilled travel mug and a paper
plate heaped with snacks.

"Are you into theater, Chase?" Laurie asked, hoping
to draw him into the conversation and get to know him
better. She had to wait for his answer as he swallowed a
mouthful.

"Nope, I've never been much into theater. I was always a music nerd."

"So do you play an instrument then?"

"Guitar. And I've noodled around with keyboards a
bit. You?" he asked, looking hopeful.

"I just play the radio," Laurie said. "And the keyboard on my laptop."

"Oh, yeah. I heard you were the literary type," Chase said.

Laurie raised her eyebrows, surprised that he knew that. She took a bite of her cinnamon roll, still thinking about his comment. "Oh, this is delicious," she said, her mouth half full.

"I love anything with cinnamon," Chase agreed.

One of the church's teens, a girl named Ashley, approached their table. "Did you bring your guitar today Chase?" she asked.

"Sure did. It's in the parlor. I was hoping to show you a few things."

"Great. I'll get mine out of our car." Ashley stopped by the table where her parents sat, and hurried out of the parish hall with the car keys.

"You give lessons?" Laurie asked.

"Yep. Ashley wants to play at the open mic at the Coffee Pot this Friday. Her parents took her and a friend there just to listen last week, and we got to talking. You ought to come some time. It's nice. It brings a lot of people together."

"Music *and* coffee," Laurie said. "What's not to like?" The revelation that Chase taught guitar made him even more interesting. And if Ashley's parents trusted him around their daughter, Laurie thought he couldn't be as bad as all that, despite what Mary thought. She made a mental note: *the Coffee Pot, Friday night.*

Chapter 3.

Laurie was the last to arrive at the Treasure Chest volunteers' meeting in St. Mark's parish hall the following Wednesday. She took a seat between Anne and Mother Barbara, and waved to Mary, seated farther down the table.

"Hey," Anne said. "I heard you have a new job. Are you still going to be able to work at the shop?"

"Yes, afternoons and weekends when I'm needed. I started working for the *Journal* Monday, but it's just part-time, mornings."

"Well you'll be right downtown, then. That's nice."

Everyone grew silent as Carol, the committee chairman, opened the meeting. "I need to tell you a few things about our new *anti-theft* measures." She said, looking over her reading glasses. Carol's southern accent and ladylike manner always made Laurie think of Blanche in the Golden Girls. "We put a lock on the jewelry display case, to stop anyone from just reaching across the counter, sliding the door open, and taking something out. Now, the key is in the cash drawer, and when a customer wants to see something in the case, just unlock it. But *please*, when they're done, make *sure* you lock it again, and put the key back in the drawer. I know it's more trouble, but if we leave the case unlocked, that defeats the purpose. Everybody got that?"

Carol paused as everyone nodded. Then she looked down, tapping her pen on her notebook. "And here's the other thing I wanted to discuss. I'm worried because we haven't made much money in the last few months. Is it just the time of year? I mean, maybe our customers have a lot to do in their yards, or they've been on vacation for spring break. But we need to get more people into the shop. I say this because we're going to have to get that old air conditioner replaced soon, and I'm not sure we have the money we need. I hope y'all can give me some ideas." She looked around the table, waiting for someone to speak up.

"We used to be the only game in town, and now there are two other thrift shops," Anne pointed out.

"Well, I checked out some of the competition, though," Evelyn said shaking her head, dangling earrings swaying. "They're smaller, and kind of disorganized. I wouldn't worry about them."

"I think we're not charging enough for clothes," Alice said. Laurie noted Alice's expensive-looking sweater, and thought she might be right, at least where *her* donated items were concerned. But Alice also used to own a dress shop, and thought the Treasure Chest should be run like a for-profit business.

Anne leaned forward. "But y'all, we have *so many* clothes! Have you looked in that back room? Everyone must have cleaned out their closets at the same time. You can't even walk in there. We have *got* to do *somethin*!"

Laurie remembered Mary's tales of when the shop first opened. Church-members feared there wouldn't be enough merchandise to keep it going. Now the back rooms were overflowing with donated items. Not just clothing, but housewares, knickknacks, and books. In fact, they made regular contributions of books to the friends of the library for their annual fund-raiser.

"I still think we should have the shop open another day of the week," Mary said. "I mean, why not open on Wednesdays too? That's just five days a week, but it would give us a whole 'nother day of sales, which would mean extra income, and we'd move that many more items. And we'd still have Sundays and Mondays off."

A few volunteers grumbled to each other. Finally Evelyn said "I think we're already stretched to the limit, Mary. I believe we ruled out that suggestion a couple of meetings ago."

Mary folded her arms and leaned back, glaring at Evelyn. Mother Barbara turned toward her and said soothingly "Wednesdays are when we hold our Bible study, and the mid-week service. Plus there's the monthly meeting of the women's group. I hate for people to miss out on opportunities for worship, fellowship, and Christian formation just because they're working in the shop." Mother Barbara tried to maintain the delicate balance between the Treasure Chest, which helped keep the church open, and reasons the church was open in the first place.

Virginia rarely spoke up in meetings. A friend of Joan's, she was not a member of St. Mark's, and some of the other women made sure she didn't forget it. This time she ventured her opinion. "We have to think about our customers. They shop at the Treasure Chest because they don't have a lot of money. Maybe we should *reduce* our prices."

Alice shook her head. "We have a lot of customers who know *exactly* what they're buying. They look at the labels, and go straight for the items from Anne Taylor or Chico's, or Ralph Lauren and those brands. We need to keep them at a higher price."

"Right," Anne agreed. "We don't want to go too low. Y'all, the church needs the money." Some women nodded their heads, murmuring about the low attendance at services the last few Sundays.

"But you just said we have so much stuff!" Virginia insisted. Laurie and a few others nodded agreement.

"Well, we can't just *give* things away," Anne snapped.

Laurie turned to Anne. "But we *do* give them away!" Laurie said. "We just boxed up a bunch of unsold winter clothes, and Don took them to the mission."

Anne folded her arms and looked away, so Laurie appealed to the others. "How much did all those clothes cost us? They were free to us! And donations keep coming in. We'll make more money if we sell more volume, instead of worrying so much about the price of each item. We get nothing if our prices are so high that we end up boxing up the clothes and giving them away at the end of the season."

The women were silent. Carol fidgeted with her notebook looking around the table. Finally Joan offered a suggestion. "We could try what we did when I worked at the shop in Atlanta. Every week we had a half-price sale. One week it was on ladies clothing, the next week men's, or children's, or maybe on kitchen items. That way there was always something on sale, which gave the customers a reason to visit more often. Prices were lower, so people bought more, and we didn't have so much stuff that just sat in the shop for months."

"That sounds confusing to me, changing every week like that," Evelyn said.

"Do it for two weeks at a time, then," Joan huffed.

"Girls, please!" Carol held up her hand asking for peace. "I think that could work. We could put up a sign telling what's on sale. And maybe Laurie could put something on Facebook for us."

Virginia nodded. "People will get the hang of it. We always tell customers when they walk through the door if we're having a sale."

"But we shouldn't have a sale right now," Evelyn protested. "We just put the new spring clothing out."

"We should put everything in the furniture room on sale," Mary said. "You know some of those things have been there for a while." She looked at Laurie, who nodded thinking of the bathroom sink under the table.

Carol agreed. "Okay, we'll start with a half-price sale in the furniture room for two weeks, and see how it goes. That'll give people a chance to hear about it and come buy things. We can go on to the kitchen room after that. But no sale on clothes until next month." She made a note and checked her agenda.

There was a pause in the meeting while a couple of volunteers worked out some schedule changes, swapping work days because of spring break and Easter holidays. Carol leaned over to Laurie. "I wanted to show you something," she said, handing over her smartphone. "Here's the picture where we donated five hundred dollars to the arts center. If I send you a copy can you post it on Facebook, and say something wonderful about us?"

"Sure," Laurie said examining the photo. It showed Carol and a nice-looking man in front of the Chinkapin Arts Center. He was smiling as Carol handed him a check. With two fingers Laurie zoomed the image, trying to guess how old he was. The man appeared medium height, clean-shaven, with dark wavy hair. His smile and his blue eyes were dazzling. "What's his name?" she asked.

"Oh, Lord, I should know." Carol looked up at the ceiling. "It's Jeff... I'm trying to remember."

"What happened to Sharon?" Anne asked, craning to look at the picture. "She's the one we usually work with at the arts center."

"Right. Well, she's still there. This is the new instructor. Sharon said to take *his* picture for a change. I *wish* I could remember his last name!"

"I'll call the arts center," Laurie said. "Or better yet, I'll stop over there. I still have that box of picture frames rattling around in my car." The picture of Jeff certainly was intriguing. *Never hurts to meet someone new*, Laurie thought.

The thought reminded her of Chase. "Say," she said as the meeting wrapped up and volunteers began to leave. "Did we ever find out anything more about the gold ring that went missing? I mean, it hasn't turned up, has it?" Laurie looked at Evelyn, remembering her accusation.

"You know what I think," Evelyn said shrugging.

"I find that hard to believe, though," Laurie said.

"What are you talking about?" Virginia asked.

"Well, what happened was..." Laurie began.

"Drop it, Laurie!" Mother Barbara said sharply. Laurie turned to her in surprise. "Would you come to my office? There's a brochure I wanted to show you. Maybe you could help me."

Mother Barbara left the parish hall. Bewildered, Laurie exchanged a look with Virginia, but quickly rose and followed Mother Barbara to her office. The priest waited at the door, and closed it behind them muttering something about little parishes having big ears.

"Sit down a minute," Mother Barbara said. Laurie waited while the priest shuffled papers on her desk. Finally she met Laurie's eyes. "Chase took the ring."

"Chase," Laurie repeated. "Wait. I thought I heard he donated it to the shop."

Mother Barbara looked out the window for a moment before turning back to Laurie. "I don't know how much you may have heard about his ... background. Let's just say he needed the money. He's been through some rough circumstances, and has little left to his name. I couldn't give him anything out of my discretionary fund, so I suggested he take the ring back and sell it. He took the ring, but he didn't want to have to tell anyone."

"Oh," Laurie said, nodding her head, still in the dark, and still curious. She wondered about Chase's "background" but it was clear Mother Barbara didn't intend to say any more about it.

"The guy is interesting, and talented. It's hard to believe he's so bad off," Laurie said. She considered her own situation. *Maybe not so hard*, she thought. "Does anyone else know?"

"I explained what happened to Carol, but no one else needs to know," Barbara replied. "I'm trying to leave him his dignity. And he's trying to get his life back in order. All the education he has is not very marketable, but he's got himself a new job, and I've let him use the parlor to give a few guitar lessons. He says he feels really at home here at St. Mark's."

Laurie nodded, remembering vaguely what Mary told her the day the ring was found missing, about Chase using the church as a home base. Laurie had wanted to get to the bottom of the "theft" to clear Chase's name. Instead she had almost embarrassed him in front of the Treasure Chest committee. She felt foolish. "Well, unless there's something I can do, I guess I'll mind my own business and concentrate on my own problems."

"How's your job at the *Journal* going?" Mother Barbara asked. "Can you tell yet whether you'll like it?"

"It's okay so far. It helps with living expenses. I work on the events column on page three - whatever people submit, I clean up."

Mother Barbara nodded. "Speaking of events, I've been working with the vestry to come up with some events the church can hold, to give us a little more visibility. I wanted to pick your brain, get a newcomer's perspective. Don wants to have a golf outing again, but I was thinking of something to bring more outsiders to the church. People associate the Episcopal church with the arts, so maybe a concert, or an art show, or something. And you could help us get it listed in the Journal."

"Definitely," Laurie said.

"Think about it for a while, and let me know if you come up with some ideas." Mother Barbara selected one of the papers from her desk. "And actually, I did have something else I was hoping you could help with today. I picked up this brochure when I visited St. Michael's. I'd like to put together something similar for St. Mark's." Laurie scanned it, nodding. Then the two bent their heads over the brochure and got to work.

Chapter 4.

By the time Laurie left Mother Barbara's office everyone else had gone. She drove to the arts center to drop off the picture frames and get the information she needed for her Facebook post.

The Chinkapin Arts Center was in the town's old armory, a block from St. Mark's. Laurie parked her Malibu in the nearly empty lot, and carried her box to the front door, finding it unlocked. In the dim foyer, there were several paintings on display, and a bulletin board covered with flyers listing dates of upcoming classes and events. In the lofty room beyond Laurie saw a few tables, and several moveable display walls hung with paintings and photographs.

"Hello?" Laurie called, her voice echoing in the cavernous space.

"In the classroom," a woman's voice answered.

Laurie followed the direction of the voice through the gallery, and found the woman in a classroom propping canvases on small easels which stood at intervals on a table spattered with paint.

"Hi. I'm Laurie Lanton from the Treasure Chest. Are you Sharon?" Laurie set the box of frames on the floor, extending her hand.

"Yes! Nice to meet you. What can I do for you?"

Laurie explained about the boxful of old pictures and frames, and Sharon bent to flip through them.

"Oh, these are terrific!" she said. "We're having a student art show in a month, and the entries all have to be framed. I know some people will be glad to use these. Thanks so much for thinking of us."

Mention of an art show reminded Laurie of what Mother Barbara had just said about an event at St. Mark's. Well, if the arts center was hosting one in a month, it wouldn't do to hold one at the church to compete. But maybe later in the summer?

Laurie pointed to the easels set up on the table. "Are you getting ready for a class? Or is this the 'Art Night Out' I've heard about?"

"This is for a birthday party tonight. The birthday girl and her guests will make paintings to take home, and then they'll have cake and refreshments in the gallery. Here's what they're painting." Sharon showed Laurie a picture of a circus dog in a tutu riding a unicycle. "Are you an artist?"

"Not hardly," Laurie said with a laugh.

"You should try Art Night Out. No experience need-ed, and we provide all the supplies. Here's a brochure," she said, and handed Laurie a flyer. "Jeff leads the art nights. They're lots of fun."

Laurie glanced at the flyer. On the back was a photo of the handsome, dark-haired man with the captivating smile. "Oh, this is the guy I came to ask about." She showed Sharon the picture Carol had sent her. "I'd like to post it on our Facebook page and give the arts center a plug, but Carol couldn't remember his last name."

"It's Williams. Jeff Williams. He's recently moved here from Atlanta, but his family is from Chinkapin." Sharon placed paintbrushes beside each easel.

Laurie noticed the short bio on the back of the bro-chure: *Jeff Williams showed an interest in art at a young age, inspired by his parents, both professional photogra-phers. He earned a B.F.A. in painting from the Savannah College of Art and Design (SCAD), and strives to convey the beauty he finds in the world around him.*

"SCAD, huh? I've heard that's expensive."

"He went to the SCAD campus in Atlanta, but I guess they probably cost just the same. If it were me, I'd want to go to Savannah, though."

"How long has he worked here?" Laurie asked.

"A couple of months. We brought him on just as April Ross went out on maternity leave. We're lucky to have

Jeff, but we're not exactly sure how long he'll want to stay."

"I guess he's just out of college then?" Laurie was digging for information, but hoped her interest in the handsome young man wasn't too obvious.

Sharon laughed. "Late twenties, I think. Nice looking, isn't he? His dad recently passed away, so he came to help his mom settle the estate and wrap up loose ends." Sharon talked as she sorted fat tubes of paint. "He said he would be in the area for a while, and asked about using the space to hold a few art classes. We put him right to work, and so far it's worked out great."

Laurie heard a sound coming from the doorway and turned to see a woman and girl carrying boxes and bags. "Hi, Sharon. We're here to set up and decorate for the party," the woman said.

"Okay. Just a minute and I'll help you move those tables." She added to Laurie, "That's our birthday girl and her mom. Was there anything else?"

"No. Thanks for the flyer and the info," Laurie said. She pointed at the box of old picture frames. "You know, we get more of those than we ever sell, so if you can use them, just call and we'll get another boxful together. I'll leave my phone number."

"Thanks. Maybe I'll send Jeff to pick them up," Sharon said with a wink.

Chapter 5.

"Y'all, it's hot in here!" Anne fanned herself with a piece of card stock.

"You can say that again," Laurie agreed. "And humid." She stood at the check-out counter in the Treasure Chest stacking old grocery bags, while Anne put prices on several pairs of earrings attached to snippets of card stock. "Whenever someone opens the door we get a blast of hot air. But every fan in the shop is already running."

"I could have sold two fans yesterday," Anne said. "I hated to tell people they weren't for sale!" She called down the hall to Mary, who was working in the children's clothing room. "Mary, set the thermostat down a notch. See if it does any good."

"I thought they were supposed to replace the air conditioner this week," Laurie said.

"They were hoping to have it done on Tuesday, but now it won't be done until Saturday," Anne said. "Actually, they'll be in today to disassemble and get everything ready, but the new unit will be installed tomorrow. You know, we're going to be closed tomorrow."

"Oh, yeah," Laurie said snapping her fingers. "I need to post that. 'Closed Saturday.'" She jotted a reminder. "And did you see what I posted about our donation to the arts center? It was mentioned in the *Journal* too."

"You do good work!" Anne said. "We never had such good publicity until you started working here. I know our customers see the sale announcements, because they mention them when they come in."

The brass bells hanging from the door jangled as four men in khaki pants and "Anderson Heating, Ventilation, and Air Conditioning" tee-shirts walked in. Laurie was surprised to see Chase with them.

"Thank God y'all are here," Anne said. "It figures this would be the hottest week of the year so far." She introduced herself to the crew leader, a young man named Bo, who removed his cap.

"We'll be hauling things in and out. I hope we're not in your way," he said.

"It's the end of the month. No one has any money left, so we're not too busy. You do whatever you have to, and don't worry about us."

Bo led the crew to the mechanical room at the back of the shop. There was banging and clattering as they disassembled the old HVAC system.

"Chase works for Anderson HVAC?" Laurie asked Anne.

"It looks like it," she answered shrugging. "Y'all in the choir probably know him better than I do. I'm always gone when you come down for coffee hour." She lowered her voice. "Watch the counter while I run to the ladies' room."

A woman with a child in a stroller laid a pile of kids' clothing on the counter. As Laurie wrote up the sales ticket, a tall workman in a *Braves* cap walked up and smiled across the counter at her. "Didn't I see one of y'alls picture in the *Journal* the other day? You gave some money to the arts center, or something like that?"

"That was Carol, one of the other volunteers." Laurie rang up the sale, handed the woman her change, and stuffed the clothes in a used grocery bag, standard practice for the shop. "There you go. Thanks, and come see us again."

She had just closed the cash drawer and turned to speak to the man at the counter. She did a double take when she noticed Chase in the staff kitchen refilling his bottle of water. "Um, yes, the Treasure Chest gave a five hundred dollar donation to the arts center." She addressed the man, but her eyes kept wandering back to Chase. "They'll use it for their children's summer art program."

"I didn't know you made donations like that. I thought you just sold stuff and kept the money," he said. "My name's Dean, by the way." He reached a grubby hand across the counter.

"Laurie. Nice to meet you." She noted the dirt under his nails. *At least he reads the newspaper*, she thought.

Chase walked over with his water bottle. "When you shop here or donate items to the Treasure Chest, you help other people in the community," he told Dean. "I'd work here myself, but I have to work someplace that pays."

"Dean! Chuck! Get back here and help with this, or nobody gets paid." Bo stood in the hallway, scowling. The curls sticking out from his cap made him look too young to be the crew leader. With another glare at Dean and Chase he slouched back down the hall.

"Yes sir, Bo," Dean said with a salute. He winked at Laurie. "You can't say 'no' to the owner's son."

Chase lingered behind, leaning a hand on the counter. Laurie's eyes flicked over to the jewelry case, thinking about Evelyn's accusation, and what Mother Barbara had told her. Apparently working for Anderson HVAC was the new job Mother Barbara had mentioned.

Something else nagged at the back of Laurie's mind. "Did that man just call you 'Chuck?'" she asked.

Chase rolled his eyes and smiled wryly. "Old nick-names - you can't escape them sometimes. Hey, did you know there's water damage in the mechanical room ceiling? Maybe you should mention it to Mother Barbara or one of the wardens, and have someone check it out. From the outside it looks like the roof has been repaired before. It might be time to replace it."

"Thanks," Laurie said nodding. "I'll be sure to mention it."

For the next hour, noises erupted periodically from the mechanical room, and men hauled items out of the building. Then they reversed the process, carrying new parts in. They left soon after, promising Anne they'd return early Saturday to finish the job.

With no air conditioning the shop heated up quickly, despite the scattered fans. Anne decided to close the Treasure Chest early.

"Thank God," Mary said, coming out of one of the back rooms where she had been tagging clothes. "No one's going to want to buy those clothes after I've dripped sweat all over them! But look at the cute onesies I found back there." She held up a couple of baby items, still baring the original tags. She wrote the items up on a sales ticket, and went for her wallet in the office.

"You want to do something this afternoon?" Laurie asked.

"I've got a little time to kill, but Pete and I are going to the movies tonight. You should come with us!" She mentioned the name of the movie, the latest suspense thriller.

"No, thanks. Come to think of it, I'd better buy some groceries. I've eaten out too often this week." Laurie ate out more often than she should. She got tired of eating in restaurants by herself, but at least it delayed going home to an empty apartment. She drove to the grocery store, purchased a few items, and took her time cooking up a stir fry.

She took her plate to her little table and sat alone with her dinner. Except for the dull sound of traffic and muffled voices from the next apartment, everything was still. Laurie thought of calling someone, just to talk, but the few friends she had in Chinkapin mostly had spouses and families to keep them occupied. And except for the Walmart and the grocery stores, most places in town closed by 6 p.m.

Briefly she considered driving up to Redding where she knew of a couple of gallery shows going on. Then she remembered open mic night at the Coffee Pot café. She checked her watch, grabbed her purse and headed to her car.

Chapter 6.

It took a while, but Laurie finally found a parking space at the far side of the courthouse. The café's front door was propped open, and she could hear music as she walked along the sidewalk. Patrons crowded the tables outside, sipping iced coffee and sharing desserts. A few sat on the benches which lined the sidewalks nearby.

Laurie squeezed through the doorway, and wormed her way toward the counter. Despite the warmth of the early summer evening, she ordered her favorite hot latte - the Southern Classic. It was flavored with pecans, and always reminded her of warm pecan pie.

She looked around the café as she waited for her coffee. A young woman with a clipboard walked over to her and asked, "Are you performing tonight?"

Laurie shook her head. "But can I see your clipboard for a sec?" She scanned the list, which already had a few names crossed off. There was Chase's name, with just two performers listed ahead of him. "Thanks." She handed back the clipboard and carried her drink outside, taking a seat on the fringe of the crowd.

Over the chatter she heard a woman singing and playing a keyboard. She sounded vaguely like someone Laurie had heard on a television commercial. Laurie thought of all the concerts she and Mary had gone to when they were in college. That had stopped when Laurie married DB. He always said concerts were a waste of money. She frowned, and put DB out of her mind.

Next came a duo on mandolin and fiddle. They sounded quite good to Laurie, and they seemed to be a crowd favorite. People outside the café clapped and whistled so long that the duo got to perform an extra number.

When their set ended, Laurie strained to hear the next introduction. It was drowned out by laughter nearby, but she soon heard soft strumming on a guitar, and recognized Chase's warm baritone. He performed a song by James Taylor that spoke of suffering, loneliness, and loss.

It reminded Laurie of the empty ache in her heart, and before she could stop them a few tears slid down her face. After what DB had done she didn't care if she ever saw him again, but her whole life had changed so completely, she sometimes had a sense of free-falling. She grabbed the napkin clasped under her cup and dabbed at her cheeks.

Chase continued seamlessly into his second number. Laurie rose from the bench and moved toward the café door, singing under her breath, "Mama may have, and papa may have..." She hummed as she eased through the crowd in the café until she could see the small stage at the back. When the song ended she set down her cup to clap enthusiastically, but the woman with the clipboard called for the next performer.

Chase put his guitar into a hard case, set it out of the way against the wall, and spoke to some people seated near the stage. Laurie recognized Ashley and her parents from church. She went to greet them just as they rose to leave.

"Did you perform already?" Laurie asked Ashley. "I guess I missed it."

"I played first, before it got too crowded."

"I bet you did great!"

The teen smiled happily. She and her family moved to go, and other customers eyed the table. Ashley's mother said "You'd better grab this if you're going to stay a while."

Laurie was unsure, but Chase said "Have a seat. I'll get a coffee and join you. Can I get you anything?" She held up her cup still half-full, and shook her head.

Her eyes followed him as he placed his order, leaning casually against the counter. There was a relaxed elegance about him that she found attractive. He said something she couldn't hear that made the cashier laugh. He seemed in his element in the café.

Chase returned, and they watched the stage where a young man tuned a guitar and played a couple of numbers. "He's getting better," Chase said applauding. "I've coached him a bit. He's played here several times, and is finally getting a handle on his nerves. That's one of the reasons I love this." His sweeping gesture took in the whole café. "The people here are easy-going, and pretty forgiving. Kind of like St. Mark's."

Laurie looked closely at him to be sure he wasn't being sarcastic. She was ready to defend the little church which had welcomed her, but Chase was smiling warmly.

"How old were you when you started playing?" she asked.

"About twelve, I guess. Somewhere around middle school I started thinking about what I had to show for myself - skills, accomplishments, you know. My older brothers were both in sports, but back then I was the little guy. I couldn't compete. Anyway, our dad was something of a musician in his younger days. We never went anywhere in the car without music playing, and Dad was always talking about the artists, and explaining how the song was put together." Chase smiled when he spoke of his dad. "He had a couple of chord books, and an old guitar lying around, so I started playing.

"When I was about fifteen, I formed my first band with kids from school. Then in college I hooked up with some other musicians, and financed my education playing in the local bars. I was Nashville-bound, but real life intervened." There was a troubled look in his eyes as he swirled the straw in his iced coffee. "And now you've heard my musical autobiography." Chase bowed in his seat, smiling again. "I'll be happy to autograph your cup for you."

Laurie moved it out of his reach. "No one's touching my latte. By the way, I liked your choice of music."

He made no reply. Another performer took the stage. "Want to go for a walk? You can take your coffee with you." His eyes twinkled as he nodded toward her cup.

Their table was quickly claimed as the two squeezed out the door. It was cooler outside now that the sun was down. They strolled up the street glancing into shop windows, and casting pale shadows under the street lamps.

Laurie wanted to get to know Chase better, and maybe crack the code on his mysterious background, but was afraid of raising sensitive subjects. "How did you end up in Chinkapin? Is this your home town?"

"No. I haven't lived here long. But I like the place, and have friends here. I spent most of the last eight or ten years up around Athens."

Laurie had never been to Athens, Georgia, but knew it was a big college town with a storied musical history. She was thinking of another question to ask, when Chase surprised her with one of his own.

"And how are *you* finding it here?" he asked. "Quite a change from your old stomping grounds, isn't it?"

"Oh, quite a change. I like the climate so far, although summer's just getting started." She smiled. "The people seem friendly. Awfully proud of being southern, with the 'sweet tea' and 'bless your heart' and all. But I don't care what they say, mac 'n' cheese is *not* a vegetable!"

"But I *love* mac 'n' cheese!"

"I do to," she admitted. "And pecan pie, and good Georgia barbecue. That makes up for a lot."

They crossed the street at the corner and turned back toward the café. Laurie's coffee was gone, but she held the paper cup tightly.

"I was surprised to see that you work for Anderson HVAC," Laurie said. It seemed an unusual occupation for a man who taught music and sang in German.

"It pays the bills," he said casually. "I'm still contemplating my next big career move. How about you? I know the Treasure Chest doesn't pay your bills. Or are you a rich Yankee girl, come to see how we do things in the South?"

"Like you, I'm contemplating my next big career move." Laurie told him about her part-time job with the newspaper, and her long-cherished ambition to earn her living as a writer.

Chase was encouraging. "Writing song lyrics is writing," he suggested. "Maybe we can collaborate sometime. It's hard to find a good lyricist."

They reached the corner and paused. Music streamed from the café. Chase stood with his back to the streetlight, his face in shadow. As Laurie looked up at him, she caught the faint scent of his aftershave. She still clutched the empty cup rigidly in front of her.

"I'd better make sure no one has made off with my guitar," he said, and touched her gently on the arm. "Do you want another coffee? Or are you in the mood for more music?"

Her writer's brain clicked into gear. Cliché's like *in the mood* and *make sweet music together* floated through her mind. She *was* in the mood, but warning bells muddled her brain. All she managed to say was "Um..."

He seized her paper cup and crushed it with a playful growl. "There. Now I owe you another latte. Don't wait too long to claim it." He kissed her cheek. Then he dashed across the street and disappeared into the crowd.

* * *

Saturday Laurie drove slowly by the closed thrift shop, and noted a couple of Anderson Heating, Ventilation, and Cooling vans in the parking lot. She never got a look at whoever was working inside.

Mentally she kicked herself for being so stiff the night before, and wondered what might have happened if she had gone back into the café with Chase. She might have had an enjoyable night. Maybe a long one, if she had been reading his signals correctly. Laurie was a healthy young woman, after all. Even if she didn't think Chase had particularly good new-husband potential, she missed being with a man.

She shook her head, wondering at her train of thought. She had been married long enough that single life and dating felt strange. People were so casual about their relationships these days. Laurie wouldn't entertain the idea of remarrying for a while, but didn't think she would feel comfortable hopping in the sack with every cute guy she met.

When you're on a diet, you can still read the menu, though, she thought. She recalled the image of Chase leaning against the counter at the café. Funny that she hadn't noticed how well built he looked before. But she usually saw him in his choir robe. A person could hide just about anything under one of those. She sighed, and drove to the Chinkapin library to distract herself with a good book.

Chapter 7.

Sunday morning Laurie stared into her closet wondering what to wear to church. Whatever it was would soon be covered by choir robes. A white surplice over a long black cassock was not what you would call figure flattering.

She thought again about Chase and her musings of the day before. Then she chose a summery dress in a rose pink and lime floral, and added comfortable ballerina flats. She wasn't completely crazy. Marching around the nave and up into the choir loft was challenging enough, dressed in a long robe, carrying a hymn book, and singing all the while. *Singers never get credit for how coordinated they need to be*, she thought.

Laurie slipped into her seat in the choir loft where Steve was warming up on the organ. Mary had arrived early, and eagerly told her about the restaurant she and Pete had tried Friday before the movie. "You should check it out! They have over ten different varieties of chicken salad!"

Laurie only half-listened as Mary described the menu. Most of the other choir members were arriving, and out of the corner of her eye she saw Chase take his seat. He was wearing a polo shirt that looked vaguely familiar. In fact she thought she remembered tagging it in the Treasure Chest. He looked her way. His eyes roved up and down her body, taking in her dress and her legs. He smiled, and Laurie felt herself turning pink. Still, she was glad she had put on something pretty.

The organist lost no time starting vocal warmups, and continued as usual with a run-through of the day's hymns. Then the choir rehearsed their offertory anthem.

Finally Steve launched into an elaborate organ prelude, and the choir robed and assembled in the narthex. Laurie and Mary followed the sopranos in the procession around the church and up the narrow staircase.

Mary took the stairs one at a time as usual. Behind her, Laurie lifted her foot to step up – and stepped on the hem of her robe. Her legs were suddenly trapped, and the top half of her body plummeted forward. She bobbled her hymnal and landed on her elbows with a thump on the carpeted stairs.

Mary turned and giggled at the site of Laurie trapped by her robe, leaning on her elbows, and struggling awkwardly. With one hand she reached for Laurie's hymnal so Laurie could push herself up and free her feet.

Already in the loft, the sopranos carried the hymn, as the men still on the stairs caught Mary's mood and started snickering. Over her shoulder Laurie saw Chase's amused smile. She hoisted her choir robe up to her knees and stomped up the last few steps, snatching her hymnal out of Mary's hands, which were shaking, she was laughing so hard.

A few parishioners gawked up at the choir loft, and Steve looked around the organ console to see what was happening. The sopranos had heard the commotion, and glanced behind them with concern. Steve pulled out all the stops on the final verse, trying to cover the lack of singing in the loft as choir members caught their breath.

Laurie buried her face in her hymnal. She was sure the heat from her cheeks made the pages glow a blushing red. Instead of catching Chase's notice, she spent the rest of the morning trying to blend into the background, and left the church as quickly as she could after the post-service practice.

* * *

Laurie was glad her awkward stumble on the stairs was only witnessed by choir members, and not by the whole congregation. Still, for a couple of days she made a conscious effort to avoid her friends in Chinkapin. She spent Sunday afternoon in Redding, where she browsed through a couple of galleries and went window shopping until it started to rain. Then she took refuge in the big downtown library, and lost herself in the periodicals section. Monday she went to work as usual, and then caught up on chores around her apartment.

By Tuesday Laurie was finally ready to show her face again. After work she drove to the Treasure Chest to tag clothes for a couple of hours. As soon as she entered she noticed how much cooler it felt inside. "There's nothing like air conditioning on a summer day in Georgia."

"Don't you know it," Anne replied from the office. "And it's really not even summer yet!"

Alice appeared with an armload of blouses. "It was supposed to reach 90 degrees today. I think it already made it." Then she added "I didn't expect to see you here, Laurie."

"I was free, and figured you could use some help."

The bells on the door jangled and a woman with two young children came in.

"Hey," she said. "I'm looking for towels. I wonder if you have any." There was something very odd about the way the woman's blouse fit. Laurie tried not to stare. She was just directing her to the linens room at the end of the hall, when the woman reached a hand into her blouse and pulled out a tiny kitten.

"Oh, my goodness! I've never seen a kitten that small!" Laurie stared at the little animal, and then looked back at the woman and laughed. "I thought something looked a little strange in there." She stretched a finger out and touched the kitten's paw. It was a skinny little thing, striped like a tiger, and the woman cradled it easily in her hands.

"This is Raindrop," the woman said. "Rainy for short. I'm Coreen, by the way."

Anne came out of the office to see what they were all looking at. "Aw, that thing is precious. It can't be more than two weeks old. It barely has its eyes open."

"We found him in front of our house," one of the kids said.

"I saw it first," the other child said.

"Yes, you did," Coreen agreed. "It was raining yesterday afternoon when I picked them up from school. I thought I saw something just as I pulled in to our driveway, and there he was, almost drowned. We have stray cats in the neighborhood that go in and out of the drains. But this little baby was by his self." She kissed the cat on top of the head.

"We don't know what happened to the mama cat," the first child said.

"Poor thing! He's lucky you saw him." Laurie gently stroked its furry head. Silently it opened and closed its tiny mouth.

"I've been feeding him with an eye dropper every three hours," Coreen said. After a moment she tucked him back inside her shirt. "It's the easiest way to carry him around, plus he keeps warm in there." Coreen smiled. "So I was looking for some old towels, if you have them, and also wondering if you have any pet supplies."

Laurie walked her and the kids down the hall to show them what little they had. After shopping a while Coreen bought Rainy a food bowl and some old towels, and bought a game for the kids. As Laurie rang up her purchases the woman talked about her husband who was on disability because of an accident at work, and how she hoped the cat would cheer him up.

Laurie was always fascinated by the different slices of life she encountered when she worked at the shop. "I hope your husband gets to feeling better. And you'll have to bring Rainy in from time to time so we can see how he's doing."

Coreen promised that she would.

"Well, that was interesting," Anne said.

Alice was still going back and forth with blouses to put out for sale. "Do you want to tag some clothes? I'll show you what I've been working on."

"Hey, since y'all are both here, I'm going to run over to the church and get things ready for the Wednesday service," Anne said. Each week someone from the altar guild checked the candles and laid the altar in the proper colors. This week it was Anne's turn.

As Laurie and Alice moved toward the workroom, the shop phone rang. Anne answered, and the others paused, listening. After a brief conversation she hung up. "That was someone from Anderson. He thinks they left some tools here over the weekend. He'll be over to check in a few minutes."

"Who was it that called?" Laurie asked, thinking of Chase.

"I don't know. Why?"

"Oh, just wondering." Laurie hoped her face wasn't turning red. She suddenly felt the air conditioning wasn't doing a very good job after all.

Anne left the shop, bell on the door jangling, and Alice led the way to the tagging room. "Come on. I'll get you started in the back."

Still trying to cool off, Laurie stopped in the staff kitchen, selected a CD from a stack of donated disks, and turn on the CD player. She and Mary were usually the only ones who thought to put music on. It did seem to make customers shop longer, though.

"Did I lose you?" Alice found Laurie still in the kitchen.

"Sorry!" she said, and trotted after her. In the work room Alice pointed out the summer clothes she had sorted into bins. Each bin was marked with the price to be charged for each of the items inside.

"The three-dollar bin is overflowing, so you may want to start tagging those. I'll go back up front and watch the counter until Anne comes back."

Laurie fetched a pile of clothes hangers from the storage closet, untangled them, and arranged them on the table so she could hang clothing as she tagged. She grabbed a tagging gun, and took a moment to find a pen that worked. Then she realized there were only a few blue three-dollar tags handy. "Why do we keep the supplies in the office, instead of back here in the workroom where they belong?" she wondered aloud, and headed back up front.

She snapped her fingers to a Chuck Mangione tune, and stopped in the kitchen to turn the volume up on the CD player as the bell on the door jangled. She crossed the hallway, expecting to see Anne back from next door.

Instead she found Alice lying face down behind the counter.

Laurie rushed around the counter and bent over the inert form, holding her breath. She put a shaky hand on

Alice's shoulder. "Alice? Hey!" There was no response. Laurie raised her head and looked over the counter.

"Hey!" she said more loudly. She felt a chill, and this time it had nothing to do with air conditioning. She crept out from behind the counter and peeked down the hall toward the utility room. There was no one in sight.

The door jangled and Laurie spun around, eyes wide. "Anne! Oh, God, look! I found her on the floor. I don't know what happened." Laurie went back to where Alice lay. This time Alice moaned, and pushed herself to a sitting position, rubbing the back of her head.

"Did you see anyone out there?" Laurie asked Anne.

"A truck just pulled away, but I didn't get a good look at the driver. He had a ball cap on." Anne stood behind Laurie a moment, and then stepped past the two of them to where the cash drawer stood open.

"All the cash is gone. We've been robbed!"

Chapter 8.

Carol called an emergency meeting of Treasure Chest volunteers the next afternoon. Laurie picked up Mary, and the two arrived in the parish hall to find the others waiting to hear what happened. Alice was the center of attention as she told the events of the previous day.

"I guess the fella came in while Laurie and I were in the workroom. I heard the door, and when I went back to the counter I saw the truck parked outside. I didn't actually see anyone inside. Anne was over at the church setting up the altar for today's service. Then there was a noise behind me. That's all I can remember - until I woke up on the floor with a knot on the back of my head." She touched it gently and winced. "It's a good thing we have those cushioned floor mats. They're the only reason I'm not *completely* covered with bruises."

"And there was how much money in the cash drawer?" Joan asked.

"Eighty five dollars."

Anne said what some of the others were thinking. "Y'all, what kind of dumb shit, pardon my French, would rob a charity thrift shop?"

"That's right. If he was going to knock me over the head it should have been for more than eighty-five dollars," Alice said. They were glad she had a sense of humor about it, although no one was laughing.

Anne turned to Laurie. "Last Friday, weren't a couple of the workmen from Anderson's asking about the five hundred dollars we gave the arts center?"

Laurie hadn't wanted to bring it up, but couldn't ignore Anne's question. "Yeah, one of the workmen - Dean, I think his name was - mentioned it. And Chase was there, too." *Please let it not be Chase*, she prayed. *Please, please, please, let it not be Chase*. "Then Bo Anderson came and told them to get back to work."

"Maybe someone thought we always have that kind of money lying around the shop," Alice said.

"Funny you should say that, because there *was* more money in the office," Carol said. "All the money from last week was in one of those bank pouches in the desk drawer. Usually I deposit the money during the week and on Saturday, or someone brings it to me at church," she explained, "but since we closed early Friday, and were closed all day Saturday, no one picked up the money."

"And we're not even talking about the petty cash in the file cabinet, y'all," Anne said. "That money has grown. The last time I totaled it up, there was over a hundred and fifty dollars in there."

"But I checked yesterday, and it's all still there." Carol shrugged, palms upward.

"We can't leave the deposits in the office like that. We're going to be in trouble with the diocese," Joan reminded them. She had been senior warden the year the church was audited, and had had to answer questions from the bishop's office.

"You know, the robber may have intended to search the office," Laurie said. "I was heading there for some tags, but I stopped in the kitchen to turn up the music. Whoever it was probably heard me, took what he could get from the cash drawer, and then ran off. When I heard the bells on the door, I thought it was Anne coming back." She looked at Anne.

"I was just leaving the church, and saw his truck pull away," Anne said. "I thought he was going to stop. I wanted to ask if he found everything, but he just kept going. So I came in, and that's when I saw Laurie here, with her eyes big as saucers, and Alice down on the floor."

"Then Anne called me, and I called Mr. Anderson," Carol said. Everyone looked expectantly at her. "He said some of their tools *were* missing, but he didn't want to call the police yet."

"So what did you do?" Joan asked.

"I called the police!" Carol assured them. "We can't mess around. You know, we're a bunch of women working over there, sometimes just two at a time. I don't want to be the next one knocked in the head for eighty five dollars! I told the police what you told me, and that it might have been someone from Anderson HVAC. I also mentioned the missing tools. I haven't heard anything back yet."

The room was quiet until Evelyn said "And we still don't know who stole that gold ring. That's two robberies."

Laurie glanced around the room at the volunteers, remembering what Mother Barbara had told her about Chase. She wondered if things had improved for him, and prayed again that he hadn't done anything stupid. It didn't seem like him, though. At least, not like the guy she thought she knew.

At the Coffee Pot the previous Friday Chase had said he owed her a latte. Maybe she should claim it, and try to find out more? She hesitated to call, and not just because of her embarrassing stumble on Sunday.

"We have got to do something." Virginia spoke for the first time. "My husband's not wild about me volunteering at the Treasure Chest as it is. I'm afraid to tell him somebody was hit over the head and the store was robbed." The shop couldn't afford to lose any volunteers. Besides that, Laurie liked Virginia, and didn't want to see her quit.

"Y'all, if the shop closed, the church would really be hurting." Anne looked around meaningfully. "I still don't think the rest of the parish understands how much we depend on the money we bring in. Pledges are still down, isn't that right, Carol?"

Carol, who was also the church's treasurer, nodded. "I tried to make that clear at the annual meeting back in January, but I'm not sure it sunk in. And we've spent just about every penny that was in the maintenance fund getting the air conditioning fixed. We don't want to stop contributing to the rector's discretionary fund, but we need to build that maintenance fund back up."

"St. James in Redding just closed," Mary said. "I hope we don't go the same way."

St. James had been one of several Episcopal churches in Redding. Its large endowment kept it going for years, but membership had fallen as the city's population shifted. In recent years the building had hosted scouts, Al-Anon groups, a soup kitchen, and a health clinic. But the diocese decided the congregation was just too small, and closed the church. Now all the other groups were scrambling to find places where they could meet.

Everyone looked glum.

"All right. First thing is, we're going to post a big sign: 'No Cash Kept on the Premises,'" Carol said. "And we're going to stick to it."

As the women continued their discussion, Laurie heard her cell phone buzz, and fished it out of her purse. There was a text from an unfamiliar number.

You working at Treasure Chest today?

Laurie replied: *Closed Wednesdays. Who is this?*

The answer came back: *Jeff - arts center. Have any more frames for us?*

Yes bunches. I'm working Thursday. Laurie held her breath.

"What's up?" Mary asked. "Is that the *Journal?*"

"No. Someone else." Laurie turned her phone over, hiding the screen.

"What are you being so mysterious about? Let me see." Mary mouthed silently *"Chase?"* Laurie shook her head. She had told Mary about Friday night at the café, and Mary warned her again not to get involved.

Mary playfully walked her fingers toward Laurie's phone, pretending to make a grab for it. "You're blushing!" she said, arching her eyebrows.

"Oh, all right. Look." Laurie handed her the phone. "It's Jeff, the guy from the arts center."

"The one with the big blue eyes? Have you met him in person yet?" Mary inquired.

"No."

The phone buzzed again, and Mary read the screen. "Looks like you'll get your chance tomorrow," she said in a sing-song voice. "He wants to come see you at the Treasure Chest."

Mary turned her back to Laurie. She started typing, and Laurie reached over and snatched the phone. Mary laughed as Laurie checked to make certain her friend hadn't actually sent anything.

As Carol summarized suggestions and ended the meeting, Laurie sent a quick text, and grabbed her notebook from the table. Mary rose, humming a familiar-sounding tune, and smiled suggestively at Laurie.

"'*Fools Rush In*'? Really? Is that what you're humming? First of all, he doesn't want to see *me*. He wants to pick up more picture frames. Second of all..."

"Yes?"

"Well, there is no second of all."

"Laurie, Laurie." Mary shook her head. "I'm just trying to help out. Here's an opportunity to meet someone new."

"What?! Who are you, and what have you done with Mary? Weren't you telling me I should stay away from men for a while?"

"Homeless broke ones, sure. Look, I know you're lonely, and I want you to be happy. This guy has a job, he's cute, and he's creative. You always liked creative types. When he stops in, you should ask him out for coffee or something!"

"We'll see," Laurie said. She fanned herself with her notebook. She'd just texted Jeff to drop in at the Treasure Chest Thursday around 12:30. Laurie planned to work from noon to 4:00, but there should be a couple of other volunteers there. She was sure she could get away for "coffee or something." If she had the nerve to ask him.

Chapter 9.

"Did I miss anything important while I was texting?" Laurie turned her car onto Redding Road, and headed toward Mary's house to drop her off. Laurie truly did care about the Treasure Chest. And even if some people didn't realize how much the church depended on the shop's income, she did.

"According to Carol, the police said they'd cruise by more often," Mary recapped. "Also, there was some discussion about who has keys to the shop. It's still just the inner circle, you know, the 'fair-haired' ones," she said making air quotes. She and Laurie both had dark hair.

"I thought I heard some talk about no cash on the premises. How are we supposed to make change?" Laurie wheeled onto Mary's street.

"We're supposed to leave fifty dollars in small bills and change when we close up each day, so we can open in the morning. Hopefully no one will burgle the place for that! And someone will have to go to the bank more often, or put the deposit in the safe at the church." Mary shook her head. "It's going to be more of a hassle."

They were in Mary's driveway. "Stop in for a visit?" she asked.

"For a few minutes, if you'll put some coffee on."

Laurie admired how Mary's kitchen always looked like a picture out of a magazine. She wondered whether her friend would be able to keep it up once the baby arrived. "How's your nursery looking? Didn't you tell me Pete painted it last weekend?

"Yes! I was hoping you would ask." After starting up the coffee maker, Mary led the way down the hall toward the bedrooms. "Here we are!" She held her hands out, beaming. "I did the sailboats."

Laurie admired the room, turning around a couple of times to take in the rocking chair, a white Jenny Lind crib and matching changing table, and the little dresser under the window. The walls were a dove gray, with pale accents of blue and sea green in the curtains. A row of little sailboats was stenciled halfway up one wall. "I don't know how you pulled off this color scheme, but it looks nice. Very soothing."

"I did take a few art classes back in the day, if you'll recall. I might add some mermaids or maybe do seashell stencils on one of the other walls." Smiling, she smoothed a hand over the changing table. "I still need to get bumpers for the crib, but I've got plenty of time yet."

They wandered back to the kitchen and Mary poured a couple of mugs of coffee. As she was getting milk from the refrigerator Laurie noticed a frown on her face. "I sure hope they catch whoever it was who robbed the Treasure Chest. It makes me nervous to know they're still out there. Poor Alice. She's not a spring chicken. She could have been really hurt."

Laurie nodded, sipping her coffee.

"And we have had some really valuable items in that shop!"

"Like what?" Laurie asked smirking.

"You never heard about the emerald necklace we had for a while?" She laughed when Laurie's eyes popped open. "I guess not. This was a couple of years ago, when I had just started volunteering. Carol and I were work-ing in the shop. It was on a Saturday, and an older cou-ple came in - nobody we recognized. They were asking questions like what did we do with the money we make, and were we affiliated with any political party. Of course Carol told them we use the money to pay our bills, you know, the mortgage and electricity, and we give some to the church, and the rest goes to charities like the food pantry and the children's art program at the arts center. So then they handed over a box, and said 'here, maybe you can do something good with this.'

"I opened the box and my eyes nearly fell out of my head. There was a beautiful gold necklace with a sparkling green pendant in a sort-of filigree setting. The guy said, 'Now that's a real Columbian emerald, so you ought to get a good price for it.'"

"An emerald necklace? He just handed you an emerald necklace?" Laurie's eyes were still wide, and her coffee was momentarily forgotten.

"*And* a gold bracelet to go with it! So the first thing we did was to get them appraised. Evelyn has a friend who is a jeweler, plus there's that guy at the pawn shop who's always good about telling people what stuff is worth. Well, they both said not to take less than six hundred dollars for the necklace, and the bracelet was worth another one-fifty or so."

"Good God," Laurie said, still incredulous. "So what happened to them? I mean, who's going to come into a charity thrift shop looking for an emerald necklace?"

"That's exactly what we thought. The bracelet we put into our jewelry case at the shop. We weren't worried about being robbed in those days. We had it for a long time, but eventually did sell it for a hundred and twenty-five. Someone got a bargain on it."

"But the necklace? What did you do with it?"

"Well, it was not too long before Christmas, and someone got the idea to sell raffle tickets and raffle it off.

We put the necklace in the safe over at the church, but we had a picture of it, and sold tickets to anyone who came into the shop and wanted to buy one, and of course we sold tickets to church members and their friends. We had the drawing a couple of weeks before Christmas that year."

"How much did you end up getting for it?"

"Over six hundred dollars from the raffle, which everyone was happy about," Mary said. "We gave five hundred of that straight to the food pantry. So when we say we get anything and everything donated to the Treasure Chest, we're not kidding."

"Amazing," Laurie said setting down her mug. "Well, listen, girlfriend. I've got some errands to take care of. I guess I'll see you this weekend, if not sooner."

"'Kay. Have fun tomorrow! Don't let Jeff paint you into a corner, or anything," Mary quipped.

"Ha-ha. I guess I'll be hearing art jokes now."

Mary laughed, and Laurie headed home. *Errands,* she thought. *Right. Nuking supper, and planning what I'll wear tomorrow.*

Laurie had been carefully conserving her part of the proceeds from the sale of her and DB's house up north. Her expenses rarely left much in her budget for extras, and she hadn't shopped for a brand new outfit since the divorce, not counting a few pairs of shorts and tee shirts she got after moving south.

Back at her apartment, she took stock in her closet. She had at least bought some cute things from the Treasure Chest. She pushed aside a few blouses, selected a red and white print one, and held it up in front of the mirror, admiring the way it set off her dark brown hair.

She always looked good in red. White too, for that matter, if only she could keep things white. White clothing usually ended up some pastel or other, depending on what else she threw in the washing machine with it. She told herself it was because washing was expensive now that she had to pay for every load. Truth to tell, though, she'd had the same problem when the laundry machines were in her own house. Her laundry skills were nothing to brag about.

And that was another reason to be glad she was shed of DB. She could never meet his laundry and housekeeping standards. Or his mother's, for that matter. Despite all of Mary's coaching and encouragement, Laurie never could measure up to their expectations.

For six years when she could have been building her career she had played house maid to DB, and piddled around at the weekly paper in their little bedroom community writing advertising copy. At least there she occasionally covered a rotary meeting or a school play, and got her byline in the newspaper. But now, when she had a chance to start over, she was just cleaning up the events column, answering the phones, and doing clerical work. Laurie sighed.

She dug in the old jewelry chest on her dresser looking for a necklace to go with her outfit. She was just shaking her head over Mary's story about the emerald necklace when a gleam of gold in the back of the box caught her eye. Reaching in deeper, she withdrew a heavy round pocket watch. She recognized it immediately. It was the watch DB's parents had given him when he got his master's degree. How it had wound up in her jewelry box, she had no idea.

She popped open the case and read the inscription. "The mind once enlightened cannot again become dark." She had always liked the quote, and tried to remember who had said it: maybe Benjamin Franklin, or Thomas Paine, or one of the other patriots from the founding of the country. She closed the case again, and admired the filigree on the outside.

She started to put it back into the jewelry box, but then set it aside. She knew the right thing to do would be to call DB, let him know she had it, and offer to mail it back. When she felt up to it.

* * *

Laurie sped through her work at the *Journal* Thursday and got to the Treasure Chest just after noon. Joan was sorting through a box of kitchen items while Carol waited on a customer. Laurie stashed her purse, and went down the hall to the eclectic room to look for picture frames.

Quickly she did a U-turn, and went to the staff kitchen for the broom and dustpan. "I saw one of our six-legged friends on the floor doing the back stroke," she explained.

"They seem to show up every time it rains," Carol said. "I had to run around mopping up some wet spots on the floor when I came in this morning. This roof..." she trailed off, shaking her head.

Laurie nodded, and returned to the eclectic room. She swept the floor, gathered the debris in the dustpan, and addressed the insect. "Don't go anywhere." Then she leaned the broom against the wall and started opening cabinets.

The eclectic room contained an assortment of items including office supplies, home décor, and knick-knacks. Built-ins along one wall held books for sale on the shelves on top, and the cabinets below were crammed with out-of-season merchandise.

Fall and Halloween decor filled the first cabinet Laurie opened. The next contained Valentine's Day items. In the third cabinet Laurie hit pay-dirt - varying sizes of picture frames. There were always too many to put them all out for sale. She hauled out over a dozen and laid them on the floor. Several still had pictures in them.

Laurie examined the pictures one by one. The first looked like an old paint-by-number. A faint smell of linseed oil clung to it. The second was a pencil drawing of a running horse.

The third, a watercolor, was under glass in an attractive wooden frame with a hanging wire stretched across the back. Palm trees leaned sinuously over an indistinct but lush tropical landscape, with turquoise water in the foreground. Laurie lingered over the painting admiring the vibrant colors, the vivid blue sky, and the sense of motion in the trees. The scene reminded her of a long-ago vacation on the Gulf Coast of Florida.

The distant jangle of the door brought her out of her reverie. Laurie emptied the dustpan and put away the broom. Then she found a cardboard box for the picture frames, and hauled them to the front where Carol was making change for a customer.

"Did I tell you Jeff from the arts center is coming by this afternoon? I told him we had more picture frames for them. These were in the cupboards in the eclectic room. I'm going to look for some others."

"Fine with me," Carol said glancing in the box.

Laurie pulled out the tropical watercolor and held it up. "I wasn't sure about this one. What do you think?" She tilted the painting toward the light. "It's kind of pretty," Laurie said. "I think it's a watercolor, but I don't know much about art. I don't see a signature or anything."

"I remember this picture. My boss brought this in." Carol still worked three days a week as a billing clerk at Marshall's law firm. She looked at the painting through her bifocals. "He brought boxes of things over after his father-in-law passed. You said this was in a cabinet?"

"Yep. In the eclectic room with a bunch of picture frames."

Carol clicked her tongue. "Evelyn must have been 'cleaning' again. She's always throwing things away, or hiding them, or putting them in the back after we've put them out to sell." She paused. "But I can't imagine it's worth anything, or the Marshall's wouldn't have just given it to us. Maybe Jeff can tell us something about it, but as far as I'm concerned, the arts center can have it."

Laurie set it back in the box, and scouted the store for more picture frames. Then she helped Carol at the counter. As they rang up clothing for a customer, Carol said

"I don't know if you heard at the meeting, but starting Saturday all bathing suits are going to be half price. Will you put something on Facebook about it?"

"Sure," Laurie answered. "Ladies'? Kids'? All swimsuits?"

"All of them. And cover-ups and flip-flops too. I don't know how you're going to say all that."

"Never fear. One picture is worth a thousand words. I'll set something up to add to the post." Laurie's posts always featured an interesting photo or some clip art.

Gathering a couple of colorful ladies' swimsuits, a pair of swim trunks, and a cute child's suit, she arranged them on the sales counter. She selected a pair of sunglasses from a basket nearby, and laced them through the shoulder strap of one of the swimsuits.

"I just put a price on these. Want to use them?" Carol offered a pair of hot pink flip-flops, which Laurie added to the display.

She grabbed her phone and took a look at the arrangement with the camera app. "It looks great except for the peg board behind the counter. Hmmm." She looked around a moment.

As Carol watched, Laurie grabbed a turquoise cover-up from a clothing rack and draped it over the peg board. Then she pulled the tropical watercolor out of the box of picture frames, and hung it where it was visible behind the swimsuits.

She checked the arrangement again. "Perfect!" She snapped a couple of pictures, and in a moment had posted one on the Treasure Chest Facebook page.

Laurie handed her phone to Carol. "What do you think?"

Carol read aloud. "'Surf's up! Shop the Treasure Chest before you hit the beach. All swimwear and beach items half price starting Saturday.' That's great! And that painting really sets it off."

"I love a happy customer!" Laurie carried her phone back into the office to show Joan, but shoved it into her purse as the shop door jangled and Jeff walked in.

Carol greeted him with a smile. "Well, hey! It's nice to see you again."

"Carol! How are you?" He reached across the counter and shook her hand. "I wanted to see where our angels live! Thank you again for your contribution to the arts center."

"You're quite welcome. You haven't been here before, have you?"

Laurie came out of the office and stood beside Carol. "Hi. I'm Laurie Lanton." She extended her hand.

"Jeff Williams. Nice to meet you." His handshake was firm and warm. His eyes were a bright cobalt blue, and his smile was more than charming, it was enthralling. Reluctantly, Laurie pulled her hand away.

"Why don't you show him around the shop?" Carol suggested.

Laurie walked around the counter feeling awkward. "You never know what you'll find here. The items change from week to week, but we have a little something for everybody."

She led him through the shop pointing out the men's clothing and eclectic room. Jeff glanced politely around, spent a few minutes looking at some craft supplies, and studied the books for sale.

While he looked, Laurie studied him, mentally comparing him to his photos, and wondering if he worked out. She didn't think painting pictures would put such muscles on a man. She was having second thoughts about her second-hand outfit, until she noticed paint on his blue jeans.

Still, Laurie suddenly felt defensive about the thrift shop. "We're a self-supporting ministry of St. Mark's. We provide quality items at low prices. And since the Treasure Chest opened we've made donations to the food pantry, the animal shelter, the arts center, and several other organizations in Chinkapin."

Jeff smiled at her again, making her catch her breath. "This place is bigger than it looks from the outside," he commented. "What were all these rooms originally? Classrooms? Or studios?"

"Uh, no. This was a doctor's office, so - exam rooms, a waiting room, reception and billing - that kind of stuff. Now and then a customer tells us they used to see the doctor here. Of course that was before my time. I've only been in Chinkapin for a few months."

"So you're new to the area." He turned to her again, and again she noted the blue of his eyes. She had planned to ask him for coffee, but was losing her nerve.

"Yep. I wasn't born in the South, but I got here as quick as I could." She smiled. It wasn't really true, but she thought it sounded better than telling people in Georgia that she came from the same state as U. S. Grant and General Sherman.

"Let me show you what we have for you. Or for the arts center, I mean." Laurie led him back to the checkout counter. Part of her wanted to gaze into those blue eyes, and part wanted to hand Jeff the box of frames and shove him out the door.

She reached for the box, which was behind the counter. "Here, let me get that," Jeff said. As he took the box from her she glanced inside. Suddenly the donation looked skimpy.

"Wait. There's one more." She pulled the watercolor down from the peg board. "You might as well take this too. We don't seem to sell many paintings."

He put the box of frames on the counter and took the painting, setting it on top of the others. He looked at it intently. Finally he asked "Has this been in the shop long?"

Carol answered. "A couple of weeks. It was in a box of things that belonged to my boss's father-in-law. The family had it for years and years."

"Hmmm," Jeff said nodding. "Looks like the Caribbean, or maybe somewhere in Florida. I wonder..."

He was still looking at the painting when the bell on the door behind him jangled and Alice walked in. "Here I am," she said. "And what are you all up to?"

Laurie glanced at her watch. It was just before 1:00. She knew this was her chance to ask, but she hesitated, and her brain felt muddled again. "Um..."

Carol jumped in. "Alice, this is Jeff Williams from the Chinkapin Arts Center. He stopped in to pick up some picture frames."

The two shook hands. "Laurie was kind enough to show me around your shop. We were just going out for coffee." He looked hopefully at Laurie, eyebrows raised.

Laurie stared. Then she smiled. "Yes, we were!"

Chapter 10.

On shaky legs Laurie darted into the office, grabbed her purse, and dashed out the door as Jeff loaded the box into the back of his SUV.

"Of course if you have other plans, I'd take a rain check," Jeff said.

"As it happens, I'm totally free. Where did you have in mind?"

"The Coffee Pot. Where else? I guess you know where it is, across from the old courthouse? Meet you there in a few minutes." Jeff said, and flashed that warm smile.

Laurie preceded him out of the parking lot. She managed to parallel-park in front of the café without embarrassing herself, and waited on the sidewalk. For a moment she thought of the open mic last Friday and the evening stroll with Chase. Then Jeff was at her side. "Ready?" he said, and opened the door for her.

After scanning the menu a moment, Jeff got a black coffee and an espresso brownie. Laurie ordered her favorite latte and a bagel with pimiento cheese, since breakfast seemed forever ago. She took a slow deep breath. "The smell of coffee always seems to calm me down."

"Funny. I feel that way about the smell of paint. It makes me relax."

"You won't be relaxed after that black coffee and espresso brownie!"

Jeff laughed. "I like my caffeine with a little sugar on the side."

They took their coffee to a table where they waited for their food. "I read your bio on a flyer from the arts center," Laurie said. "I understand your parents were photographers."

"Yes, they were. Well, my mother still is, of course. Dad just passed away a couple of months ago."

"I'm sorry." Laurie hoped she hadn't opened a painful subject.

"Well, it happens. He was older than Mother, but still." He looked at his hands and scraped some paint off a fingernail. "That's why I'm here. Helping Mother go through everything. She wants to put the house on the market and move up near my sister in Knoxville. She wants to be able to enjoy the grandkids."

"Do you think her house will sell quickly?"

"I don't know. It's one of the big Victorians on King Street, so it needs a buyer who's willing to take on all the upkeep a house like that needs." He sighed. "I'll have to get some tradesmen in to work on a few things."

"Lucky you could get away from work, or whatever you had going on." Laurie was curious, but didn't want to seem nosy.

"Well, I was ready for something new. I was the fine art director at a small gallery north of Atlanta. I curated a bunch of shows there, and founded a community arts festival. Seemed like my responsibilities kept increasing, but my salary never did, even after I finished my degree." His shoulders sagged. "So it wasn't too hard to leave the gallery behind. When I got to Chinkapin I stopped in at the arts center, and offered to teach a few classes there. We'll see how long I stay around."

"You don't have any firm plans, then?"

Jeff narrowed his eyes. "Am I being interviewed here? I'm not running for public office, you know."

Laurie laughed, hoping she wasn't blushing as usual. "I guess my journalism training is showing. In school we were encouraged to ask questions, but I've been told I interrogate people when I think I'm just making conversation." The server arrived with their food, and Laurie busied herself with her bagel, pulling it apart and taking a bite. *Harder to put your foot in your mouth when there's food in it*, she thought.

DB had often accused her of interrogating him. Her ex never liked to be questioned about his whereabouts, or what he was doing. He always made Laurie feel she was not being trusting enough.

"That's okay." The scowl was gone and Jeff was smiling again. He took a bite of his brownie and chewed for a moment. "I haven't made firm plans. I'd like to own a gallery of my own somewhere. Really it depends on selling the house. That may take a while, especially to get what I want - that is, what Mother wants - for it. Maybe one of her cronies at the Presbyterian church will buy it."

"So you're Presbyterian then," Laurie said matter-of-factly. She knew there was a big Presbyterian church on Main Street, a couple of blocks beyond the courthouse. Immediately she wished she could retract her statement. Jeff would probably think she was grilling him again.

"Well..." Jeff took another bite of brownie and shook his head, waving his fork around. "I'm not sure I can swallow all the doctrine. This brownie is really good, by the way," he said, changing the subject. "So what brought you to Chinkapin?"

"Oh, you know. Or maybe you don't know." She blurted out, "Have you ever been married?" She realized too late she was grilling him again. And what an awkward question! But he just shook his head, so she rushed on. "Well, I was, for six years, until my former true-love-until-death-do-us-part decided he liked someone else better. So - surprise! Suddenly not married anymore!" Laurie couldn't seem to stop babbling. "And Mary - she works at the Treasure Chest too. We've been friends since middle school, but she's lived here with her husband for several years. She convinced me to move here. New start, new state, everything."

"Ah-hah," Jeff said, watching her with an amused smile. "Well I'm glad you're here. And did you say you're a journalist?"

"Well, sort of. I studied journalism in college. And I just started working part time for the *Journal*. What I really want to do is write fiction."

"So why don't you?" he asked.

Laurie squirmed, thinking about what a procrastinator she was. "Actually, I do have a couple of things in the works," she exaggerated. She'd spent some late nights at her laptop, and written a few scenes for a novel. "And I just joined a writers group in Redding." At least that part was true - she had been to one meeting. "But don't look for my book in the library any time soon."

"I'd love to read your stuff sometime," he said. "Creative people are the best, aren't they?" Jeff finished his brownie and looked down for the napkin in his lap.

"Wow. It looks like I was in a paintball fight this morning. I didn't realize how much paint I got on myself."

"What have you been working on?" she asked.

"Trying to get a few paintings ahead for Art Night Out. I teach a different painting every Friday." He turned to her, eyebrows raised. "You should totally come!"

Laurie protested. "I got an F in elementary school art class."

"No special skills required. It's fun, and we supply everything, including refreshments. Look." He pulled out his smart phone. "This is what we're painting this Friday." He showed her a picture of a mare and a foal running in a pasture, with blue sky, trees, and a white board fence in the background.

"And here's the one I was working on this morning, hence all the yellow and orange paint on my jeans." A bright field of sunflowers extended across the canvas.

"Wow. These are nice," Laurie said. She swiped her finger across the screen looking at more paintings. "You really did all these?"

"Are you surprised?" Jeff sat up straight, pretending to be offended, and looked down his nose at her.

"Oh, no." She looked at the images again. "So what do you paint just for fun, when it's not for a class or something?"

Jeff sighed, and Laurie looked up, surprised to see a dispirited look on his face. "I hardly know anymore. If I want to keep up with my bills, I can't spend much time painting for fun."

She handed back his phone, and tried to sound encouraging. "Well, I would never be able to paint like this."

"Au contraire, ma chérie," he said. Suddenly he leaned close and looked deeply into her eyes. "Let me show you just how talented you are." He waggled his eyebrows comically, and looked at her through incredible lashes.

For a moment Laurie was unable to breathe. Her eyes were locked on his.

Jeff sat back to glance at his watch, and air returned to Laurie's lungs. "Like I said, this Friday we'll do the painting of the two horses." He stood and moved away from the table, tugging at his pant legs and smiling boyishly. "I should go back to the arts center. I left things in kind of a mess."

Still flustered, Laurie wiped imaginary crumbs from her lips and reached for her purse. Out on the sidewalk, she thanked him for stopping by the thrift shop. Then a thought flashed through her mind.

"Wait a minute," she said. "What if I write an article about you for the *Journal*?" Her heart pounded. She wasn't at all sure the editor would approve, but her mind was moving fast. "You know, a feature story about the new artist in town, and put in a plug for Art Night Out. Classes like that are all the rage. It would be good publicity for the arts center. And I'd love to see my by-line in a newspaper again." She gave him what she hoped was a persuasive smile.

"Sounds great to me. Come to the class on Friday." With a quick wave he crossed the street, and in a moment his SUV pulled away.

Laurie moved toward her car. Her mind was full of questions to ask and angles to consider. This type of art class did seem to be a popular pastime lately. She needed to do some research. Or should she go back to the Treasure Chest? *When in doubt, drink more coffee*, she thought, and returned to the café.

Chapter 11.

Fueled by caffeine, Laurie drove home and peered into the apartment building's first-floor laundry room. The washing machines were completely full. Reluctantly she dragged her laundry and her laptop to the laundromat in town.

After cramming everything into a washer, Laurie fired up her laptop to do some research for the article she was planning to write. She wanted to find out just how popular this type of painting class was, and details about some other studios and galleries in the area. She had ideas of possibly expanding the article into a larger feature about the trend in general.

Forty minutes later, she put the wet clothes in a dryer, and let her mind drift back to her meeting with Jeff. He was every bit as good looking as his photographs. She ticked off the items on her "perfect-man" checklist. Educated? Check. Employed? Sort-of. Right age? Truth be told, she thought he might be a year or two younger than she, but what did that matter these days? Family-oriented? Well, he apparently had a sense of duty, and was here when his mother needed him. Laurie definitely liked a man who took care of his family.

Too bad he isn't Episcopalian, she thought.

Laurie wasn't what they called a "cradle Episcopalian," having grown up in a different denomination, but when she was a child church had felt like a second home to her. She loved the candles and the flowers near the altar, the mighty organ, the choir, and the stained glass windows. She even remembered the paintings in the Sunday school room - the gentle Virgin in her blue robes, and the good shepherd carrying the lamb.

Church was never a part of her lazy Sunday mornings with DB. And after the divorce, when she tried joining a church before moving south, it just didn't seem welcoming. Maybe it was just her, but Laurie had felt awkward with the singles group. She wasn't accepted by the married women either. They seemed cold and distrustful because Laurie was a divorcée.

At St. Mark's no one seemed to care whether she was divorced or not. And married people didn't always attend church as a couple. Everyone was welcome, and everyone was treated the same. Though they might disagree with each other on some points of dogma, they were united by that beautiful prayer book.

But what was it Jeff had said? He couldn't swallow the doctrine? Well, there were a few things Laurie had a hard time comprehending. But somehow, when she let her doubts get the better of her, she felt like something precious had been taken from her. Then she would set aside the doubt, and trust again, and all was right with the world.

The dryer buzzed, and brought Laurie back to the laundromat. She dragged her clothes out of the dryer, folded and stuffed them into the clean laundry bag, and headed for home.

Stopping for the traffic light at the corner of Main and King Street, Laurie thought about the Victorian house Jeff's mother was selling. Impulsively she turned and drove slowly up the street, scanning lawns for a *for sale* sign.

Then she saw it - a beautiful three-story wooden mansion with a wide porch and tall double doors. Elaborate woodwork decorated the porch and the gables. Laurie was sure if she went inside she would find high ceilings, plenty of fireplaces, oak or chestnut woodwork, and heart pine floors.

Around the back she saw some kind of outbuilding, and a dark SUV like Jeff's. She sped up, hoping he hadn't seen her. Glancing again toward the yard, she noticed an older woman gathering hydrangeas.

Laurie wove through some back streets and finally arrived at her apartment. Such a difference, in just a few blocks! Her nearest neighbors were a pawn shop on one side and a store-front evangelical church on the other. She wheeled into the lot at the back and found a parking spot.

Laurie popped the trunk to retrieve her laundry, but quickly ducked behind the trunk lid. A man had just gotten out of a beat-up car parked one row over. She watched as he approached the apartment building, and waited until the door closed behind him. Then, holding her laundry bag so it blocked her face, she dashed in and up the stairs, taking refuge in her apartment.

She had no idea what he was doing there, but she had just seen Chase enter her apartment building.

Chapter 12.

The next morning Laurie peeked out the door at the apartment's parking lot. There was no sign of the car Chase had arrived in the previous evening. Feeling foolish, she drove the short distance to the *Journal* office, and got a cup of brew from the communal pot.

She pondered a moment over her plan to write an article about Jeff's art classes. After all, she had been hired just to work on the events column. The paper didn't take many articles from free-lancers. But Laurie knew she had writing talent. She sighed over how rusty her skills had grown, and all the time wasted when she was married to DB. Finally she scrawled a note about the article she hoped to write and left it in the editor's empty office. Then she got comfortable at her desk.

Considering the short amount of time Laurie had been working at the *Journal,* she had collected a surprising number of pens. Most of them bore the logos of *Journal* advertisers, and they were stuffed in a large mug that read "Given enough coffee, I could rule the world." Likewise, she had several small tablets for jotting notes, all bearing company logos and slogans. The only other things on her desk were a telephone and a laptop – a much nicer laptop than the one she owned.

She picked up a copy of the morning's paper to check if the events column looked okay, but a photo on the front page stopped her cold. It showed a familiar-looking young man with curly, light-brown hair. She read the accompanying article twice. "Thank God it wasn't Chase," she breathed.

For the next few hours Laurie flew through her daily tasks. To her delight her boss approved her proposed article about Art Night Out, and even spent some time chatting with her about it. After work she drove straight to the Treasure Chest to share the morning's news.

Evelyn and Anne were behind the counter when Laurie sailed through the door waving her newspaper. "Did you see the article in the *Journal? 'Man arrested after foot pursuit in Chinkapin'*?"

"No. Who was arrested?" Evelyn asked. Then her eyes widened. "Oh! The guy who parted Alice's hair Tuesday?"

"The very same," Laurie said. "Listen to this. 'A foot pursuit following a traffic stop resulted in the arrest of a Chinkapin man.'" She scanned quickly down the column. "Blah-blah-blah, 'Sheriff's office said a vehicle was speeding on Interstate 75 and was pulled over by Deputy Paul Jones at approximately 3:30 p.m.'

"Let's see... 'The driver, Bo Anderson, 27, of Chinkapin...'"

Anne and Evelyn exchanged a glance, mirroring raised eyebrows and a look of surprise. "Remember Mr. Anderson didn't want Carol to call the police right away?" Anne said. The two nodded, and Laurie continued.

"'Bo Anderson, 27, of Chinkapin, got out of the vehicle and fled on foot toward Walmart, where he was apprehended. Deputies on the scene searched the vehicle and found some items which are part of an ongoing investigation.'" Laurie lowered the newspaper. "The tools, perhaps?"

"There's more." She continued reading. "'Anderson was charged with speeding, financial transaction card theft, *and* possession of a firearm by a *convicted felon*.'"

"Wow. He's in deep trouble," Evelyn said. "I'm glad he didn't use the firearm when he robbed us." She laughed nervously.

"Right? All he needed was to add armed robbery to the other charges," Anne said.

"I'm glad the police caught him," Evelyn admitted. "I felt a little nervous coming into work today, after what happened. So many people are messed up these days, I'll tell you." A customer laid a pair of jeans next to the cash register and joined their discussion about the sad state of the world.

Humming a cheerful tune, Laurie looked around the shop to see what needed attention. She felt light-hearted. She still wondered what Chase was doing at her apartment building the previous evening, but thank goodness it wasn't hiding out from the law.

Her phone buzzed. She was surprised to see a text from Jeff: *Help! Sharon bailed on me. Need help setting up tonight. Come at 6:30? I'll make it worth your while...*

Laurie had planned to attend Art Night as research for her article. She wasn't all that interested in painting, but she was interested in Jeff. She wondered what he meant when he said he'd make it worth her while.

She texted back: *Sure. See you at 6:30.*

The afternoon went by quickly as Laurie tagged clothes and hung them in the back room. As she worked, she shopped for a "new" outfit. She tried on a few things and settled on a pair of tan shorts and a white cotton peasant top with navy embroidery.

When Laurie put the "closed" sign in the shop window at 4:00, she was ravenous, and sped home for a bite to eat. Then she changed into her new outfit, and looked in her jewelry box for something to go with it. Suddenly she was sick of the jewelry DB had given her over the years. Most of it was costume junk, and she just wanted it out of her life. She selected a simple birthstone necklace her mother had given her, fluffed her hair, and applied her favorite lipstick. Then she grabbed a notebook and a couple of pens and drove to the arts center.

The front door was unlocked and all the lights were on, but the building was quiet. In the lofty gallery Laurie saw a couple of standing easels, and tables set in rows. There were paintbrushes and paper towels on each table, along with easels holding canvases primed with sky blue acrylic paint.

She placed a hand over the middle of her stomach hoping to still the butterflies, and took a deep breath. "Hello," she called.

"Hey! I'm in the kitchen." Jeff appeared in the kitchen doorway, and quickly disappeared again. Laurie followed, and found him behind a pile of grocery bags. His dark, wavy hair looked windblown. "I just came from the store," he said. "Sharon usually handles the snacks. I hope I've remembered everything."

"I'd say more than everything. It looks like you're serving a buffet dinner."

"Maybe I have overdone it." He laughed at himself. "Here, help me set up the refreshments. Plastic cups on this end." He handed her a package. "Beverages will go next to them. I'll start getting the snacks out."

Laurie set out stacks of cups, and arrayed soda bottles and jugs of iced tea next to them. "Ice?"

"There's an ice machine in the mop closet. How about filling that little cooler over there."

Jeff set out paper plates, napkins, and a plate of cubed cheese. He extracted a platter of cookies from a plastic bag and set it in the middle of the table. "Look in the cupboard up there for a plate. We'll put out some olives and pickles and stuff." Glancing at his watch, he said "Good grief! Here, do something with these. I've got to get the paint ready."

He left Laurie alone to finish. She opened the jars he'd indicated and made up a small platter, snacking on pickled okra as she worked. She poked her head out into the gallery again, counting easels to get an idea how many people would be there. Jeff was squeezing dollops of acrylic paint onto paper plates.

"Hey, do you have crackers, or anything?" she asked.

"Damn!" He struck his forehead with the heel of his palm. Laurie was glad he didn't get paint on his face. "Look around in the cupboards. Maybe there are some left from earlier this week."

Laurie opened cupboards at random, and found a box of wheat crackers and some cheesy goldfish. She added them to the buffet, and tweaked the layout. She had hosted many receptions for DB's oh-so-important coworkers, so this was easy.

She returned to the gallery to watch Jeff's final preparations, taking notes and snapping a few photos. At seven fifteen people started to arrive. They took seats or strolled around the gallery examining paintings for sale.

Jeff set palettes in front of most of the easels. "I don't want to put out more paint than we need," he told Laurie. "We have reservations for eighteen tonight, but we usually have a few walk-ins. Can you help, if more people arrive? All you have to do is grab the tubes of paint and squeeze some of each color onto a Styrofoam plate, like this." He indicated the plate near the easel where she was standing, and Laurie nodded. He looked at her white blouse. "Go in the classroom and get an apron. I don't want you to hate me if your clothes are ruined."

Obedient as usual, she went to the classroom and found a bib apron where he had indicated. She appreciated his thoughtfulness. He didn't have to know she'd only paid four dollars for the blouse.

As she put the apron on, her eye fell on the box of frames and pictures she had given him at the thrift shop the day before. The tropical watercolor was still on top. The colors were beautiful - so clear and fresh. And there was something about the scene that was at once peaceful and alive. She was sorry she hadn't bought the picture to brighten up her dull apartment.

Out in the gallery Laurie heard Jeff greeting some guests, so she returned to mingle and chat. Several people were grouped around the tall easel set up in front of the tables, admiring Jeff's painting of the two horses.

Laurie noticed she was one of the few painters who appeared to be there by herself. There were an older couple, a grandmother and her granddaughter, a pair of siblings and a few others who appeared about high-school age, and several groups of friends, a few of whom looked like they had already been enjoying some liquid refreshments.

Jeff took Laurie aside. "Looks like we'll need three more plates of paint. Can you fix them up, and put them wherever people sit?" All the materials were on a rolling cart outside the classroom. Using her own as an example, she carefully squeezed out dollops of paint onto three Styrofoam plates.

"Okay, everyone," Jeff said, calling for their attention. "If you'll find a seat by an easel, we're ready to get started." He paused as people settled at the tables. "My name is Jeff, and this is my lovely assistant, Laurie." He flourished a hand in her direction, and Laurie waved.

It was interesting to watch Jeff lead the class, demonstrating on the primed canvas set up next to his finished example. He told jokes as he worked, exchanged banter with the students, and between times wandered among them, checking their progress and answering questions.

Laurie felt distinctly out of her element. The last time she had painted was with a roller, on the walls in her old house. She wasn't even sure how to hold the brush. She followed along, poking and dabbing at her canvas as Jeff described what paint to use and what shapes to make, but whatever she did, it didn't look much like a horse.

Jeff made a few suggestions to the woman next to her, and then stopped behind Laurie. She looked over her shoulder, caught him smirking, and shook her head. "I can't do this."

"No, no. It's fine. Curve this around here." He took her brush, and changed the line on the back end of the mare. Instantly it looked - well, not anatomically correct, but at least she could tell what it was supposed to be.

Jeff moved on among the students. "Remember, the beauty of acrylics is you can paint over something if you don't like it." He returned to his easel.

Laurie was glad when Jeff announced break time. It grew noisy in the gallery as people grabbed refreshments and strolled around inspecting each other's artwork. Laurie wandered among the tables scrutinizing the paintings. Suddenly Jeff was beside her. "Are you enjoying yourself?"

"I'm finding it a little frustrating. I think I'm putting the paint where it should go, but my painting doesn't look right."

"Don't expect it to look like a photograph. And every now and then, stand up and take a look from a distance. If you're too close it's just pigment on canvas."

Laurie walked back to her own painting. Jeff was right. From a distance it looked a bit more like a horse. She thought about her own life - up close, just a stream of mundane acts, individually meaningless. But if you stepped back from it to view it as a whole... She wondered what the grand sweep of her life would look like from a distance.

Jeff resumed his spot at the front of the gathering. "Okay, everyone, find your seats again please." He began instructions on painting the foal.

Laurie kept at it, but grew increasingly dissatisfied. Finally she decided her painting would have just one horse in it. She was okay with the way the mare looked, and didn't want to ruin the picture by blobbing more paint on it. She covered over her attempt at the foal with green paint, hoping it would look like grass.

She left her seat and observed the people around her. The high school students were the most serious, listening intently to Jeff's instruction and quietly working away, occasionally comparing paintings.

The four women at the front table were the loudest. More than once Laurie had seen the flash of a hip flask tipping over their cups of soda. They flirted with Jeff, calling him "Sugar". Laurie noted that he seemed to really enjoy the attention, and flirted right back.

Finally Jeff made an announcement. "As you're finishing up, please help yourselves to more snacks. If you want to continue with your painting at home, here's a list of the paints we've been using. Feel free to take one. And be sure you check out the paintings we'll be doing at upcoming Art Nights. They're all on display in the lobby."

The volume went up again as chairs scraped on the floor and people snacked and compared paintings. Laurie spoke to several of the painters. She explained about the article she was writing for the *Journal*, asked a few questions, and jotted down their names and comments about the class.

"Before you leave, would you all please bring your paintings and line up over here? I'd like to get a group photo." Jeff indicated a raised platform at the end of the gallery. Some stood on the platform, others on the floor, and a few sat on chairs in front. "Laurie, would you do the honors?" he asked, handing her a camera.

Laurie composed the image in the viewfinder, noting again how photogenic Jeff was. She snapped several pictures with the camera, and a couple more with her cell phone.

Students gathered their personal items and departed in small groups. The rowdy gang of girlfriends was the last to leave. Laurie kept her eye on a strawberry blonde who didn't seem able to talk to Jeff without touching him. Laurie walked among the tables, gathering trash and eavesdropping on their conversation. At last the women left, and Jeff noticed her cleaning up. "Thank you so much for helping me. I've got to visit with everyone, but really, I just want to get off my feet."

Quickly he gathered all the brushes and put them in a pan of water. "We can leave the tables and chairs out, but I need to put the paints away." He cleaned the paint tubes and checked the seals, and then rolled the cart with the supplies into the classroom. Laurie followed to put away her apron. Again the tropical watercolor caught her eye.

"The more I look at this painting the more I like it," she said, holding it up. "I wish I could paint this way."

Jeff moved closer, putting a hand on the picture frame. Laurie could feel his breath on her hair. Her shoulder brushed his chest. She wanted to lean her body against his. "I could give you some private lessons," he said. Her pulse quickened. She looked up, and found him smiling. The five-o'clock shadow on his cheeks made him look rough and exciting.

He looked at the painting again. "I'd like to show this to an instructor in Atlanta, to see if she can tell me more about it." He took it from her hands and set it down on top of a book on American painters. "Hey, you know what we should do?" he asked.

She looked into his eyes. "What?" she asked, breathlessly.

"Put away that stuff in the kitchen, and go somewhere we can relax."

Laurie felt too wired to relax. She made short work of capping bottles, stashing plates and cups, and washing up, while Jeff refrigerated left over food.

Finally the kitchen was tidy. "Fancy a beer? We could run over to Rancher's," Jeff said.

"Sounds great," Laurie lied. She actually didn't like beer much, but she wanted to spend more time with Jeff. "I live out that direction. Maybe we can drop off my car, and ride together."

She gave him directions to her apartment, and glanced nervously in the rearview mirror as he followed her down the main drag. Suddenly she swerved. Her car had drifted over the yellow line. Glad he wasn't there to see her blush, she forced herself not to look in the mirror again until she parked her car outside her apartment.

Margaret Rodeheaver

When he arrived she hopped into his SUV, and minutes later the two were at the restaurant.

Chapter 13.

Rancher's was a western-themed steakhouse near the interstate. The only steakhouse in Chinkapin, it was popular for dinner, and Laurie had eaten there once with Mary and Pete. She'd never been there this late on a Friday night, though, and never in the bar. Jeff led Laurie to a booth in a corner and they ordered a couple of beers.

As they waited for their drinks, Laurie looked around at the other patrons. Tonight the clientele was different from the usual couples out for a nice dinner. Men in boots and jeans leaned against the bar, heavy key chains spilling out of their pockets. The women seemed a little too "fixed up," wearing tight clothing, low-cut blouses, and heavy eye make-up. Laurie felt underdressed and childish in her shorts and peasant blouse.

Jeff took a long pull on his beer and sank deeper into the cushioned bench. "So you enjoyed the class?" he asked.

Actually, she hadn't. She'd found painting awkward and frustrating. She chalked it up to inexperience, and avoided answering directly. "You have such a knack for teaching," she said. "You're so relaxed with the students. They liked your jokes. And some of their paintings were really impressive!"

"We had a good turnout tonight."

"What else do you teach at the arts center?" Laurie asked, remembering the article she planned to write. She started to dig in her purse for her notebook, but decided against it.

"I teach one of the weekday painting classes, and the occasional party. There's also a weekly sketching session held at the Chinkapin library that Sharon and I alternate leading. That doesn't pay anything, other than donations, but it's usually enough to make the evening worthwhile." He shrugged. "I should sketch more anyway."

"Are you into photography at all?"

"Funny you should ask that. I was thinking about it recently. You know, I inherited a bunch of photography equipment from Dad. Thing is, it's all the old-school stuff. It's primo equipment - if I wanted to shoot with film. But all the commercial photographers have gone digital. If I did photography, it would be for the cash, so I'll probably just sell the equipment. I don't want to sound mercenary, but I have loans to pay off. Art school wasn't cheap. What I'd like to do is open my own place, sort of a combination gallery and frame shop, if I can get the funds together." He picked at the label on his beer bottle.

"It's hard earning a living in the arts. People in the writers group in Redding were talking about that last time." She smiled sympathetically. "Maybe you can sell more paintings - find some rich clients who need portraits done. Or who need a portrait of their poodle, or something."

He laughed. "Trust me - I've done a few of those, especially when my bank account was gasping. There's money in painting pets and children." He pointed his bottle at her. "And in painting houses. Not walls, and things, I mean house portraits. I had a friend who sort-of specialized in that. It's popular with the folks who own historic homes, like Mother's, or like some of the houses up in Redding."

Laurie waited for Jeff to say something else, but he grew silent. It occurred to her that he hadn't asked her anything about herself. He'd seemed so personable and chatty with his students, but now she felt like she had to pull the conversation out of him. Maybe he was just tired.

She glanced over at the bar, and watched a man run his hand along the hip of the woman next to him. The woman wore a tight, satiny dress and towering heels, and spoke quietly in his ear. The man downed his drink, and the two left the bar. Laurie had the feeling she'd just seen a financial transaction. Or maybe she was thinking in those terms because Jeff seemed so focused on money.

He was still peeling the label from his empty bottle when Laurie decided she'd had enough. She'd gotten up early for work, and had been on her feet too long. Plus she was tired of hearing Jeff talking about himself.

She rose from the table, abandoning her beer. "I hate to cut this short, but if you don't mind I have to get moving. I have an early morning tomorrow." She hoped he wouldn't ask about her plans, because she would have to invent something. Luckily Jeff seemed as ready to go as she was.

The two rode in silence. As Jeff pulled into the lot at her apartment he startled her by suddenly asking, "Do you know where that watercolor came from? I mean specifically who donated it, or anything else about it?"

Her mind was a million miles away, and it took her a moment to remember which painting he was talking about. "N-no," she stammered. "That is, Carol said it belonged to her boss's father-in-law. Something like that."

"Try to find out for sure for me, please?" His charming smile was back, making her feel confused. Her head had started to ache. She nodded as she got out.

Jeff opened the window as she rounded the car. "Bye, Love," he called. "Thanks for everything. It was fun."

Laurie winced at his comments. She was surprised when he pulled away before she even got into her apartment building, and stood a moment watching as his SUV turned onto the main road.

A moment later she glimpsed a man lurking between two cars in the dim parking lot. Her heart pounded as she scurried to the building clutching her keys.

She turned her key in the lock, pulled the door open, and took a final look over her shoulder. Only then did she see the guitar case - and Chase, looking right at her.

Laurie couldn't pretend she hadn't seen him. She waved a hand just before letting the glass door slam behind her, and scampered up the stairs and into her apartment. She stood a moment with her back to the door, catching her breath. By the time she walked across the room and twitched the curtain aside, there was no one in the parking lot.

Chapter 14.

Laurie's alarm sounded early - too early for a Saturday. She hit the snooze button, but lay awake mulling over her evening with Jeff.

She showered and dressed, and was midway through her second cup of coffee, still wondering why she felt so irritated. Was it just because Jeff had flirted with the other women in the class? As if she had a right to feel jealous!

She thought back to her marriage with DB. Had she been a jealous wife? DB really had been a dirt-bag. It had just taken a few years for her to see it. Years while she helped to pay off his student loans, and turned down job opportunities while he got his career established. She had tried to be the perfect wife, but it just left her feeling tied down and smothered. If she had been jealous, she was just jealous of his male privilege. She was over DB.

As she gathered her old costume jewelry to take to the Treasure Chest she saw DB's pocket watch. *Might as well call him, and get it over with,* she thought. *I can't get much more irritated than I am already.* She supposed DB would be awake and at home at this hour on a Saturday morning - though she didn't care if she *did* wake him - and dialed his number. A woman answered.

Laurie looked at her phone. She was pretty sure she had dialed the number for DB's condo. Then she realized the person who answered must be the new Mrs. Monroe. Maybe Laurie could get more irritated after all. "I'd like to speak to DB, please," she said.

"Who's calling?" the woman asked.

"Laurie Lanton."

"What is it in regard to?" Now the voice on the other end sounded cold.

"I have something of DB's that got mixed up with my things. It's a pocket watch. I'll be glad to mail it if -"

Mrs. Monroe cut her off. "I'm sure David doesn't want anything you have."

"I'd like to talk to him myself, please. Is he there?"

"He can't come to the phone."

Laurie was getting exasperated, and started pacing. "Look, I just need his new address," she said more loudly, trying to get through to the woman.

"I'm sure he wouldn't want to be bothered."

Now Laurie was steaming. "Oh, you're sure, are you? Well, let me give you a piece of advice. Don't be so sure about anything where DB is concerned, because he'll use you up and throw you into a corner like –"

The little icon on Laurie's phone winked out. The woman had hung up.

Laurie threw her phone on the bed and it bounced to the floor. She picked it up and set it on her dresser. Then she grabbed a pillow off the bed and screamed into it as loud as she could.

* * *

She arrived at the Treasure Chest thirty minutes later, only slightly calmer. A few customers were browsing in the shop. Mary sat on a stool at the counter while Carol put out a few newly tagged blouses. Laurie set her purse down in the office, and dumped the jewelry she'd brought onto the counter.

Carol was excited to see it. She grabbed a pen and some tags, and the women discussed what prices to charge. While they worked, Laurie asked about the watercolor painting.

"Oh, I did find out more about it," Carol said. "My boss Mr. Marshall mentioned it because he saw the photo you posted on Facebook with the painting in the background. He said it used to hang in his in-laws' den. Their name was Hinson or Hansen, something like that. Their family had a cottage on the Gulf coast of Florida below Crystal River for years and years. They all used to go fishing there. Anyway, the story was that some famous painter gave his wife's great grandmother the painting, sometime around the turn of the century. But then nobody could remember who the painter was. It wasn't signed or anything."

"Hmmm. A little vague," Laurie mused. "But that's more than we knew before."

"I was surprised nobody in the family wanted it," Carol said. "But you know, people are that way. None of my kids wanted Kenny's mother's china, so it's sitting in boxes in our garage."

"If people don't want their family heirlooms, they can bring them here," Mary said from her perch. "We'll be happy to sell them, won't we?" The other two agreed.

Carol continued to tag jewelry. Suddenly she stopped. "Well, this here looks like a family heirloom! Look at this watch." She held up DB's pocket watch, and opened the case to examine it. "Lord, I hate Roman numerals, but the face is beautiful." Slowly she read the inscription aloud. "'The mind once enlightened cannot again become dark.' Laurie, surely you don't mean for us to sell this here."

"Let me tell you about that watch," Laurie began. "DB's parents gave him that watch when he got his master's degree, and somehow it got mixed up with my jew-elry that I brought down with me. I tried to call DB, but instead of him answering it was that ... *Nasty Word*." Laurie meant the "B" word, but was trying not to be vul-gar. "That witch was so rude! I told her I had the watch, and would be glad to mail it back, but she was sure he wouldn't want anything I had. Then I texted his old cell number, but who knows. She probably reads his texts and deleted it. Anyway, I haven't heard from him, so the heck with him. The Treasure Chest can have the watch, and more power to us." She punctuated her story with a slap of her hand on the counter.

"Well, it's right pretty," Carol said. She still looked doubtful. "What price do you think we should put on it?"

Mary was peering over her shoulder. "I don't remem-ber this at all. He must not have carried it very often." She took the watch and looked at it more closely. "It doesn't have his initials on it, or anything. I was going to say, if it had his monogram, it wouldn't be worth as much."

"I just want to get rid of it," Laurie said. "Put twenty dollars on it and let it go."

Carol looked at her for a minute. "I'll put twenty five, and put it in the display case."

She finished tagging the jewelry, putting some in the display case and hanging the rest on the bulletin board with the other costume jewelry they had for sale.

Laurie took up a post next to Mary at the check-out counter. "How's Thumper?" she asked, indicating Mary's belly. She had been calling the baby "Thumper" ever since she went with Mary to a doctor visit, and got to hear the baby's rapid heartbeat through a stethoscope.

"We're both fine. He's pretty quiet lately. Kicks once in a while." Mary smiled. "I found some more cute stuff today. Here, look." Mary held up an infant-sized baseball uniform, and Laurie laughed.

"You don't know whether it's a boy or a girl yet!"

"Well, boys and girls can both play baseball! Besides, this little outfit is soft and adorable." Lately Mary had a hard time not buying every cute baby item that came into the shop. She had already purchased a baby's bath-tub, a swing, and a boatload of clothes.

"With the amount of clothes you've bought you'll be changing that baby four times a day. And you know Pete's folks are going to be buying tons of stuff, since it's their first grandchild. But, whatever. Everyone has their vices."

"At least it's not costing me much." That was true. Pretty much anything at the shop could be had for a bargain price. "I'm determined this baby is not going to have a huge impact on our budget, or our lifestyle. Life will go on just as before."

"Uh-huh. We'll see about that," Laurie said, smiling. She had no experience with babies either, but thought her friend sounded a little naive.

"Y'all, I'm going to run over to the Tasty Chick and bring back something for lunch," Carol said. "Anyone want anything? A co-cola or anything?"

The two declined. "Stay together, now," Carol said. "I don't want to come back and find one of you knocked in the head. I'm serious!"

When they were alone in the shop Mary turned to Laurie. "So, you saw that cute guy Jeff last night, didn't you? Details, girl!" She smiled impishly.

"Nosy, aren't we? I wish it had been as fun as you're imagining." Laurie recapped the events at the arts center, and at Rancher's afterwards. "Bottom line is, I feel like I was taken advantage of. Especially after I bought a new outfit for the evening."

"That you probably paid a whopping seven dollars for," Mary said teasingly.

"Plus tax!" Laurie said. She stuck her tongue out at Mary, then leaned her elbow on the counter, her chin on her hand. "I got there early and helped him set up and all. He couldn't have gotten everything done without me. At least, I definitely made it easier. But Jeff pretty much ignored me during the class, *and* I had to watch while he flirted with that redhead."

"I'm sure he was just being friendly. After all, he wants people to have a good time, come for more classes, and tell their friends. It's just good business."

"Whose side are you on?" Laurie faced Mary with a hand on one hip and her nose in the air. "So then he took me to that sleazy bar at Rancher's." Mary rolled her eyes and grinned. She and Laurie both knew she would not have called Rancher's a sleazy bar before last night. "He was only interested in talking about himself. It was disappointing."

"Well if you needed info to write your article, and all he talked about was himself, I guess you got it. What did you expect?" Mary asked. Laurie felt her face growing hot, and both of them burst out laughing. "Don't answer that! But honestly, was he going to take you back to his *mamma's house* and make passionate love to you?"

"Hmph," Laurie grunted. "Yeah, I guess that's true. At least *I* have my own place, pathetic as it is." She changed her tone. "That's not fair, though. He is here to help his mother move. And his father just passed away."

"Well," Mary said, "you can always go to another Art Night."

"Please shoot me first. I don't think I'm cut out to be a painter. That's not the end of the story, though." Laurie told her about Jeff dropping her off at her apartment.

"He said '*It was fun,*' huh?" Mary shook her head. "That's probably what the cowboy at the bar told his 'friend' in the satin dress."

"That's what I thought too!" Laurie laughed, and then looked puzzled. "But what do you think about Chase being there? This is the second time I've seen him near my apartment." Laurie wondered if he was stalking her, but thought the idea was a little too crazy to say out loud.

"Well, duh. Maybe he lives there," Mary answered. "It's not the most exclusive address in town."

"Oh!" Laurie's eyes widened.

"You know, you really should move into some nicer digs, now that you have a job." Mary rattled on, but Laurie wasn't listening. Why had it not occurred to her that Chase might live there? She had imagined he was homeless, but couldn't remember if that was because of something Mary said, or what Mother Barbara had told her. Could he be sharing an apartment with someone? Or have his own place? Chase did have a job, after all, and rent at those apartments was really cheap. "Affordable," as the real-estate ad put it.

Mary was still giving her advice. "You should ask him tomorrow at church. You've seen him in the parking lot twice now, and he's probably seen you. It would be weird *not* to say *something*, if you live in the same building."

"By golly, you're just full of suggestions, aren't you?"

"Yes, I am. And you should *listen* to me once in a while." Mary was thoughtful for a moment. "I guess he's getting his life together, which is good. But be careful you don't get too nosy. He'll think you're *interested*." She made air quotes around the last word, got off her stool, and walked down the hall to the ladies' room.

The bells on the door jangled as Carol returned with her lunch. "Y'all, the Tasty Chick is doing a good business today! I should have guessed, with all the cars in the parking lot." She settled with her food at the worktable in the office, and laid a paper napkin across her lap.

"That sure smells good," Laurie said. "One of these days I'm going to have to break down and get some for myself."

"Have one!" Carol held out a chicken tender.

"No, thanks. I'll stick with my peanut butter crackers." Laurie rummaged in her purse. She sat in the chair by the desk, and as she opened the pack of crackers, she saw something out of the corner of her eye. "Oh my gosh! Did you see that?"

"What?" Carol saw the expression on Laurie's face and froze, her cup of soda midway to her mouth. She swept her eyes from side to side trying to see the whole office without moving. Suddenly a little brown mouse scurried out from under the table and disappeared under the cabinet near the door.

"Ew!" Laurie said, jumping up. Carol scooped her food into her lap and scooted her chair into the middle of the room.

Mary had just come back from the restroom and stood in the doorway. "What's all the excitement?"

"We just saw a mouse!" Carol said, a note of hysteria in her voice.

"Well, no doubt! Those tenders smell so good I'm surprised you don't have all kinds of critters fighting over them. I was hoping I might swap my salad for them without you noticing."

Laurie still had a worried look on her face. "It came from under there," she said pointing to the table.

Mary leaned over slightly and peeked under the table. There were two large boxes stuffed with bags and bits of paper used to wrap fragile items. "You guys, anything could be living under there. Snakes, spiders, who knows what." Carol gave her a nasty look. "Well, I would have straightened that stuff out," Mary said defensively, "but in case you haven't noticed, I can't bend over."

"Thanks for cheering me up, Mary. Lord, just wait until Virginia hears about this. Bless her heart, she was about ready to quit after Alice got whacked in the head. This might just put her over the edge."

"You sound pretty nervous yourself," Mary said. "I guess we need to find some mousetraps."

"Ooh! We could get a live trap and sell it as a pet!" Laurie said.

"Right, you do that." Mary rolled her eyes.

"Come to think of it, we have some mousetraps," Carol said. "I priced them the other day. They're in the furniture room, next to the fishing poles. Watch my lunch while I go get them." Carol left, and Mary and Laurie looked uneasily around, squealing simultaneously as the mouse ran back across the room.

"Did you see him again?" Carol crept back into the room with a two-pack of mouse traps.

"Yep. He's back under there." Laurie pointed under the table.

"Well, here. Let's get these baited." Carol pulled the plastic wrap off the mousetraps. Laurie and Mary baited them with pieces of chicken, careful not to pinch their fingers.

"Guys, I've read that mice can't see very well, so they run along next to walls and things," Laurie said. She placed the traps against the wall on either side of the office door.

"This one must have better eyesight than most. He was out in the middle of the room," Carol observed.

"I wish we had another trap or two," Mary said. "Because you know, if we saw one mouse, there are probably several more."

It was almost closing time and, as usual on Saturdays there was a rush of customers. Mary waited on them and Carol helped bag the items. Laurie looked around the shop for another trap, and came back to the office carrying a bird cage.

"Look. What do you think? We can put some food in here and rig the door so it slides down if something goes in."

"You're serious about catching them alive, aren't you," Mary said.

"Catch and release. Like I do with my men."

"Wow!" Mary raised her eyebrows and smiled. "You go, girl. Do you have any bait left?"

"You mean for man-catching?"

"Honey, you've got all the bait you need for that!" Mary said.

"I still have a peanut butter cracker. Seeing that mouse took away my appetite." Laurie separated the cracker sandwich into two halves, put them inside the cage, and set the cage on the floor. She propped the door open with a pen, testing it a few times to make sure it would shut if a mouse went in.

"Y'all, we'll need to check after church tomorrow and see if we've caught anything," Carol said.

"I will if you'll come with me. In fact, you'll have to let us in, because Mary and I don't have keys."

Chapter 15.

Laurie helped Carol and Mary close up the shop at 2:00, and spent the rest of Saturday doing research for her article. On Sunday morning she crept through the parking lot, eyes darting back and forth, looking unsuccessfully for Chase's car. It was only nine o'clock, and the temperature was already in the 80's. Finally, she gave up the gumshoe routine and drove to St. Mark's.

She could hear the organ from outside the church as she walked across the front lawn past the shady courtyard where the columbarium stood. Someone had freshened the flowers in the urns, and had weeded the flower beds. It was a tranquil, soothing space. Laurie said a prayer for the departed, and then pulled open the old church doors and climbed the stairs to the choir loft.

Mary beckoned Laurie to her usual seat. "Be extra careful when you climb the stairs in your choir robe," she teased. "You don't want to get tangled up again."

Laurie wrinkled her nose. "No kidding," she said.

"Do anything fun last night?" Mary asked.

"Nope," Laurie sighed. "You?"

"Nothing much. Pete and I watched some TV, and then floated in our pool. I like to swim after dark with the pool light on. The water's been so warm!"

"You skinny-dip with the pool light on?" Laurie teased, trying to keep a straight face.

"Shh," Mary said with a finger to her lips. "It's very private back there."

They broke off their discussion to join in the vocal warm-ups. Then Steve called out hymn number 458.

"'*My Song is Love Unknown*,'" Laurie heard Chase say in the row behind her. "One of my favorites." She half-turned and saw him smile as he looked up from the bulletin.

She flipped to the page in her hymn book, and read the words of the first verse as Steve played. One line seemed to jump out at her.

"'*Love to the loveless shown, that they might lovely be*.'" She read the words under her breath. Then she closed her eyes, and listened as the choir sang. She thought of Chase, and whatever was in his past. She thought of herself, suddenly single again when she'd thought she would be married forever. *Love to the loveless shown, that they might lovely be*. She blinked rapidly to clear her eyes, and joined in singing the second verse.

Laurie made it through the service with no embarrassing stumbles. Afterwards the choir remained in the loft long enough to run through a spiritual Steve wanted them to sing at some point in the summer. They left the choir loft chattering, hung their robes haphazardly in the robing room, and went to join the parishioners still mingling in the kitchen and parish hall.

Halfway down the hallway Mary slowed and whispered to Laurie, "Remember, you were going to ask Chase whether he lives in your apartment complex."

"Yes, 'Mother.' When I get around to it," Laurie added under her breath.

"Ah - coffee! There's still coffee." Laurie poured a cup and got behind Mary in the snack line. Chase and Rob fell in behind them.

Mary shimmied awkwardly, her pregnant belly swaying, as she sang the refrain from the spiritual. "Quit holding up the line," Laurie growled. She poked Mary in the back with a plastic fork. Mary squawked and scurried along, putting snacks on a paper plate.

"You two are in a good mood," Chase commented.

"Why not? This is the best party in town." Laurie selected a couple of cookies and some grapes, and she and Mary waited as Chase loaded his plate. Mary nudged Laurie, and gave her a meaningful look. Laurie shook her head slightly. She wasn't ready to interrogate Chase about his living arrangements.

They joined Pete in the parish hall, and Rob and Chase took seats at the same table. Mary clucked softly like a hen to her chicks. Laurie suspected she was calling her a chicken, and kicked her under the table, which produced a yelp from Mary.

"Why are you making animal noises?" Pete asked her. He put a hand to her forehead, checking whether she had a fever. "My wife is a little strange," he stage-whispered to the others.

"We've noticed." Rob nodded.

"Hopefully it's just her delicate condition, and she'll be back to normal soon. I think it's best to ignore her." The two started discussing Atlanta traffic. Pete was supposed to attend a conference at his company's head-quarters there the following week, and had just about decided to drive up that evening to avoid Monday morning's rush hour.

Laurie busied herself pulling grapes off the stem. Mary gave her a threatening look. Before she could start clucking again, Laurie blurted to Chase "Hey, I thought I saw you over by my apartment building the other day. You don't live out that way, do you?" She hoped that left him enough wiggle room to answer noncommittally if he was homeless or couch surfing.

"You live over on Hodges, next to the pawn shop? Then yes, we're neighbors."

She pressed on. "Your roommate – is she also a musician?"

Chase laughed. "I don't have a roommate. I live in that big apartment all by my lonesome." Mary laughed too, at Laurie's clumsy attempt to find out if Chase had a girlfriend.

Laurie changed the subject, indicating his plate. "You must have a hollow leg, or something."

"I got up too late to eat breakfast. I deejay-ed for a private event at the Coffee Pot last night, so I was out late." After a moment he said "I was hoping I'd see you there Friday for open mic."

Laurie wondered if that was all he was thinking. "Well, you know, the Treasure Chest has made donations to the arts center, so I thought I should check out their Art Night Out. I'm writing an article about it for the *Journal.* I'll have my byline in a newspaper again. " She pumped a fist in the air.

"Woo-hoo," Mary said, giving Laurie a high-five. She knew what it meant to Laurie that she was writing for publication.

"Yep. I proposed the idea to the editor, and he liked it. The story should be printed this week."

"Bravo." Chase nodded.

"Anyway, I helped the art instructor set up for the event because Sharon couldn't be there, and he took me for a beer afterwards." She didn't like the way that sounded, and added, "I don't have much knack for painting. It's not really my thing."

"Does that mean you'll be donating your painting to the Treasure Chest?" Mary asked.

"Um, sure. Someone might buy it to line the bottom of their parakeet cage," Laurie said.

"That good, eh?" Chase asked.

"Hey!" Laurie suddenly exclaimed, jumping in her seat. "The bird cage! We need to check the traps at the Treasure Chest!"

"Oh, yeah," Mary agreed, turning to Pete. "Remember I told you about the mouse?"

"Is Carol still here? We need a key to the shop." Laurie spotted Carol, and went to talk to her as Mary filled Rob and Chase in on the excitement at the shop Saturday.

Laurie returned to the table. "Carol said as soon as we're done eating she'll let us in next door. We might need reinforcements." She looked at Pete.

"I'll help," he said.

"Not me," Rob said. "I can't bear the thought of small animals being tortured."

"Can I come?" Chase asked. "I wanted to shop for a few things yesterday, but didn't get there in time."

"Sure. Eat up!" Laurie said, and Chase hurried to clean his plate.

Minutes later the small group crossed the parking lot and Carol unlocked the door to the thrift shop. She flipped on some lights, and Mary and Laurie tip-toed around the counter toward the office.

"Why are you tip-toing?" Pete asked. "If the mouse is in a trap it's not going to jump out at you."

"It's the ones we *haven't* caught that we're worried about. There could be a nest full in there," Mary said. "And why are *we* in front? You should be in the lead." She gave her husband a push, but Laurie was already in the office.

"Look! We caught one dead and one alive." A mouse lay in one of the traps, the metal bar across its neck. "This one didn't even get to finish his chicken tender."

"You wasted a chicken tender on a mouse?" Chase asked, easing past Mary to watch as Pete picked up the trap and headed outside to the dumpster.

"My live trap worked! I wonder what it says about me that the mouse and I both like peanut butter crackers." Laurie knelt on the floor near the bird cage. A mouse scurried nervously inside, and then stopped and stared at her with large black eyes. "Aw, look at this little guy. He's kind of cute."

"He reminds me of a dog I used to have," Chase said.

"A dog?"

"Well, he was a small dog."

"Oh, good grief," Mary said shaking her head. "That thing could have fleas or God knows what. Before one of you names him, will someone please take him outside and put him out of his misery?"

"Can't we just take him out and turn him loose?" Laurie asked.

"Only if you want to trap him again later," Mary answered.

Laurie looked at Chase. He backed away, hands raised in surrender. "I can't," he said, shaking his head. "Sorry."

Pete returned with the empty trap. "What did you do with it?" Laurie asked.

"I blew taps and tossed his furry butt in the dumpster. What did you think?"

"Here," Mary said handing Pete the cage. "Everyone else is too tender-hearted. Can you euthanize this one and blow taps again?"

Pete left with the cage while Mary looked for the remaining trap. "Well, the bait's gone from this one. And we'll want to rebait the other one. If there are more mice in here, I'd like to catch them before any customers get here Tuesday. Do we have any more bait?"

"I'll check the kitchen." Laurie left as Mary poked around under the worktable with an umbrella. On her way to the staff kitchen she saw Chase at the counter. Carol was writing up a sales slip for a blanket and a few other items he was purchasing.

Laurie returned to the office. "I found some crackers and a fast-food packet of mayonnaise." She started to smear mayonnaise on the crackers, and noticed Mary had a faraway look in her eyes. "What's wrong?"

"I was trying to remember a song we did in choir, back in college. Something about a mouse with great personal valor." She hummed uncertainly.

"Oh, we did that one," Chase jumped in. "And there's something or other about 'my cat Jeoffry.'"

"Yes!" Mary exclaimed. "Except I can't remember how it goes." She looked thoughtfully at Chase.

"I remember you used to sing something about a mouse that gnawed down a tree," Laurie said.

As if on cue Chase and Mary both sang out "The mouse that gnawed the oak tree down."

"Okay, guys, you're scaring me," Laurie said.

Then Chase spoke normally. "What happened to Jerry?"

"Who's Jerry?" Mary asked, startled.

"You know, Jerry the mouse. That's what I named the one in the cage." Mary still looked clueless. "After *Tom and Jerry*? Don't you watch any educational television?"

Laurie laughed, taking the cage from Pete, who had just returned. She put a cracker in the cage, propped the cage door open with the pen as before, and placed the cage in the middle of the floor. "I hope mice like mayonnaise. I'm not much of a fan."

"If they like the same things you like, then you should put a latte in the cage," Chase said.

"Speaking of which, you still *owe* me a latte." Laurie raised her chin and stared at him with her hands on her hips. She didn't feel bad about claiming the drink, now that she knew he was working and had a place to live.

"I do indeed," Chase said with a bow. "The Coffee Pot is closed Mondays, but I'll be glad to buy you a latte Tuesday. I should be off work at 5:00."

"I'll meet you there Tuesday," Laurie agreed with a nod.

Mary had a worried look on her face as she glanced from Chase to Laurie. Laurie had the feeling she was about to say something, when Pete began steering Mary by the elbow. "Let's go home, Mary. If I'm going to drive to Atlanta this evening I have to pack sometime today."

Driving home from church, Laurie wondered what she expected from this "date" with Chase. She thought maybe she should be dating guys with deeper pockets, or at least better prospects. She remembered what she used to think about Episcopalians – that they were all rich, snobbish bankers, lawyers, politicians, or Daughters of the American Revolution. It certainly wasn't true at St. Mark's.

And then there was Chase's "problem" with drugs, whatever that was. Laurie didn't know any details, but the "d" word frightened her. She tried not to judge people who turned to alcohol or drugs seeking escape from emotional trauma or personal tragedy. And she felt sorry for people who needed relief from physical pain, and ended up addicted. But Laurie had a hard time imagining Chase in either of those categories. He sure looked healthy enough.

She thought again about his lithe figure as he leaned against the counter at the Coffee Pot that night – more like a dancer's than a manual laborer's. Laurie tried to remember the last time she'd been out dancing, or had a man's arms around her. She felt a warm tingle as she imagined a man's body molded to her own.

This line of thinking is not going to help me write that article, she thought. She stopped at her apartment, packed up her laptop and the little mouse she always preferred to use, and left again for the Redding library, hoping for inspiration.

* * *

Redding's public library was housed in a massive, granite building on College Street. Laurie liked libraries in general, and she liked this one in particular because of its large selection of periodicals. It seemed to have them all, unlike the smaller Chinkapin library.

She entered from the sunny parking lot and paused as her eyes adjusted to the dimness inside. Then she walked past the newspaper racks, scanned the display of magazines, and picked up the latest issue of *Writer's Digest*.

"Well hey, Ms. Laurie." She looked up, surprised to hear someone in Redding address her by name. She could barely see his face for the sunlight pouring through the window behind him, but she recognized Jeff's voice coming from deep in one of the leather armchairs.

"Hi," she said, waiting for an invitation to sit down. It never came, but she took the chair beside him anyway. "Don't tell me you can paint *and* read."

He laughed. There were those blue eyes again. Why did she find Jeff so alluring?

"Are you here to see if anyone has checked your novel out of the library?" he asked.

"Not today. Just doing some research." She waved the magazine. "How about you? Looking for inspiration?" She saw copies of *The Artist's* and *Watercolor* magazines on the low table in front of him.

"Like you. Research."

"Speaking of which," Laurie said, "I have more information on that painting you were asking about."

Jeff shot forward in his chair, suddenly alert. "Do tell! What did you find out?"

Laurie repeated Carol's information, and Jeff looked pleased. "So it came from Florida, somewhere around 1900 or a little later?"

"That's what Carol said. It was given to her boss's wife's great-grandmother – something like that – but no one can remember who painted it. Did you find any markings on it?"

He gave her a blank look and shook his head. "None at all. I'm thinking of taking a trip to Atlanta sometime this week, to see what my old professor has to say about it. It's probably nothing to get excited about, but I owe her a visit anyway."

"Well, I'd be curious to know what you find out. If it's worth more than just the value of the frame, you could sell it, and the arts center could use the proceeds for more kids' art classes."

"Sure," Jeff said, nodding. "That's just what I was thinking."

Laurie thought there was something off about his tone.

"Are you coming to Art Night Out next Friday?" he asked abruptly.

Laurie looked past Jeff out the window, trying to decide whether to tell him how little she had enjoyed painting. "We'll see. Look, I'm going to find a quiet corner where I can set up my laptop." She indicated the bag she was carrying. "I've got some writing to do. See you!"

She wove through the stacks and found a desk in a corner far away from Jeff. *Why didn't I just tell him 'no'?* she wondered.

She set up her laptop, dug out her notes, and worked on her writing until the library closed.

Chapter 16.

Laurie was happy with the writing she got done that afternoon. First, she completed her article on Art Night Out for the *Journal.* She added information she had gleaned through research, phone calls, and some interviews she had done at a couple of art studios Saturday afternoon, and was pleased with how thorough it was. She emailed it to Scott, her editor, crossing her fingers.

Then she leafed through one of the library's magazines to the page with the writing prompts, and lost herself in drafting a bit of flash fiction to submit to her writers group for critique.

She left the library and was considering rewarding herself with a trip to the Dairy Queen when her cell phone buzzed. "Come over and watch a movie with me," Mary begged over the phone. "I'm bored."

Laurie hoped Mary wasn't planning to lecture her about getting coffee with Chase. She might have turned Mary down. Mary was used to Pete being out of town, but tonight she sounded unusually whiney and forlorn. *I'm such a pushover*, Laurie thought. "I'll be over in a few. Need me to pick up anything? Lemonade and pick-led okra, or anything?" Mary's food cravings had become strange and unpredictable.

"Nope. I'm good. I ate some scrambled eggs a while ago."

When she arrived at Mary's house a short while later Laurie was surprised by how deserted the place looked. Pete's pick-up was missing from the driveway, and the front curtains were drawn. She knocked on the door, found it unlocked, and let herself in.

The flicker of the TV was all that lit Mary's dim living room. Laurie could just make out her friend's lumpy outline curled on the sofa. "Hey, lazybones. Have you picked out something for us to watch? Not that natural childbirth video again, I hope," Laurie said, wondering if Mary had fallen asleep.

"No. I don't care. Whatever you want." Mary stirred, stretched her legs, and sat up yawning and blinking when Laurie switched on the light next to the couch.

"When did Pete leave?" Laurie asked.

"A couple of hours ago. He's probably almost at the hotel." She rubbed a hand over her belly. "I just can't get comfortable this evening."

"What, is Thumper kicking you in the bladder again?" Laurie grabbed the remote from the coffee table and busied herself searching Netflix.

"Something like that. I don't know. Actually she hasn't moved in a while. I just feel kind of crampy." Mary slipped a hand behind her back, pulled out a pillow, and thumped it with a pained expression. "I guess it's probably that Braxton Hicks, or whatever it is."

"You probably just need to have a BM," Laurie joked, trying to make her friend feel better. "You're getting anxious because you have less than a month to go. How about a good comedy, or a fun girl-power movie to take your mind off things."

"I wish Pete didn't have that conference this week."

Laurie was only half paying attention as she scanned the list of movies and settled on one she had been wanting to see. "Here we are. I'm going to steal a soda from your fridge. Can I get you some water or juice?"

"No." As Laurie helped herself to a soda and some ice from the kitchen she heard Mary thump her pillow again. "On second thought, I should probably have a glass of water," she called.

Laurie reached into the cupboard for another glass, and heard a sound in the living room. She looked around the corner and saw Mary getting up off the couch. Suddenly Mary stiffened. "Oh, no. Laurie? Laurie, I think..." Quickly Mary waddled toward the powder room.

Laurie froze, listening. Her gaze flitted between the glass in her hand and the powder room door. She filled

Mary's glass with water, carried the drinks to the living room, and paused the movie, which had just started playing. "Mary? Are you okay in there?"

A moment later the powder room door opened and Mary appeared, wide-eyed. "Help! I think my water broke!" she quavered.

Laurie heard the words, but somehow they didn't register. She stared at Mary.

"Help me! I need another towel to wipe this up."

Finally Laurie grasped the situation, and ran back to the kitchen to grab some dish towels. As she mopped the floor she glanced up at Mary's frightened face. "It's okay. You're going to be okay. I'm taking you to the hospital."

"I can't go in this." Mary indicated her wet clothing. "Go upstairs and get me something." Uncertainty must have showed on Laurie's face. "Anything!" Mary cried frantically.

Laurie ran up the stairs, and Mary called after her. "And my go-bag. Get my go-bag. It's on the floor in the closet."

Laurie grabbed a clean-looking pair of pajamas she found lying on the bed. Then she threw open the closet door and snatched up a pink-striped tote bag. It was bulging with items Mary thought she might want at the hospital. Laurie had watched her friend pack and repack it several times in the preceding weeks.

With Mary finally clad in dry clothes, the two climbed into Laurie's car. "You have your cell phone, right?" Laurie asked. Mary nodded, and fumbled the phone out of her purse. "Call your doctor's office," Laurie instructed "and tell them we're on our way to the hospital."

Mary called the number. After a brief exchange she said "Well, that was the answering service. They just told me to go to the emergency room. I guess the doctor will show up eventually. They act so blasé about this stuff! It makes me feel like I'm getting worked up over nothing." She forced a smile.

Laurie tried to keep her mind and her eyes on the road but she wasn't really seeing the traffic. She just wanted to get to the hospital as fast as possible without getting pulled over. Mary let out a soft moan from the seat next to her. "What's happening? Are you having labor pains?"

"I don't know," Mary whined. "It's too soon! But it hurts. It's been hurting for hours."

"You must be having contractions. I guess it's supposed to hurt. Do you think you were off on your calculations? I mean, you've been saying you're not due for another three or four weeks, but..."

Mary shook her head. Laurie sped up to make it through a traffic light just as it turned red. "Don't worry," Laurie said. "We'll be there in just a few more minutes."

"It's fifteen minutes from here on a good day!" Mary said. "Slow down before you get the three of us killed."

"Yes, 'Mother.' I can tell you're fine. You're still bossing me around." Laurie smiled in spite of the situation, but then felt a stab of worry. What if there was something wrong with Thumper? What if Mary lost the baby? "Call Pete. He'll want to know what's going on."

Laurie pressed harder on the accelerator, wishing Pete were in town. Mary let out another moan, and rubbed the side of her belly. "Hang in there, Thumper," Laurie said. "I'm looking forward to seeing you, but not on the front seat of my car!"

Mary punched the numbers into her phone, and Laurie heard her leaving a message. "Hi. Call me back. I'm on my way to the hospital." She hung up and held the phone, willing it to ring. "His phone went straight to voice mail. Maybe he's still driving, or went out for dinner or something." She looked out the passenger window, and Laurie saw a tear trickle down her cheek.

"Well, that message ought to get his attention. 'I'm on my way to the hospital.' Sheesh!" Laurie turned onto the old state route and let out a long breath as the red "emergency room" sign came into view. She careened into the circular drive, slammed the car into park, and jumped out to help Mary into the hospital.

Moments later Laurie dashed back out, and moved the car to a legal parking space. Then she jogged back into the hospital to find out what had become of Mary. The person at reception directed her to "Maternity," and Laurie rode the elevator up tapping her fingers against her thighs. She almost crashed into three people as she bolted out of the elevator.

She found Mary lying on a bed clothed in a white hospital gown, her hair encased in a floppy hat that looked like a shower cap.

"How are you feeling now?"

"About the same. The nurse told me I'm in labor, but they're not saying much else."

"Well, maybe that's good. I mean, maybe that means there's nothing particular to say, and it's just a matter of waiting." Laurie tried to put a hopeful spin on the situation, but Mary looked solemn.

A couple of people bustled in and Laurie turned away as a woman reached a hand up Mary's gown. *No dignity in a hospital room*, Laurie thought.

"You're just a few centimeters dilated," the woman said. "You have a long way to go. Hang loose, and we'll check you again in a little bit."

Laurie moved a plastic chair next to Mary's bed. She sat down and pulled the cell phone out of Mary's purse. "What do you say we make a few phone calls, eh? You want to call your mom?"

"I guess." Mary left a voicemail and let her phone drop onto the bed. She knew she wouldn't be seeing her parents any time soon, since her father had just had a hip replacement. "I wish Pete would call me back." She panted as another spasm clenched her belly, then dialed Pete's number again, with no success.

"What about your in-laws?"

"Oh," Mary moaned. "I really didn't want them here watching me give birth. I wanted Pete!" She grimaced and moved her legs as another spasm rolled over her.

A nurse bustled in, and Laurie watched as the woman attached a monitor to Mary's belly. *This has the makings of a long night*, she thought.

Chapter 17.

Laurie looked curiously at the monitor strapped across Mary's abdomen. "So what's that for?" she asked.

"Making sure everything's still fine with the baby. So far, so good, they said," Mary answered. But she didn't have a "so far, so good" look on her face.

"Is that standard procedure?" Laurie asked. "You don't look too happy, considering you're about to see that baby you've been hoping and praying for."

"Well, I didn't tell you this before, but Thumper's not in the right position. I know she *was*, a couple of weeks ago, head down and all, because I could tell by the kicks and the hiccups." Laurie still found it amazing that babies in utero had hiccups. "But a week or so ago, Thumper shifted around the opposite way. I just thought there would be plenty of time for her to turn again. I have a feeling I'm not going to have the natural childbirth I wanted."

Laurie was sorry her friend was disappointed, but honestly she didn't think anesthesia was such a bad thing. She felt the same about "natural childbirth" as she did about "natural dentistry." Bring on the pain-killers! Then again, it wasn't her baby, and she hadn't read up on childbirth like Mary had. Laurie watched silently as Mary breathed deeply through another contraction.

"So the baby's breach, then," Laurie said.

Mary closed her eyes and nodded. "It wasn't supposed to be this way!" she wailed. "I was going to have a natural childbirth, in that pretty birthing suite with the rocking chair!"

"Can they turn her around, do you think?"

Mary turned her head away, but Laurie saw the tears coming again. For a change, her friend was not in control. The woman who was always telling other people what they should and shouldn't do, and how to run their lives, couldn't control her own body, or her baby.

"Oh, Mary, I'm sorry," Laurie said, taking her friend's hand. "Hey, the point is a healthy baby, right? Whatever way that happens is a good outcome, I say."

Laurie felt hopelessly ignorant as she tried to console her friend. She regretted envying Mary, realizing anew how dangerous pregnancy actually was – sometimes life-threatening, to mother and baby. Much as she had dreamed of motherhood during her friend's pregnancy, she knew she had to learn to slow down and take life as it came, appreciating every day. She said a silent prayer for a safe delivery and a healthy baby.

She jumped when Mary's phone suddenly rang. Vibrating, it slid off the bed, and clattered to the floor. Laurie picked it up and slid her finger over the screen to answer. "It's Pete," she said, handing the phone to Mary.

"Where are you?" Mary demanded. A second later she started to cry. Tears filled Laurie's eyes too. She stood and paced the room until finally Mary ended the call.

"What did he say?"

"He's in Atlanta. I was hoping he had got my message and turned around, but he said when he checked in at the hotel he just dumped all his stuff and went straight to the fitness room. He just got my message. I hope Thumper waits until he gets here."

Laurie added another phrase to the prayer that had been cycling through her mind. *Safe delivery. Healthy baby. Pete here in time.*

Mary's labor progressed slowly, if painfully. According to the monitor, the baby was not in any danger. The nurses told Mary the doctor would arrive in the morning, and she would probably have a C-section.

Through a couple more hours of waiting, punctuated by Mary's contractions and Laurie's attempts to encourage her, Laurie stayed with her friend, only excusing herself for necessary breaks and a trip to the vending machine. She was running on adrenaline, and wished she could sleep in the next day.

Pete arrived more quickly than Laurie thought anyone could drive from Atlanta to Chinkapin, and took over the vigil at his wife's side. Laurie made him promise to call as soon as Thumper was born. As she left, she heard Mary chiding Pete for speeding.

Laurie dragged herself out to the parking lot and looked around dazedly for her car, struggling to remember where she'd parked. Had it just been a few hours ago? It felt like days. Somehow she made it to her apartment, brushed her teeth half-heartedly, and fell into bed.

* * *

Laurie's phone buzzed noisily beside her bed. Dazed, she poked at the screen, trying to make the alarm stop. After several unsuccessful tries she realized it wasn't the alarm. It was an incoming call from Pete.

She wiped drool off her chin, hoping not to get it on her phone. "Hello?" Her voice was fuzzy.

"It's a boy!" Pete hollered into the phone. Laurie moved it away from her head and massaged her ear.

"What? A boy? That's great. How's Mary?"

"Mary's fine. Everyone but me is sleeping, and I'm going to find a place to curl up as soon as I make a few more phone calls."

"So, she had a C-section then?" Laurie asked.

"Right. Well, they had to do what was best for the baby, and Mary agreed. So she'll be in the hospital for a day or two, at least. She didn't get her natural childbirth, but the baby's beautiful, and thank God I got here in time."

"I'll have to come visit. How big and all? How much did he weigh?"

"Six pounds, five ounces, nineteen and a half inches. He was a little early, but not as early as Mary thought. Started breathing on his own, and everything. Guess she was a little off on her calculation."

"Thanks for the info. I know you have other calls to make, and would like to get to sleep, so... Hey, wait! What's his name?"

"Richard Leonard Roster. Richard for Mary's dad, and Leonard for my grandpa. RLR."

Laurie hung up the phone and fell back onto the bed. "RLR," she said aloud. "Roller. Hmmm." Suddenly she shot back up again, realizing it was Monday and she was supposed to be at work. She looked at the clock, dialed her office, and made her apologies.

She jumped in and out of the shower, swiped on a little make-up, and let her hair drip-dry as she threw her clothes on and stuffed a granola bar in her purse. At the office she tipped her head through the editor's door.

Scott was banging away at the computer on his desk. "Hi," she said with a little wave. "Thanks for your understanding about this morning. That baby just wouldn't wait, and my friend's husband was in Atlanta, so..."

Scott waved away her apologies, and pointed to the chair beside his desk. Laurie sat, wondering about the big smile on his face. "This story you emailed is great! I didn't know you'd done so much research on this painting fad, and all those other studios in the area."

"Yeah, well, I can cut some of that, to shorten the article if you..."

"Just what I was thinking," he said. Laurie sagged in the chair, remembering all the leg-work she'd done to get the extra interviews. "If you can cut it down to a feature just on the Chinkapin Arts Center and this Jeff guy, we'll run it this week," Scott continued. Laurie nodded, wondering why he still looked so excited. "Then we'll run the entire article as the front-page feature on the summer edition of the *Southern Oaks* supplement."

Laurie froze a moment as that sank in. *Southern Oaks* was the quarterly supplement that went out to all the newspaper's subscribers. She'd also seen copies of it at the Chinkapin welcome center near the fairgrounds, in doctor's waiting rooms, and in racks in restaurants all around town. Every real estate agent in the area gave a copy to their clients. *Southern Oaks* was everywhere.

And her story would be on the cover. For a whole quarter.

She sat up straighter, a smile replacing the stunned look on her face. "Really? That – that's awesome!"

The two discussed details and a deadline for the shorter version, and Laurie left his office, feeling peppier than she had all morning. She sped through cleaning up the events column submissions, and stayed a little later than usual to start revising her article.

By early afternoon she was ravenous. She felt like she hadn't had a proper meal in days. She planned to go visit Mary at the hospital, but stopped by the Coffee Pot first for a bite to eat.

As soon as she pulled open the door she saw a familiar face. "Mother Barbara," Laurie said. The priest was next to the cash register, stirring a packet of sugar into her coffee. "How are you? Have you heard the news? Mary had her baby."

"Pete called me this morning," she nodded. "I just came from the hospital."

"How did Mary look? And how's the baby?"

"Typical new mother," Mother Barbara said shaking her head. She had two grown children of her own, and a grandchild on the way. "Poor Mary is so anxious for everything to be perfect. It just never is! But she's fine, and the baby's precious. So tiny!"

"I'm going to run by the hospital as soon as I have something to eat. I'm starving! Want to sit and drink your coffee with me?" Mother Barbara found a table while Laurie gave her order to the person at the counter.

"I'm glad I caught you," Mother Barbara began when Laurie took a seat. "I never get to talk to you at church, because you're busy with the choir, and then yesterday of course with the mice."

"Right! Oh my gosh. So much has happened in the last twenty four hours, I almost forgot! I hope someone checks the traps today."

"I'll make sure someone goes over there."

"And, I got some good news today!" Laurie's face lit up as she told about her upcoming articles in the *Journal* and in the *Southern Oaks* quarterly.

"Wonderful!" Mother Barbara exclaimed. "I've seen the *Southern Oaks* magazine everywhere! And your article will be on the cover? Excellent. Well then, you are just the person I should talk to. You're so good with publicity and have gotten so involved in the community. The vestry and I have been discussing ways to give the church a little more visibility, and to bring more people through the doors."

Laurie nodded. The priest had mentioned this before, and now was bringing it up again. Laurie really did love the little church. In some ways she didn't want anything to change, but she knew that without some new members the parish would die. Plus, she had other, more spiritual reasons for wanting to help bring people to St. Mark's. "Have they come up with anything new?"

"So far, mostly the usual. We'll definitely do the golf outing and barbecue, but not until the fall when the weather cools down. They are great fun, but they tend not to bring in many newcomers – usually just members and their friends, who already know about us. I'm looking for something different." She took a sip of her coffee.

"Hmmm. I remember you were talking about something in the arts. You don't think people would turn out if Steve gave an organ recital?" Laurie suggested. "Or, maybe Chase could put something together. Maybe a jam session, or something like what they do at the Coffee Pot!"

Barbara shook her head. "Here's what I've been thinking. I know I've said this to you before, but I keep coming back to the idea of an art show." Laurie could tell the priest really wanted this art show to happen, and was just looking for someone to take it on. And with Laurie's new-found expertise, she might have a hard time *not* volunteering.

Barbara's eyes were wide with excitement. "We can hold it in the parish hall. We have several talented artists at St. Mark's, including a couple of our youth. In fact, they gave me the idea in the first place. One of them just had a painting on display in the governor's office. An art show could be something to keep the youth engaged."

"You know," Laurie said shrugging, "they're having an art show at the Chinkapin Arts Center in like, a week. They've been advertising it in the *Journal's* events column."

Mother Barbara's face fell. "But," Laurie went on holding a hand up, "it's only open to their current students. If you're talking about an art show open to the whole community, say a month or two from now, we might even get the arts center to help us set it up, considering the donations the Treasure Chest has made to their children's programs."

Barbara sipped her coffee as the wheels turned in Laurie's head. "If we opened the show to basically anyone who wants to enter, we'd probably get entries from people in our parish, plus the students at the arts center, and who knows who else. I've got some contacts at a few local studios, after writing that article. That probably would bring us more artists. And maybe the kids you mentioned could get some of their school friends to exhibit." Laurie paused to eat a bite. "I think this could work. Have refreshments, an artist's reception – that would bring in the artists and some of their friends and family." She tapped her lips with her fork before adding

"We probably want to hold the show a little later in the summer, to give us time to publicize it in the newspaper. We could make up a bunch of flyers and get them out around town. It would be nice if we could come up with a theme." Laurie took another bite of her food and continued thinking.

"I like it. The church could donate a few prizes, for winning entries," Mother Barbara suggested. "Should it be free to enter, or charge a small fee to cover the prizes?"

"Hmmm. I guess I'm not sure how these things typically run. If we want to bring more people in, free is probably best. Unless we collected something: canned goods for the food bank, or something like that. I'll tell you what. Let me think about it some more, and maybe ask around a bit. This could be something really fun, though. And good for the community."

Chapter 18.

After Mother Barbara left, Laurie continued brainstorming, jotting a few notes in the small notebook she always carried in her purse. Then she left for the hospital to visit Mary.

She rode the elevator up to the maternity wing, paused at the nurses' station to get her bearings, and found her way to Mary's room. Through the open door she could see a pair of legs covered by a white blanket. She knocked softly, and entered.

Mary was sitting up in the hospital bed, a tray of half-eaten food next to her. On the other side of the bed was a rolling hospital-style bassinet with clear plastic sides.

Laurie crept over to the bassinet and peeked in at the tightly swaddled little bundle sporting a light blue knitted cap. "Oh," she breathed, "How sweet." She reached a finger over the side and stroked the baby's velvety cheek.

Mary folded her arms over her stomach, watching Laurie and the baby. "Hi, Mary," she said in a mocking tone. "How are you? Oh, I'm fine, thanks, just had my belly sliced open and half my guts pulled out."

"Oh, hush," Laurie said. "You knew the baby would be the center of attention for a while. No one's interested in the momma, even if you did all the hard work." Laurie finally gave her friend a good look. Mary had obviously had a rough night. She had circles around her eyes, her face looked sweaty, and her hair was plastered to her head. "You do look like you've been through the ringer. How are you feeling?"

"Like I've been through a ringer. Pete was teasing me a while ago. You just missed him. He finally went home to get some sleep. Anyway, I kept hitting the button on the pain pump, thinking it wasn't working, but he said 'oh, it's working, all right. If you'd seen what they did to your stomach you'd *know* it was working.'"

"Fun stuff, huh," Laurie said, pulling a seat over next to the bed. "Sounds like I left just in time last night."

"Yeah. The bad thing is, I know I'm going to pay for using these pain drugs. They make you so constipated!"

"Yikes! TMI," Laurie said, making a "time out" sign with her hands. "So how's the food?" she asked pointing to the tray.

"It's okay. I've had worse." Mary was interrupted by a whining little wail from the bassinet. "Uh-oh. Someone's waking up."

"Want me to bring him to you?" Laurie asked. She didn't wait for an answer. Sliding her hands under the swaddled baby, she lifted him to her shoulder and patted him softly. "It's okay, little Roly. Mommy's right here."

"Roly?" Mary asked. "What happened to Thumper? Where'd you come up with Roly?"

"Pete told me his name, Richard Leonard Roster. RLR. His initials make me think 'roller', so – Roly. As in roly-poly."

"Oh, jeez. You try to give a kid a nice normal name, and look what happens." She held her palms up looking exasperated, and then took the baby from Laurie's arms. "It's okay, Ricky," she cooed. "We won't listen to what that crazy lady says."

"Crazy godmother, you mean. How's the nursing going?" Laurie asked, watching Mary struggle with the top of her gown.

"Not very well. I couldn't get anything out this morning. My boobs were tight as drums and big as cantaloupes. I think with the baby being three weeks early, I wasn't really ready to start. And Ricky wasn't ready to nurse, either. But finally the *lactation consultant*" – she said the words in a snooty voice – "came in and helped me out. Actually, she *was* very helpful." The baby latched on, and Mary let out a sigh. Laurie watched with frank interest.

"I hope Ricky does get a little more roly-poly," Mary said. "You haven't seen his skinny little legs. He should have fattened up in my womb for a few more weeks. As it is, I'm afraid the fat is all mine."

"Well, he looks like he's eating pretty good to me," Laurie said. "And I'm sure you'll be out jogging before long."

"Six weeks, girlfriend. I'm going to be a lady of leisure as long as possible, or at least as long as I can keep Pete on diaper duty."

"Changing the subject, since I don't want to even think about messy diapers, guess what St. Mark's is going to do?"

"What?"

"Hold an art show." Laurie told Mary about her discussion with Mother Barbara at the Coffee Pot that afternoon.

"Sounds like lots of fun," Mary said. "Maybe you can get your artist friend to help you." She waggled her eyebrows.

"Jeff?" Laurie asked. "Hmmm. Maybe I can *avoid* getting my artist friend to help. I think I'd rather work with Sharon. But we'll see. It's all still in the planning stages. I really do think it would be a nice event, and maybe attract some new people to the church. At least they'll figure out where we are."

"Yeah, when you write up the advertising, be sure it says 'right across from the Tasty Chick'."

"Right!"

* * *

Laurie left the hospital before she had to witness a diaper-changing. She felt a mid-afternoon slump coming on. She wanted to get out and stretch her legs, and decided to do a little shopping downtown before supper.

Most of her friends in Chinkapin knew Laurie was strapped for cash. Still, she didn't like to keep showing up in clothes that came from the Treasure Chest. It was time to check out the competition, and look for some new threads in one of the other thrift shops that had opened recently.

"Top Dog," run by the friends of the animal shelter, was down the street from the Treasure Chest in the middle of a small shopping plaza. The storefront was painted to resemble a dog house, and cheery flowers bloomed in planters on the sidewalk outside.

Laurie stepped in and eyed the two rooms which made up the shop. In the front were pet supplies like collars, leashes, dog and cat toys, and animal-themed gift items. The large room beyond was lined with shelves holding a hodgepodge of donated items. Kitchen ware was stacked next to toys, hats sat on top of lamps, and old videos were mixed in everywhere.

In the center of the room was a long rack of clothes. Everything was jammed together, and nothing was arranged by size. Laurie pawed through the clothing with difficulty, and finally found something she liked. She carried it back to the cash register, and looked again at the gift items.

"The stuffed toys are half price today," the volunteer at the register said. In a lower voice she added, "some of them are left over from Christmas."

Laurie looked up and recognized a woman she'd seen at the Coffee Pot. "I know you. You sang 'How Much is That Doggy in the Window' at open mic night a couple of weeks ago." Smiling, Laurie extended a hand across the counter. "Laurie Lanton."

"My name's Megan. Nice to meet you."

"A friend of mine plays at the Coffee Pot a lot. Chase Harris. Maybe you know him."

"Sure, I know Chase. He helps set up the mics and things sometimes. He's a nice guy."

Laurie nodded. "Half price, eh?" she said, eyeing the toys. "My bestie just had a baby boy. In fact, I'm going to be his godmother. It'll be a while before he plays with anything like these toys, but they are awful cute." She picked up a stuffed dog that reminded her a little of Blue from *Blue's Clues*.

"That one is four dollars. Three if you brought in a can of dog food."

Laurie dug the money out of her wallet. "So what happens with the money you bring in here?"

"We use it to support the animal shelter," Megan explained. "Everything from utility bills and transportation costs to food, medicine, and veterinary care. Some of the vets in the area donate their services, and people bring in food, and supplies like bedding and such. But we still have to buy different types of food, like puppy chow or special food, and medicine."

"So is this place self-sustaining? I mean, does the money brought in cover all the costs of the dog shelter?"

"No. It's doing very well, but ... no. Some of the volunteers have been brainstorming some kind of fundraiser, but..." She trailed off again.

Laurie remembered one of the Treasure Chest volunteers mentioning other thrift shops in town, but Laurie would not have even known where this one was if she hadn't driven by it every week on her way to church. She wondered who was working on Top Dog's advertising and publicity. An idea for an article stirred in her mind. "I understand this shop hasn't been here very long."

"About six months." Another customer came in, and Megan told her about their special on stuffed animals. As Laurie continued to look around the small shop, a painting of a pug caught her eye. She never thought pugs were the most attractive animals, but this picture was engaging. The dog's eyes shone with an inner light, and its long pink tongue unrolled from its mouth. Between its tongue and the angle of its head, the dog looked like it was just waiting for someone to start a game of fetch.

Laurie was suddenly startled by barking behind her. "Hi, Sparky," Megan said, coming out from behind the register to pet the dog.

Laurie turned to look, and did a double-take. "That looks just like the dog in the picture," she said, pointing at the picture and staring at Sparky.

"Not quite," said a woman in tight, stretchy jeans and a bouffant hairdo holding Sparky's leash. "The wrinkles on Sparky's head are darker, and his ears are a little darker overall. But I *love* that picture. If I could find out who the artist was, I'd pay them to paint Sparky." Laurie noticed the dog's collar, which looked a lot like the diamond bracelet around the woman's wrist.

Laurie looked at the picture again, and saw a scratchy, illegible signature. She remembered something Jeff had said, that there was a lot of money in painting children and pets. Sparky was snuffling around her ankles, curled tail waving over his back.

"He sure is friendly," Laurie said, smiling and crouching down to scratch him behind his ears.

"Laurie, this is Glenda." Laurie rose as Megan introduced them, and the two shook hands. "Glenda is the current chairperson for the friends of the animal shelter. I was just telling Laurie that we're thinking of some kind of fund-raiser, but not sure what. There's no space to really do much here. Maybe something in conjunction with a dog show at the fairgrounds, but those tend to be pretty commercial."

"What would you think about an art show?" Laurie asked.

"An art show?" the others said it together, and exchanged a glance. Megan shrugged.

Laurie pointed to the painting of the pug. "Take this painting. How cute it is! What if you had an art show, and all the artworks featured pictures of pets? These days that covers a lot of ground. I mean, I've heard of people keeping chickens as pets. Even farm animals."

"But where could we hold an art show? I know it costs money to rent the arts center, unless they had a hand in running the show. We surely don't have the space here, and the animal shelter itself ...Well, the new shelter is nice, but I still don't know how that would work."

"I have just the place," Laurie said with a smile. By the time she had given them a rough outline of her proposal, they were both on board. She promised to set up a meeting with Mother Barbara within the week.

Chapter 19.

Tuesday morning Laurie put on the blouse she had bought the day before, a summery Hawaiian print. She added a loose-fitting pair of cotton slacks, and casual sandals. Curling her hair was a waste of time in Chinkapin's early-summer humidity, so she tied it in a short ponytail low on one shoulder, and fluffed her bangs.

She hoped her ensemble would be appropriate for both her job and her afternoon plans. She would be seeing Chase later, but since he was coming from work she didn't think she needed to be "dressed up." Laurie's mind drifted to the image of Chase leaning against the counter at the café. She closed her eyes, and took a deep breath.

Her job was a welcome distraction. First, she was thrilled to see her article about Art Night in the morning's paper. Her editor complimented her work, and was interested in more story ideas.

Second, Laurie truly enjoyed the mental exercise of editing the events column. She had felt her writing skills improving as she edited and reworded the information

submitted by members of the community. Announcements ran the gamut from church events, plays, and concerts, to gardening classes and festivals. Learning about
all the goings-on in Chinkapin made her feel a part of
the action.

Laurie noted the picture submitted for this week's
Art Night Out at the Chinkapin Arts Center. Jeff's
painting of the night sky with fireworks reminded her
that Independence Day was coming up in a few weeks.

Another announcement caught her eye for an estate
sale on King Street, to be held the third weekend in
June. Laurie plugged the address into the navigator on
her phone. As she expected, it was the house she had
driven by the day she went looking for the Williams' res-
idence: Jeff's mother's place.

Even at work, she didn't seem able to get away from
Jeff.

She finished her work for the day, grabbed a quick
lunch, and headed to the Treasure Chest to kill time before her date with Chase. She was happy to see Virginia's car parked outside. Virginia's husband had planted a
big vegetable garden that spring, and it yielded more
produce than one family could eat. They couldn't let it
go to waste, and wouldn't hear of selling it. That meant
all their friends got to enjoy the fresh vegetables.

"What did you bring today?" Laurie asked Virginia, peering at the bag on the counter in the staff kitchen.

"Tomatoes, yellow squash, and zucchini. You and Alice divide them up. Anne took all she wanted this morning."

Laurie's mouth watered at the sight of the lovely tomatoes. She selected a couple of squash, a zucchini, and half a dozen ripe tomatoes, and made her way to the shop's office. Alice came in and sat in the desk chair with a sigh.

"I had to come up for air. I've been tagging clothes for an hour," she said.

"You look pooped. Have you had some lunch?" Laurie asked.

"I did! I brought a sandwich, and added a couple slices of fresh tomato. It was *so* good!"

"Speaking of food, I don't see the bird cage." Laurie noted the empty spot where the cage had stood, and looked cautiously around the office.

"We checked for mice first thing this morning. Something ate the cracker in the cage without springing the door. But we did catch a mouse in one of the traps. Virginia disposed of it."

"I rebaited them. See?" Virginia pointed to the two traps against the wall. "I was going to rig up the bird cage, but someone bought it!"

"Isn't that funny?" Alice said. "That cage has been here for three months, and finally someone wanted it."

"Sometimes all it takes is moving items around for customers to show interest in things," Laurie said.

"I hope that was the last of the mice, but we need to keep checking for a while," Virginia said. "By the way, Carol called earlier to remind everybody not to leave any food out. And I reminded *her* about the problems with the roof. We had that little rain shower last night, and I had to mop up a couple spots on the floor again, mostly in that back hallway."

"Speaking of mopping up water," Laurie began, and launched into details about Mary's emergency trip to the hospital and the new baby. The older women reminisced about their own birthing experiences. Laurie listened with interest, but felt rather left out. She tried not to think about her current, partner-less state. She helped Alice pick out several cute baby items from the children's room to take to Mary once she got out of the hospital.

A rush of customers in the early afternoon kept the three women busy. An older couple was outfitting a vacation cabin they had just purchased, and brought item after item to the counter. They started with linens, buying two sets of sheets, a comforter, a shower curtain, and a bath rug. Next they shopped in the kitchen room. As

Alice rang up the sale, Laurie and Virginia wrapped glasses, dishes, silverware, and a coffee maker.

When they left, the women collapsed in the office. "Did you hear what that couple said?" Alice asked, looking at Laurie. "They said they found us on the web. They saw your post about the half-price sale in the linens room, and that's why they came in. And then they bought all that other stuff too." She held up her hand and high-fived Laurie.

Immediately the door jangled and Alice groaned, starting to rise. Virginia glanced through the doorway and called out "Good timing Mother Barbara. We could have used you about five minutes ago. We just made a seventy-five dollar sale."

Mother Barbara leaned across the counter to see the three women sitting in the office. "That's great! You all earned your paychecks today. One more sale like that, and you can close for the rest of the week." Then to Laurie she said "I thought I'd find you here. Can you come over to the church and we'll talk business for a few minutes?"

Laurie rose and walked with Mother Barbara across the parking lot and into her small office. "Have a seat. I was working on my homily for Wednesday's service and saw your car over here. How's everything going?"

Laurie smiled at Mother Barbara. More than once she had confided in the priest about the dramas of her personal life. Although Laurie knew she was well rid of DB, the years of dysfunctional married life sometimes left her feeling blue. It helped to hear Mother Barbara's words of reassurance, particularly since the woman had also been through a marital break-up.

"I'm doing fine. Never a dull moment," Laurie said.

"Nice shirt, by the way." Mother Barbara indicated the colorful tropical print Laurie was sporting.

"Guess where I got this."

Mother Barbara waited for the big reveal.

"Top Dog. It's one of the competing thrift shops in town, and it's run by the friends of the animal shelter."

"Ah," Mother Barbara said. "Well, we can't think too badly of them, since they're working for a worthy cause."

"Right. Well, I don't think their shop is much competition, really. It's small, and not very well organized. But, I was talking to a couple of people there, including Glenda, their chairperson. Remember we were looking for a theme for our art show, and wondering whether to make it a fund-raiser, or something? It so happens that the friends of the animal shelter were also contemplating some type of fund-raiser. How about partnering with them on our art show?" Mother Barbara narrowed her eyes.

Laurie leaned in. "Listen. Who doesn't like helping out poor homeless animals? So they're automatically a good charity to partner with – good will, and all. And it'll help us to narrow the focus of our art show. The theme can be pets, or animals; something like that. I think we can be ready by mid-July, and – get this – call it the Dog Days art show, benefiting the Chinkapin Friends of the Animal Shelter. What do you think?"

Mother Barbara had a big smile on her face. "Dog Days art show. I love it! I was thinking summer, before people get tied down with school, and sports, and everything."

"School starts earlier and earlier every year, so we don't want to wait any later in the summer. I think mid-July should work out fine."

"What about the arts center? I don't want it to seem like we're moving in on their territory. I'm not sure we could compete with them, in any event."

"I'll call Sharon to double-check, but they're busy with the kids' summer art camps. I don't think they have another show scheduled until a lot later in the fall. Plus, if we ask them to judge the show ..." Laurie smiled, eyebrows raised.

"That'll make them a part of it. Perfect!" Mother Barbara really did look pleased. "Well, I'll leave it to you, then. If you can get a few rough details down on paper, and maybe a draft of a flyer, we can present it to the vestry."

"Will do!" Laurie jotted some notes in her little notebook. Her smart phone beeped, and she looked at the calendar reminder displayed on the screen. "Oh, what time is it? I have to get out of here. I'm meeting a friend at the Coffee Pot." She looked at Mother Barbara, blushing a little. "See you later!"

Chapter 20.

Laurie ran across the parking lot and got in her car. *Alice and Virginia can close the shop on their own*, she thought, driving to the Coffee Pot.

Although it was a little early for her date, she didn't have much time to feel nervous. Chase was already waiting at a table outside the café. Apparently he hadn't come directly from work, because he was cleaned up and wearing a shirt from the Treasure Chest – a blue golf shirt Laurie had tagged a few weeks ago. With a pang she wondered if she should be letting him spend money on her. Then she smiled to herself, considering she wore clothes from the thrift shop all the time.

Chase rose and held the door for her. "We were working a residential job, and finished up early. Boy, were the homeowners glad, too. The temperature in their house was over ninety degrees."

"I bet they were glad! It's been a hot summer so far," Laurie said.

"And it's just getting started! Maybe you'll want an iced coffee today." He smiled at her.

"An iced mocha latte. I'm going to live dangerously."

"You only go around once," Chase said. "Two large iced mochas please, Amber."

He evidently knew the young cashier, who gave him a toothy smile, flashing braces. The barista waved, calling out "Hey, Chase. Good to see you."

Laurie sat at a bench behind a long table against the wall, and watched Chase as he paid for the drinks and chatted with the cashier. Though not exactly handsome, he was still very appealing. She wondered why she didn't feel jealous over him talking to the ladies in the café, like she had felt jealous with Jeff. With Chase it seemed less about flirting and more about just being friendly.

After a moment he handed her a frosty glass and took a seat next to her on the bench. "So, business is good then?" she asked, returning to what she thought was a safe subject.

"Oh, yeah. Everyone's running their air conditioners at warp speed this time of year, so some of them are bound to break or just wear out. It means lots of over-time for us. We're a little short-handed right now. If we'd finished that last job any earlier in the day, we would have started another one."

He took a sip of his latte, and seemed to remember something as he swallowed. "Hey, I saw your article in the paper this morning! It was really good."

"You liked it?" she asked, glad someone had noticed it. Apparently no one at the thrift shop had read the paper.

"Yeah, I did. I liked that it was so descriptive! I feel like I know exactly what goes on at one of those classes now."

"Thanks." She was pleased he appreciated something she had written. DB never complimented her on her writing.

"Anderson HVAC was mentioned in the paper last week," she said, thinking of the article in Friday's newspaper. "What's the story with Bo Anderson? Is he out on bail or anything?"

Chase let out a long breath, shaking his head. "That young man has made some poor decisions. And that's probably the understatement of the year. He's not likely to see the light of day for a while. I feel sorry for his daddy."

"That's too bad. Have you known them long?"

"Oh, I've known the family for about ten years. I was never great friends with Bo – he's several years younger than I am. But old man Anderson, as everyone calls him, had really pinned the future of his business on that boy, so he's especially disappointed. He was hoping to retire this year, and now he doesn't know what he'll do."

"There's no one else working for him who would want to take over the business?" she asked.

"One guy that might have been interested moved down to Valdosta and started a business of his own. Most of the other guys really couldn't handle it, or they're older themselves, and don't want to take it on."

The two sipped their drinks, chatting about work, the upcoming holiday, and the tentative plans for the art show at the church.

"This place makes the best lattes," Laurie said finally, stirring the bottom of the glass with her straw to get the last bit of chocolate. "I thank you for the drink. I don't mean to run out on you, but I know these ladies want to close." The café was only open late on the weekend. "And I've got a bag of fresh produce in the car that doesn't need to get any riper."

"Got any tomatoes in there?"

"Maybe," she said temptingly. She remembered how he heaped his plate full of food during the Sunday coffee hour, and wondered if he was getting enough to eat. "I might be talked into sparing one or two."

"Have you ever tried tomato pie?" he asked.

"I've never even *heard* of tomato pie."

"You have been missing out! It's simple, really – basically like a quiche. The main ingredients are eggs, cheese, and tomatoes. Do you like cheese?"

"Are you kidding?" Laurie asked. "If I liked it any more I would turn into a mouse. And it's not safe to be a mouse around here." They both laughed, remembering Jerry the mouse at the Treasure Chest. She quickly filled him in on the day's mouse tally.

"Let the record show, I did not harm any mice at the Treasure Chest," Chase said. Laurie thought how pleasant he looked when he smiled. His good mood was infectious. "We could make a tomato pie tonight," he suggested. "That is, if you don't have plans."

It sounded good, and Laurie certainly did not have plans. "Won't it take a long time, like, to make the pastry and all?"

"Not the way I do it, with pre-made pastry dough that you just unroll into the pie pan. Grate the cheese, whip up the eggs, add a little onion, the sliced tomatoes, some freshly ground pepper, throw it in the oven, and..." He made a smacking sound with his lips. "Plus if you can keep yourself from eating the whole pie in one sitting, the leftovers are great for breakfast."

Laurie laughed at his enthusiasm. "Okay, do we have everything we need? I've got the tomatoes, and probably enough eggs. Not sure about the cheese, and definitely not the pie crust."

"I'll run out and get the cheese and pie crust. Meet me at my apartment in thirty minutes. I'm in unit 103."

They walked out of the café together and Amber turned over the "closed" sign behind them.

Laurie drove straight back to her apartment and gathered the necessary groceries. She redid her ponytail, fluffed her bangs, and looked at her watch three or four times. Finally she trotted downstairs and knocked on the door of apartment 103.

The apartments in the 100's were partially below ground level, so the windows in Chase's apartment were higher up on the wall, and smaller than those in Laurie's apartment. Otherwise, the units were much the same.

"This place looks eerily familiar," she said, as he took the bag from her and offered her some iced tea.

"Don't tell me they made more of this furniture," he said.

"'Fraid so. My windows are bigger than yours. I guess that makes up for me having to climb stairs to the third floor."

"You must have a great view from up there," he said.

"Yeah, I can see *over* the roof of the pawn shop." She laughed. "On a clear day, I can see all the way to the Oil Lamp Restaurant."

"Ah, the Oil Lamp. Best meatloaf in town."

"Okay, chef, you're making me hungry. How do we make this tomato pie?"

He turned on the oven light, beckoning her to look inside. "Observe." The pie crust was browning.

"What's that stuff in the crust?" she asked. It looked like stone marbles.

"Those are pie weights, grasshopper," he said. "The crust has to pre-bake. If you don't put something in the pastry to hold it down, it'll bubble up, and then there's no room for the filling." He pointed to a cutting board on the small kitchen counter. "Can I trust you with a knife?" When Laurie nodded he said, "Slice these toma-toes nice and thin."

Chase grabbed an old iPod, connected it to a small stereo system, and music filled the apartment. Laurie recognized the swing era chanteuse. "That sounds like Helen Forrest," she said, pausing with the knife in the air.

"That's right! I'm surprised you've heard of her."

"I love that kind of music – the 1940's, World War II, the swing era. My grandparents had a bunch of old rec-ords they let me play with. That's one of the things I like about the Coffee Pot. They play all that great old stuff. Benny Goodman, Artie Shaw, Harry James..." She swayed her hips to "Melancholy Mood."

"I'm glad to hear that. I set up the sound system for them, and I program the music." Laurie stared, lips parted. Chase added "Of course the music goes with the décor and the whole atmosphere they have going on."

She resumed slicing, and Chase placed an onion next to her. "Chop this, and I'll grate the cheese."

Finished, Laurie watched Chase assemble the cheddar pie. He carefully layered the ingredients in the crust, totally focused on his work. "Are you always such a perfectionist?" she asked.

"Only when I'm trying to impress the ladies." He smiled without looking up, and put the pie in the oven. Then he took up his iPod again. "Here's something more modern you might like – Mary Louise Knutson." Smooth piano jazz flowed from the speakers.

The apartment was warm from the oven and the slanting rays of sunlight glancing through the window. Suddenly Chase took Laurie by the hand, placed his other hand on her waist, and danced her around the small living room. Laurie let him lead as she listened to the music.

Another song started. Laurie looked up as they continued dancing. "Is this the same, Mary Louise whoever?"

"No, this is Bill Charlap, another jazz pianist." Laurie closed her eyes, swaying in Chase's arms, listening as upright bass and drums joined the piano.

It felt nice to be held again. It felt natural. The music was mellow and smooth, and one song blended into the next until Laurie wasn't sure how long they danced. "I love this," she murmured.

Chase pulled back to look at her. His angular features softened. Laurie caught her breath, glanced down, and then back at his face. "I love this music," she said. He smiled, but the look was gone.

"Let's check the pie. We don't want it to burn." Businesslike, he grabbed a pair of oven mitts, pulled open the oven door, and examined the pie.

"A few more minutes." He grabbed his glass of iced tea and sat at one end of the saggy sofa.

Laurie cast her eyes around the room and pulled a book at random from a small bookcase nearby. "*Driving the Scenic Back Roads of Georgia*," she read aloud.

"That's a good book," Chase said. "It's full of history about some of the smaller towns and scenic areas. Maybe you haven't had a chance to explore much, but this is a beautiful state. I travelled a few of those routes, before moving to Chinkapin."

She sat on the couch as he got up to check the pie. Idly she turned the pages, not really reading. She knew she'd said the wrong thing when they were dancing, but wasn't sure if that was good or bad. She was attracted to him, there was no doubt. Was Mary right when she cautioned her not to get involved? What if they did get involved, and then broke up? It could get awfully uncomfortable in the choir loft.

"Do you want to see something beautiful?" Chase brought the pie over for her inspection. The crust was golden brown, the cheesy filling looked nicely set, and it smelled delicious. He set it on a hot pad, and pulled some dishes from the cupboard.

"How can I help?" Laurie asked.

"Silverware in that drawer," he indicated with a nod of his head. He sliced a rustic loaf of bread. Then he held up a bottle of red wine. "Want some?"

"A small glass," she said, promising herself she wouldn't have more than that.

They sat together at his little table and Chase served generous slices of pie. It was as good as he had promised. The bread and wine complimented it nicely.

"An absolute feast," Laurie said. "How is it that I never heard of tomato pie before? You seem to know a lot about tomatoes."

"I beg your pardon, madam, you mean the *love apple*," he corrected her.

She laughed, relaxed. Chase was interesting. Companionable. Even attractive, the more time she spent with him. She wondered again about his past. Maybe what she thought she knew about him was wrong.

Laurie turned down his offer of another slice of pie, but when he held the bottle of wine above her glass, she nodded.

After supper she bagged the bread while Chase covered the leftover pie. As he tidied the kitchen, she perched on the couch with her wineglass. Finally he came and sank into the couch next to her, massaging his temples.

"Long day, huh?" Laurie said.

"Yeah." He leaned back, then turned his head to look at her. "More wine?"

"No, thanks." She swirled the contents of her glass, finished the last sip, and then set it down on the floor.

Chase took her hand and laced his fingers into hers. He reached across with his other hand and trailed his fingertips along her forearm. Music streamed from the speaker with a woozy melody and the shushing sound of brushes on cymbals.

Laurie moved nearer, her forehead against his shoulder. Chase stroked her hair, twirling a loose lock softly with his fingers. He brought his face close to hers, and she looked up at him through her eyelashes.

That's when his cellphone rang.

The sound clashed crazily with the moody music. Laurie pulled away slightly, but Chase ignored the phone. He drew her close again. She placed a hand on his chest, sketching little circles with her fingernails across his muscular shoulder. Their lips met softly, and her body warmed as they relaxed into each other. She pulled him closer, and their kisses grew deeper.

And his phone rang again.

"Crap," he breathed, reaching over to the little book case to snatch it up. He looked at it and made an exasperated growling sound. "I have to see what this is about."

Pulling away, he stood and walked into the kitchen talking on the phone. Laurie groaned inwardly, slouching back on the couch, and closed her eyes. She opened them again, looking around for a clock. She watched Chase pacing in the kitchen, rumpling his hair with one hand, talking indistinctly into the phone. He glanced occasionally at her, a pained look on his face. Finally he nodded and ended the call.

"I have to go," he said.

Chapter 21.

The next day Laurie finished her shift at the *Journal* and drove to Mary's house for lunch. Mary had left the hospital that morning, and texted Laurie that she might manage to make some coffee if Laurie would bring her a pimento cheese sandwich from the Coffee Pot. Laurie suspected Mary was really hoping for a report on her date with Chase.

Mary met her at the door, walking slowly and holding a hand to her stomach. "I fibbed about making the coffee. Pete did it just before he left. I told him go ahead and go to work this afternoon, because I'm mostly just going to lie around. I can't believe I'm home already! I kind of feel like if I move too fast my staples will pop out and my guts will fall onto the floor. But the nurse said that's not likely to happen."

"You're better off at home," Laurie said. "Hospitals are dangerous places." She placed the bag with their lunch in it on the kitchen table and poured two mugs of coffee.

"By the way, that's decaf," Mary told her.

Laurie's shoulders slumped, and she groaned.

"I know, but – you know," Mary said, pointing at her rounded breasts. "I want to nurse as long as I can, and I don't need little Ricky getting all spun up on caffeine."

"I hope some of your family comes to help you out. Didn't you tell me your in-laws wanted to visit as soon as the baby was born? I guess everyone was thrown off schedule when he came a little early."

"My in-laws are coming in a few days," Mary said. "I sure can use the help, so I'll be glad to have them, at least for a while." Laurie looked around the kitchen and nodded. There was a dish in the sink, and a cereal box left out on the counter. Mary would never have let that happen before the baby was born.

"So where is little Roly?"

"Asleep. He loves his new nursery," Mary said, gently lowering herself to a seat.

"Oh, he told you that, did he?" Laurie asked with a smile, noting the nursery monitor at Mary's elbow. Laurie had always wanted children, but the timing had never been right for DB. Now, without a man in her life, she tried not to think about it, which was not easy under the circumstances.

Laurie sat at the table, dove into the paper bag, and pulled out two sandwiches.

"So, you have to dish in exchange for coffee," Mary said, pouring creamer into her mug. "How was your get-together with Chase yesterday? Did you behave your-self?"

"You know, I could have stayed at the Coffee Pot and had a *real* cup of coffee, and not had to answer any intrusive questions."

"And I could have stayed in bed and let Pete wait on me! Come on now, out with it."

"Well," Laurie began, smiling, "our little date at the Coffee Pot was pleasant enough. Afterwards was great too, but..."

"Afterwards?" Mary raised her eyebrows. "Do we need to have our little talk again?"

Laurie set her friend straight. "Nothing like that. After we left the café we went to our apartment."

"*Our* apartment? Girl, you do move fast!"

"I mean our apartment *building*! Remember we live in the same building? Anyway, I said I had vegetables in the car – you know, from Virginia, because she was at the Treasure Chest yesterday. And Chase got all excited and told me about something called tomato pie. Have you ever heard of it?"

Mary shook her head. "I've eaten onion pie, but not tomato pie."

"Well, after he described it I wanted to try it, so we met back at his place and made the pie and ate supper together." She took a sip of coffee to hide her smile.

"Tomato pie, huh? I see that smile. Are you sure you just had supper?"

"Well, we were getting cozy on the couch afterwards, until his cell phone rang. He didn't answer at first, but then he saw it was his boss, Mr. Anderson, who sounded really upset. I could hear the guy through the phone. His wife fell and hurt herself, and the ambulance was there, and Mr. Anderson wanted Chase to meet them at the hospital."

"Really! That's weird. I mean, why call Chase?"

"I know, right? But I guess there's no other family in the area. And he and Chase go back farther than we realized," Laurie said. "Chase told me he's known the Andersons for, like, ten years."

"But he hasn't lived here that long, has he?"

"No. But Chase's wife – ex-wife, whatever – is from here, so I guess he's been in and out of Chinkapin for a long time."

"Hmmm. There's more to that story than we know." Mary looked thoughtful. "So did you hear anything more from Chase last night?"

"Yeah. When he left I went back to my place, of course, but he texted me later. They were still in the emergency room, but it looked like Mrs. Anderson was going to be admitted. Evidently she broke her hip. I don't know if Chase took Mr. Anderson home then, or what happened. I wonder if I should call."

"Wouldn't he be at work now?" Mary asked.

"Yeah. And he said they were super busy because of the hot weather and people's air conditioners going out."

Mary still looked thoughtful, but brightened as Laurie reached into the paper bag again, pulled out a small container of fruit salad, and handed it across the table. "Yum!" she said. "Well, let me tell you *my* news. My sister and her family are coming to visit for the fourth of July, and staying through the following weekend. I've talked to Mother Barbara, and we're going to do the baptism while she's here."

"Wow. Already? I thought you were going to wait a little longer. I mean, you won't exactly be ready to host people. Or is she coming to help you too?"

"To help, and to visit, I guess. She wants to see the baby, and her kids can swim in the pool. She better *not* expect me to wait on everyone. Anyway, do you want to go shopping with me? I won't be able to fit into a lot of my old tops for a while." She sighed. "I didn't plan this whole motherhood thing very well."

"They just tagged a bunch of cute summer clothes at the Treasure Chest. What exactly are you looking for?" Laurie asked.

"I'll need something pretty for the baptism. Whatever it is, it has to be cool and flowy. Holding Ricky makes me sweat. Then, my sister said something about us going to the fireworks at the fairgrounds on that Saturday, and then having a luau pool party Sunday afternoon. She promised to do all the work. You'll come to the luau, right?"

"I've got the perfect shirt for it," Laurie said, thinking of the Hawaiian shirt she'd worn the previous day. "And you know I enjoy seeing your sister and her kids. Besides, where else would I be?"

"Maybe we can find something like a Hawaiian shirt for Pete, too."

"I'll check for you next time I'm at the shop." Laurie tucked into her food, and the two ate in silence for a moment. Then Laurie updated Mary on the mouse situation, and the art show.

"It's definitely a go. You know, art is not actually up my alley, but Mother Barbara wants me to coordinate the show with the other groups involved, and publicize it. There'll be other people handling snacks, and setting up and stuff. I'm counting on you to help, or at least to provide moral support."

"Oh, sure. I'll be glad to help. Maybe I'll even get my old drawing pencils out, and enter something myself. I did win that junior high school art competition, you know." A few squawks erupted from the nursery monitor, followed by a high-pitched wailing. "Question is whether Ricky will cooperate." Mary put a hand to her abdomen, and started to rise.

"Stay put. I'll go get him." Laurie disappeared down the hall, and returned cradling Ricky gingerly in her arms. "I'm not used to holding a little guy like this." As she gazed fondly at the baby, she patted his bottom and unconsciously swayed from side to side, feeling like a balloon had inflated inside her heart. "I need one of these. He's so soft and sweet. I could just eat him up! Oops – wait – I think he's trying to eat me. Mary!" As the baby turned his head trying to nurse, Laurie handed him carefully to his mother.

"I thought someone else would be getting hungry about now. Yes, I thought so," Mary crooned to the baby. She fumbled under her blouse a moment. Then she stuck the baby's head under her shirt tail and he started suckling. "It's convenient not to have to mix up formula and clean bottles and all, but the down-side is the feeding is all up to me."

"You don't look too unhappy about it," Laurie observed, watching Mary's face as she caressed her infant's legs and feet.

"But back to your art thing," Mary said. "You told me there are going to be prizes. Who's going to judge the show?"

"Well," Laurie hesitated. "I called Sharon at the arts center today, hoping I could get just her to do it. But she insisted it should be both her and Jeff. So ... I guess I'll have to make nice with my old friend again." She sighed.

Mary smiled. "Hmmm. Well, I've known lots of couples who started out hating each other, and then fell in love. Anything can happen."

"Don't get your hopes up. Just because you think I *should* go for this guy doesn't mean I will." Laurie popped the last bite of her sandwich into her mouth and took a moment to chew and swallow. "But speaking of Jeff, I came across an announcement today for an estate sale at his mother's house on King Street later this month. I bet there's some beautiful furniture in that old house. What do you think?"

"I'd be surprised if there wasn't. I would love to see inside the house. It depends on how I'm doing, but we should try to go to that sale," Mary said.

"Who's going to watch Roly?"

"His name is Ricky," she sniffed. "And I'll just plop him in the stroller. He should be good for a couple of hours, if I feed him first."

"Want to go that Friday morning then? I'll ask if I can get off work early, and pick you up."

Mary nodded, and the two made plans to check out the estate sale and go clothes shopping afterwards.

* * *

Mary's in-laws came to visit, and her mother-in-law stayed behind for two weeks to help Mary with the baby. Laurie made a point of staying away. She had met Mary's in-laws a time or two before. How two such awful people could have raised a nice guy like Pete, Laurie never could figure out. But Mary got along with them well enough, and that was what mattered.

With Mary temporarily out of commission there was one less volunteer to work at the Treasure Chest, and Laurie did her best to pick up the slack. She was working with Anne the following Saturday when Chase came into the store.

"Hey," he said, and paused at the counter where the two women were bagging glassware for a customer. "Where do I find the tee shirts?"

"Back in the back," Laurie pointed "just around the corner from the utility closet."

Chase disappeared down the hall. "I haven't seen him in here since they fixed the air conditioner," Anne said. "I guess you see him all the time, though, don't you."

"Yep, every Sunday in the choir loft, but we're usually pretty busy up there," Laurie answered. She didn't volunteer any information about meeting Chase at the Coffee Pot, or having dinner with him. "Actually I run into him more often because we live in the same apartment complex." She used the term "complex" loosely. Laurie was sure Anne was not aware that her complex included exactly one building hunkered next to Chinkapin Gun and Pawn. Anne lived in a nicer part of town.

"Well, how about that," was all Anne said. After their customer left with her purchase, Anne went into the back room to sort through donations. Laurie was glad to have the counter to herself, since she was hoping to talk to Chase when he was through shopping.

It wasn't long before he returned with four tee shirts and a pair of khaki pants. "How's our friend Mary doing?" he asked. "I heard she had her baby already. We all thought it wasn't due for another few weeks."

"It wasn't, but she and the baby are doing great. I saw them just the other day." She filled him in on a little of the excitement surrounding the baby's pre-mature birth.

Then she asked after his boss's wife, who was in a rehab facility nursing her broken hip.

Finally Chase said "I was hoping you had some more pants like these. I wear them at work, and I always seem to get caught on something and rip them to pieces."

"If you didn't see any more in the men's area we might have some in the back. I can check and see. Actually you can come with me." Anne had come back with some vases to price and set out on the shelf in the hallway. "Watch the counter, will you Anne? I'm taking Chase into the back to look for more khakis."

Laurie led him to the back room where tagged items were hanging ready to be put out for sale. "Here are the men's pants," she said, pointing to the rack. "The sizes should be listed on the tags. Looks like a lot of heavy winter stuff here, though." She started checking tags on one end of the rack while Chase started on the other.

"Been busy at work?" she asked casually.

"Busier than a one-eyed cat watching two mouse holes," he answered. "Speaking of which, have any more mice shown up over here?"

Laurie's lips curved. "No, thank heaven, but Alice did see a snake crawling up the wall when she unlocked the door yesterday. It was a little black one, nothing dangerous."

"Poor Alice. If it weren't for bad luck she wouldn't have any luck at all." Chase had reached the middle of the clothes rack, and turned to look at Laurie. "My uncle used to say there are just five kinds of dangerous snakes."

"Five?" she said. "I thought there were six types of venomous snakes in Georgia."

"Five kinds of dangerous snakes, my uncle said. Big ones, little ones, medium size ones, live ones, and dead ones."

Laurie laughed. "Dead ones?"

"Dead ones because you might think they're alive. And even if they're not venomous, they'll make you hurt yourself trying to get away from them."

Chase and Laurie stood inches from each other. He leaned toward her and she reached for his hand, pulling him close as his lips brushed hers.

Just then Anne's voice sounded in the hallway, and they stepped apart. "Hey, your phone's ringing. I think someone really wants to talk to you, because it stopped and then rang again."

Laurie sighed, and headed back toward the office. Her phone was ringing as she dug it out of her purse. She was shocked to see DB's name come up on the screen, and hesitated before answering. "Hello?"

"Hi. How are you?"

She hadn't heard his voice in over six months. It sounded the same as always, brisk and businesslike. She tensed, and felt the sweat under her arms. "I'm doing great, thanks," she answered. She wasn't about to ask how he was. She really didn't care.

"A while back, you sent me a text about my pocket watch. I want it back."

The clenching in Laurie's stomach eased just a little. "Your watch. Okay. Let's see." Laurie knew she'd seen it in the shop just a couple of days ago. She walked over to the jewelry display case near the cash register. Chase laid a pair of blue jeans on his stack of clothes on the counter, and Anne started writing them up on a sales slip.

Laurie looked for the watch where it had been in the center of the display case, but didn't see it anywhere. Beads of sweat started on her forehead. She searched the case again, but still didn't see it. Then she started rifling through sales receipts, to see if it had been sold in the last couple of days, and came up empty.

"Look, I'm going to have to look around for it. It might have been sold."

DB's voice came harsh and loud through the phone – loud enough for Anne and Chase to hear. "Sold? What do you mean sold?" he demanded. "You sold my watch?

Why didn't you send it to me? You know that watch is important to me!"

Laurie cringed under the barrage. She wondered why it had been thrown into her jewelry box if it had been so important to him.

"I said *might* have been sold. Look, when your *lady* friend, and I use the term loosely, said you wouldn't want anything that I had, I figured it was mine to dispose of." Her voice was rising and she was starting to shake. She wondered why she owed him an explanation at all.

Her comment elicited another angry explosion. "You idiot! How could you get rid of my watch? My parents gave me that watch, and when they hear that you ..."

No one heard what DB was about to say concerning his parents, because Laurie had the presence of mind to end the call. She stashed the phone in her purse, and immediately it began to ring again. She removed it, put it on silent, and tossed it back into her purse.

With trembling hands she pulled her hair back away from her face, closed her eyes, and blew out a long breath.

"What was that all about?" Anne asked, looking wide-eyed at Laurie.

"That, friends, was my ex. And now you know why I divorced his ass," she added with a nervous laugh.

"I thought I heard him asking about a watch," Anne said.

"Well, yeah. I texted him a while back that I had his pocket watch, but he never responded, so I donated it to the shop. I guess it must have sold." She looked helplessly toward the display case. "I saw it just a couple of days ago, but..."

"It's not sold," Anne said. Laurie spun around to face her. "Evelyn took it to one of her friends who's a jeweler to have it appraised. She thought it might be worth a lot more than twenty-five dollars, so she took it Thursday to find out."

"So she still has it?" Laurie asked.

"I know she does. I'm sure you can call her and get it back."

Laurie was suddenly relieved. Then tears started to spill from her eyes. "DB, that jerk," she said, wiping at her cheeks. "I don't know whether I feel like sending it to him or not. He's such a ..." She stopped.

"Such a prick," Chase filled in.

"Yeah, that'll work," Laurie nodded.

"You're well rid of him, if that's how he treated you," Anne said, patting her shoulder as she walked past her. "I'm going back to the tagging room."

Laurie took another deep breath. "Let's see what you have here," she said, briskly sorting through Chase's stack of clothes. She finished writing up the sales ticket Anne had started, and rang up the sale on the register.

"How did you end up with such a creep?" Chase asked.

"Oh, you know. They're always on their best behavior until after they get you hooked." She looked a little suspiciously at Chase. "Then they show their true colors. By that time they have you buffaloed into thinking it's somehow your fault that they're yelling at you all the time." She swallowed, and wiped at another tear.

Chase nodded. "I'm glad for your sake that he's found someone else to torture."

"And he couldn't have picked a more deserving woman," she added shakily. "She's a ... real piece of work."

"He's a butt-head," Chase said.

Laurie smiled. "That's what my brother calls him."

"You want me to mail the watch to him? I'd write him a real nice letter explaining what happened. 'Dear Butthead.' Then again, I bet I can find some more appropriate names to call him."

"Kind of you to offer, Chase," she said, still smiling. "First I have talk to Evelyn, and get that watch back. But I'll let you know if I need your services." She bagged his clothes, and handed them to him.

He lingered a few moments as if he wanted to ask her something. Then finally he said "See you tomorrow up in the loft."

"Yep," she said. "See you."

Chapter 22.

The morning of the estate sale on King Street Laurie got permission to leave work an hour early. She parked in Mary's driveway, and was at the front door when she heard a baby crying inside. She knocked on the door and let herself in.

"Mary? Hello," Laurie called, and followed the wailing toward the nursery. Roly was crying in his crib waving his arms, red in the face. Baby clothes were hanging out of the little clothes hamper, and a stack of clean onesies sat on the dresser.

"What's all the fuss about, little man? What's the matter," she crooned, picking the baby up. He turned his head and started rooting around Laurie's chest, his mouth open like a baby bird's.

"Mary?" she called, turning from the crib just as Mary ran into the nursery. "There you are. What's going on?"

"Oh, my God. I fed Ricky this morning, and put him in the crib so I could put on some make-up. Then I had to go to the bathroom. I swear I was in there for two minutes, and he started screaming."

"Well, the poor thing's hungry. Look at him." She laughed as the baby rooted desperately, trying to nurse.

Mary pushed a blanket off the rocking chair and onto the floor, took a seat, and eased the baby's head under the hem of her loose shirt.

Laurie looked at her friend's face and noticed one eye with purple shadow and the other plain. "I guess we're not quite ready to go yet, are we." She took a seat on a step stool.

"He shouldn't be hungry! He ate like a pig this morning, and took forever about it," Mary said, rocking frantically, trying to get the child to eat faster.

"Calm down, Mom. Aren't you supposed to relax or something when you nurse? You're so used to telling people how they should and shouldn't act, but a baby's got to do what a baby's got to do. Roly's in charge now. I'm going to see if you have any coffee."

Laurie went to the kitchen and warmed a cup of coffee from the carafe under the coffee maker. She came back to the nursery with the steaming cup. "Let me guess. Is this decaf?" Mary nodded, and Laurie took a sip, screwing up her face in disgust. "Are you sure going to the estate sale today is a good idea?"

Mary sighed nodding her head. "We'll get there eventually. I really want to see inside that old house."

Finally the baby seemed satisfied, and went to sleep in his mother's arms. Careful not to wake him, she put him in his car seat carrier, slapped on the rest of her make-up, and the two finally got underway.

"I wonder if Jeff will be there," Mary said. "I'm curious to see if he's as cute in person as everyone says."

"I'd just as soon not run into him, but more than likely we will."

"I'm also hoping for some affordable antiques. I'd love an old vanity, or a nice armoire for the spare bedroom. An armoire would be more practical. Or something cute for the baby's room!" Mary clapped her hands.

"I wish I had a house to furnish." Laurie had gotten rid of just about everything she and DB had bought together, but kept some furniture that was given to her by her parents and grandparents. It was still in storage up north. She wondered if she would ever be able to afford a nice old house like the ones in Chinkapin.

She looked around as they entered the historic neighborhood. "I wonder how much upkeep these old places need."

"Lots, I'm sure. But you're too late for this house. It was barely on the market, and it sold right away. Lots of people knew that Mrs. Williams wanted to move, and someone made her an offer."

Laurie was surprised, considering what Jeff had said about needing to fix the place up. Her eyes widened further as she turned onto King Street. Cars lined both sides of the road. "Wow! I hope we can find a place to park. I'll go around the block."

They parked a block over, put the sleeping baby in the buggy and slung the diaper bag over the handle, then walked back to the Williams house. Mary spotted a neighbor and stopped to chat while Laurie looked at items for sale out in the yard. There was a table set up as a check-out counter, and a sign indicating more sale items out back. Laurie signaled to Mary and walked around the house.

She saw a patio set, and peeked through the windows of what appeared to be a guest house or studio. A sign on the door read "contents not for sale."

Eager to see the main house, Laurie followed the crowd into a bright country kitchen. The vintage white cabinetry had old-fashioned bin-pulls, but the appliances were modern and top-of-the-line. Someone who liked to cook would appreciate the large center island and all the storage.

Laurie noted the double oven and thought of Chase and the tomato pie. She wondered what might have happened if the evening hadn't been cut short. He'd texted a couple of times since she saw him at the thrift shop, but was busy with work, and Laurie hadn't seen him near the apartment.

Mary caught up with Laurie as she was peering into a pantry. "Wow. Look at this – a gas stove, and *two* ovens."

"Where's Roly?" Laurie asked, noticing Mary was by herself.

"My neighbor is watching him outside. It's okay, she's in no hurry," she said defensively.

"Well, come on then, before he wakes up," Laurie prodded. "I think the dining room is through here."

A cherry dining table and eight chairs occupied the middle of the room. China and crystal covered both the table and a long side-board. A few things were already marked "sold". Laurie paused to study a painting marked "not for sale," and decided it must be of Jeff's father. He was an older man, but had the same striking blue eyes.

"This crystal is lovely," Mary said, looking at a footed compote. "I like crystal more than silver. You never have to polish it. Just wash it in hot sudsy water and it sparkles. And listen." With her fingernail she flicked the edge of the compote to hear the pure ringing tone.

"Look," Laurie said, pointing at a tarnished tea service. "Like you said. Ready?"

Mary's eyes still roved over the crystal. "Where could I put some of this? Oh, well. Let's see the rest. I only have so much money. And time."

They passed into a small parlor. Over the fireplace's carved wooden mantle hung a family photograph. It showed the same man whose picture was in the dining room, plus a woman and two attractive children. Laurie pointed it out to Mary.

"Nice-looking family," Mary said. "I guess the girl is the sister in Knoxville. The woman looks familiar too, but ..." Mary shook her head. "I don't think I've ever met Mrs. Williams."

She moved on to examine a few small tables while Laurie admired the room's high ceilings and hardwood floors. She walked through a pair of pocket doors, crossed a wide center hall, and entered a larger parlor. The front windows opened directly onto the porch. She noted the blue-painted ceiling outside, and admired the intricate woodwork.

Suddenly Laurie heard a familiar wailing coming through one of the open windows. A woman outside jiggled the handle of the stroller and looked helplessly up at the house. Mary had heard the sound too. She dashed into the center hall and out the front door. Laurie watched a moment as Mary lifted the baby and checked his diaper.

Turning her gaze indoors again, she took in an antique piano, more lovely furniture, and finally the fireplace. Next to it, an older version of the woman Laurie had seen in the family photo sat in a large wing chair looking rather bereft. Laurie went over to speak to her.

"Mrs. Williams?" The woman nodded, and Laurie extended her hand. "Hi. I'm Laurie Lanton. I wrote the article about Jeff and Art Night Out for the *Journal.* Please accept my condolences on the loss of your husband."

"Thank you. That was a lovely article you wrote. Call me Bea." She indicated another chair near the fireplace, and Laurie sat. "I had to take a load off my feet for a minute. We were pricing like mad yesterday, and I've been up since 5:00 this morning."

Laurie commented on the home's high ceilings and beautiful woodwork.

"This home is over 150 years old," Bea told her. "Of course it's been updated over the years, but a lot of the original features are still intact. The studio in the back was once the carriage house." More quietly she said "I never thought it would sell so fast."

"I understand you're moving to Knoxville," Laurie said. "It's beautiful in Tennessee."

"Yes. Well, I'm moving to be closer to my daughter Sandra, and the grandchildren. One of them is disabled, you know. The money from this house will go a long way. Jeff wasn't happy about it, but ..." With more certainty she said "It's the right thing to do."

"Did Jeff hope you would stay in Chinkapin?" Laurie asked, wondering what Bea had meant.

"Jeff's been living in the carriage house, so he'll have to find a new place. And I think he's disappointed I can't give him more from the sale of the house. But I'll be buying a small place of my own, and then Sandra really needs the money." Bea seemed to think she had said too much. "It'll be fine." She watched as strangers browsed around the room, turning things over and examining furniture.

Laurie was startled to think Jeff would be angry with his mother for aiding his sister, if that was what it was. She had assumed that since he was in town to help his mother it meant... Well, she really didn't know what his motives were, or what kind of relationship he had with his family.

"It's hard to leave everything behind," Laurie said. "I moved here recently from out of state. I still miss my old house, and all my things. Quite an adjustment."

Bea gave her a sympathetic look. "Ah, well. I knew this day would come eventually. I'm not getting any younger. You never realize how much you accumulate! I'm thankful that Jeff has been here to help sort through everything."

"Is Jeff here today?" Laurie asked.

"He had some errands to run. You know, he's teaching the Art Night later tonight, and then flying to New York tomorrow morning."

"New York?" Laurie's eyes widened.

"He's meeting some people he knows concerning selling a painting at auction."

"Selling one of his paintings? That's great!" Laurie exclaimed.

"Actually, it's an old watercolor that belonged to someone here in Chinkapin. Something from the turn of the 20th century, and valuable, I believe."

Laurie's brow furrowed. She was going to ask if Bea had seen the painting, when one of the estate sale workers entered from the hallway. "Mrs. Williams, can you come outside and answer a question for us please?"

"It looks like my break is over," Bea said, rising stiffly. "Be sure to look upstairs. There are a couple of nice bedroom suites up there."

Laurie's mind whirled. Was the painting to be auctioned the watercolor from the thrift shop? Had Jeff already been to Atlanta to have it appraised, and if so what had he found out? Could this be a different painting? Or could his mother be confused about his plans?

Mary entered the front door, and browsed in the large parlor for a few minutes. Then she sat beside Laurie in the chair Bea had vacated. "Roly's diaper – I mean Ricky's diaper – good grief, now you've got *me* calling him that." She looked more amused than irritated. "Anyway, now he has a clean one. I saw you speaking to Mrs. Williams. What did she say?"

"She said be sure to look upstairs. There are a couple of nice bedroom suites there."

Laurie led the way up the wooden staircase, stopping on a landing halfway up to admire the way sunlight poured through a leaded glass window, flooding the foyer with sparkling rainbows. At the top of the stairs several doors opened off a central hall.

Mary debated which room to enter first, but Laurie stopped her. "Guess what else she told me," Laurie said, not waiting for an answer. "Jeff is leaving for New York tomorrow to auction a watercolor painting."

Mary's face lit up. "I knew he was talented! Just think – New York. How exciting!"

"Mary, it's not one of his paintings, it's the watercolor we gave him, from the Treasure Chest."

"Really! Is that what Mrs. Williams said?"

"She said it was an old painting from someone here in Chinkapin. An old watercolor from the turn of the last century. It *has* to be the one."

Mary shrugged, shaking her head. "Laurie, you don't know that. It might be a painting someone gave him a while ago. Or maybe it's one they came across getting ready for the estate sale, and he decided to sell it. Didn't you tell me he was selling some of his dad's old photography equipment?"

Laurie nodded.

"And if he had a painting that he thought was valuable, he probably couldn't get what it was worth here in Chinkapin. I mean, he'd have to go somewhere like New York."

"Maybe you're right," Laurie said doubtfully.

"Or maybe it's something he's selling on behalf of the arts center. He is working for them, after all. He's a professional." Mary put her hands on her hips. "I think you're still mad at Jeff because you had a lousy time at the painting thing a few weeks ago."

Mary entered a room on the right. Laurie followed, but her brain didn't register the furniture and antique linens. She couldn't shake the feeling that Jeff was headed to New York with "her" watercolor. "Listen, Mary, I'm going down to look at something I saw in the kitchen. When you're done up here just look for me out front."

Laurie descended the stairway but went straight out the front door and found Mrs. Williams at the check-out table. "Bea, did Jeff tell you when he would be back from New York?" she asked.

"He won't be back until more than a week after the holiday. I believe he's flying back that Tuesday," she said. "He's got some sketching class or other to teach that evening."

Laurie thanked her. Then she took over babysitting duty from Mary's friend, and waited for Mary.

Chapter 23.

Laurie sat in her apartment that evening pondering what to do. Part of her wanted to attend the painting class at the arts center that evening and pump Jeff for information, but she knew she would feel foolish if she was wrong about his intentions.

Another part of her wanted to go to the Coffee Pot for open mic. Music really was more her thing, and maybe she would run into Chase there. Finally she put on a fresh blouse, fluffed her hair, and drove downtown.

Parking was tighter than usual in Chinkapin, and Laurie swatted mosquitos as she walked a block and a half to the café. She shouldered her way through the door, scanning the crowd for Chase, but never saw him. She listened to a few performers, sipping slowly on an iced coffee. Finally she gulped the last of her drink and drove to the arts center.

She parked, and checked her watch. The class should only just have started. She hesitated another moment, then brushed back her hair and walked through the front doors.

The first person she saw was Sharon, and Laurie felt instantly more at ease. "Here to paint? We've got a seat for you right here!" She indicated an empty spot at a table in the back of the group, next to a gray-haired woman wearing round glasses that made her eyes look huge.

"You haven't missed anything yet. I'll fix you up with a palette." Sharon scooted off as Laurie introduced herself to her table mate, a woman named Opal. Then she looked around.

The crowd appeared similar to the one at the last painting class she'd attended, with the exception of the rowdy group of girlfriends, who were absent. This was a quieter group, with more couples, the old woman next to Laurie being the exception. In front of Laurie was a canvas already prepped with a dark wash.

Sharon returned with a palette of paints, and Laurie looked toward the front of the room at the sample painting everyone would be copying. It was one Jeff had shown her previously, of the full moon shimmering over a lake, with ghostly willow branches trailing in the water.

Then her eyes found Jeff. Picking up his paintbrush and loading it with paint, he turned and said something to the guests at the table up front. Laurie didn't catch it, but the front tables burst out laughing. Just then Jeff looked up and caught her eye. He hesitated, raised his eyebrows and smiled at her before he turned back to his canvas and painted a ghostly arc. Laurie felt a flutter in her stomach.

A few painters started roughing in their outlines of the full moon, and Laurie followed suit. She had decided that tonight she would just relax, go with the flow, and not get worked up over her painting. She loaded her brush and globbed paint on the canvas.

"Slow down, dear. A little goes a long way," Opal said next to her.

Laurie looked over at the woman's canvas. She had the moon already outlined and was placing paint on what would be its reflection in the water. "Yours is looking good. Do you do a lot of painting?" Laurie asked.

"Yes. I enjoy painting. And, I like looking at that handsome instructor."

Laurie glanced at Jeff again. "He is nice to look at," she agreed. He had a crisp polo shirt and tailored pants under his painter's apron. Laurie pulled her eyes away, and smeared her glob of paint around in a circle.

"I like to tease him," Opal said. "I've known Jeff since he was a small boy. I'm a friend of his parents. Or, of his mother, I should say now."

"Too bad about his father," Laurie commented. "And of course his mother will be moving soon."

"That's right," Opal said. "What a talented man his father was." She sighed, and continued painting.

"I'll bet Jeff was a hellion when he was little," Laurie said. She still felt she didn't know him at all, and was hoping to learn something interesting.

"Actually, I've always thought of him as an old man in a young body. Now, his sister was a little firecracker, but Jeffrey was always more serious. I think he'll do well for himself in Chinkapin. He's opening his own gallery here, you know."

Laurie wondered exactly what Opal meant by that. She wanted to ask more questions, but Jeff was talking to the class as he demonstrated painting the pond or lake or whatever it was. Laurie looked at her copy, and saw that it was woefully unlike the example at the front of the room, or even the paintings other students had in front of them. She checked her watch. The coffee she had downed at the café wanted out. "I hope it's almost break time."

She dabbed at her painting a little more as Jeff made his way around the room, pausing here and there to offer comments or assistance.

Finally he made his way to her table. "Miss Opal, I'm sure your painting is looking lovely as always." He smiled at the old woman and circled around the table to see Opal's progress. It was impressive: not exactly like the picture in the front of the class, but hauntingly beautiful in its own way. Jeff smiled and nodded. Evidently he didn't have any comments, other than his silent approval.

"Class, if you'd like to take a break, you'll find refreshments in the kitchen. Feel free to get up, stretch, and look around at everyone's progress."

Opal got up from the table, straightened out a crick in her back, and walked slowly toward the kitchen.

Jeff sat in the chair Opal had vacated. "Well Laurie, aren't you a sight for sore eyes! Pretty as a picture, and I would know. I have the degree to prove it."

Laurie stuck out her tongue at him, but smiled.

"I wasn't expecting you tonight," he added.

"Oh, you know. Friday night in Chinkapin." She shrugged. "It's not the most happening place."

Jeff threw his head back and laughed. The overhead lights sparkled in his intense blue eyes. "Let's see how you're doing." He turned his attention to her painting. "Hmmm. Well, just remember. The beauty of acrylics is you can paint over things." There was mischief in his eyes now as he glanced slyly at her.

"That good, huh? Maybe I should just give up," Laurie said, laying down her brush and pushing the canvas away from her.

"Now, now. Don't be like that." Jeff picked up her brush, and in a few strokes evened out the artist's marks on the moon she had painted. He touched the brush into a couple of colors on the palette, blended them, and stroked deftly over the canvas, adding depth and shimmer to the moonlight reflected on the water.

"Amazing," she said, shaking her head. The man really did have a way with a brush.

"Amazing what *you* could do, if you just hang in there." With a final smile he pushed back his chair and went to the kitchen.

She made her way to the ladies' room where, thankfully, there was no line to wait in. Then she stopped in the kitchen for some iced tea. Sharon was just outside the kitchen door, talking on her cell.

Sharon returned to the kitchen in a huff. "That child of mine, I swear I'm going to kill him, if he doesn't get himself killed first."

"Uh-oh," Jeff said. "Trouble on the home front?"

"How does a kid run out of gas these days? Didn't he wonder what that little light on the dash was, and the awful dinging noise? Or was he playing the car stereo that loud again?" She balled her hands into fists and made growling noises through her teeth. "Jeff, I have to go rescue my offspring. Do you think you can handle the clean-up yourself tonight?" Sharon had been addressing Jeff, but now was looking hopefully at Laurie also.

"I'll help him," Laurie said.

"You will? Bless you! I'd better go before something else happens." Sharon dashed into the classroom for her purse, threw off her apron, and trotted out the kitchen door.

Jeff and Laurie walked back into the gallery. The other students were still milling around and chatting. "Thanks for offering to help," he said.

"No problem. I don't have to be anywhere tomorrow." Suddenly she remembered what Bea had told her, about Jeff flying to New York. "But I hear you're headed out of town," she said, hoping to learn more about his plans.

"News travels fast!" He seemed surprised, and just looked at her.

"I met your mother at the estate sale. She mentioned it," Laurie told him.

"Ah," he said nodding. "Yes. Well, I'll be going to an art auction."

And that explains nothing, Laurie thought. Students were looking at Jeff, waiting for him to resume the class.

"Back to work," he said. Placing his hand on her back, he steered her gently toward her seat. Laurie felt a tingle at his touch.

She took her place next to Opal, who gestured toward her painting. "It's looking better," she commented.

"I had some expert assistance," Laurie said, and then focused on Jeff's instruction for adding the trailing foliage in the painting's foreground.

By the end of the class Laurie's canvas looked a bit like a mud puddle, but she didn't care. She left it on the easel, and walked around the gallery clearing away trash. Jeff was making a final round among the students. Finally he asked them to gather for a group photo. Laurie was glad to do the honors with the camera, since it meant she didn't have to pose with the group and be captured, along with her hideous painting, for posterity.

She continued cleaning away the remains of the class, and as the last of the students left with their canvases Jeff joined her. There were a lot of questions she wanted to ask him, but didn't know where to start. "You're a little dressed up for leading a painting class. Were your painting jeans at the dry cleaners?" She pointed toward his dress slacks, still covered by the apron.

"Since you noticed, I'll let you in on my news. You know I had thought about opening a gallery and studio here in town. Well, I went to talk to a realtor today, and put up the earnest money on a property I've had my eye on."

"Fabulous," Laurie said. Her next question popped out before she could stop herself. "Where are you getting the money for this?" Immediately she regretted asking. "That was awfully rude. Don't answer that." She looked away, ducking her head, and carried some trash to the big bin in the kitchen. She could hear him behind her.

"That's okay. Let's just say I came into a windfall. I think it'll be enough to get me started, at least."

Suddenly the kitchen seemed very small, and Laurie's face felt hot. She tried to hide it with small talk. "Well, you have some fans pulling for you to succeed. Opal, for one. She told me you were opening a gallery. Like you said, news travels fast."

Jeff just laughed. "Never tell my mother anything if you want it to remain a secret. And Opal and Mother are old friends. I don't know what the two of them will do once Mother moves away. Burn up the telephone lines gossiping long distance, I suppose."

He looked around the kitchen as Laurie put things away. "If you've got a handle on this," he said spreading his hands, "I'll go out into the gallery and make sure the paints are put away. I don't know where Sharon was with all that. I'm sure she's not having a fun night."

Laurie quickly put away the leftover snacks, washed up a few serving pieces, and wiped the counters. She returned to the gallery for her purse as Jeff came out of the classroom.

"Hey, I want to show you the draft flyers I made up for the art show at St. Mark's. Tell me if I've got everything." She pulled a couple of sheets of paper out of her purse. "I did one with all the info for artists, telling how to enter and all that, and another flyer just to advertise the show. I think that one came out cute. What do you think?"

She glanced up hoping he would be pleased, but saw a shocked look on his face as he stared at the ad for the art show.

"What?" she said, looking from his face to the flyer.

"This pug ... Where did you get this picture?"

"It's a photo I took of an old painting that was for sale at Top Dog. You know, we're partnering with them, and proceeds from the show will benefit the animal shelter. Do you recognize the picture? Am I going to get in trouble for violating copyright laws, or something?" She looked again at the picture on the flyer.

"Do you mean to tell me that painting is at Top Dog thrift shop? Well, what do you know?" Now he was starting to smile.

"What? What is it?" Laurie was completely baffled.

"I painted that picture. Lord, it's been years ago, fifteen at least, but that's a picture of Amy Tidwell's pug. His name was Lemon. I painted his picture and gave it to her for her birthday. Then she caught me at a high school football game kissing Pam Cahill, and she never spoke to me again. I didn't know what happened to that picture. I'm surprised she didn't take a razor to the canvas."

"One of the women at Top Dog has a pug really similar, and she loves the painting," Laurie said.

"Well, it's really not that good. Look here." Jeff began pointing out flaws and errors in perspective. "But then again, I was just getting started with painting. I did a lot of drawing and stuff with markers in those days. I've done some much nicer animal paintings since then. In fact," he said turning to her, "I've been meaning to give you one, if you wanted to auction it off. I mean, anything for a worthy cause. Plus I have to clear everything out of the studio. Here, I think I have a picture of it." He pulled his cell phone from his pocket and scrolled through photos.

"Sure," she said. "Why not?" She was really hoping to make this show a success, both to generate goodwill and visibility for her church, and to benefit the animal shelter. "If we're going to auction it, I'd like to get it early, and include all the details about it and a picture of it in the publicity."

He scrolled back and forth on his phone, shaking his head. "Oh, I can't find it. But I'm sure you'll love it. I'm leaving town early tomorrow. Do you mind stopping at mother's house tonight and picking it up? I'm afraid with so much turmoil there, with the sale and all, things might start disappearing."

"Sure, I can come, if you're ready to leave now."

"Just let me get the lights. I'll see you in the parking lot, and you can follow me over."

Laurie jumped in her car and waited with the engine running while Jeff locked the double doors at the front of the arts center. She felt awkward going over to Mrs. William's house that late, and intended to just wait in the car while Jeff ran in for the picture.

She followed his car down the street, remembering the night she had gone with Jeff to Ranchers. Then, his future had been so up in the air. Now his prospects seemed brighter. Laurie tried to picture Jeff as a successful gallery owner, a mover and shaker in the small town of Chinkapin. Someone who might help promote her writing career. One day.

Jeff pulled into the driveway at the house on King Street and parked in back by the studio. He stood in the beam of her headlights, waving to her to park her car next to his. She rolled her window down. "Come in for a second, and I'll show you my etchings," he said with a wink. "Nah, but there are some interesting things in here." He went to unlock the door. She parked, and followed, her heart beating rapidly.

Once inside, Jeff switched on a few lights, and Laurie took in her surroundings. Bea Williams had told her the building was once the carriage house. It still looked rustic inside, but cozy too. Heavy wooden beams crossed the high, wood-plank ceiling. The walls were whitewashed shiplap. Large arched doorways that had stood at both ends of the building were now French doors.

Colorful rugs softened the wooden floor. A kitchenette filled one corner opposite an old suite of living room furniture. Part of the building was partitioned off into smaller rooms, which may once have been stalls, with a loft above them.

Jeff pointed toward the living room area. "Take a seat, and I'll get the painting I was talking about." He disappeared into one of the smaller rooms. Laurie set her purse on an end table, and perched on the edge of the couch. Jeff returned carrying a large painting.

"Oh, that's amazing," she exclaimed, reaching for the canvas he held.

"Wait. It's best viewed from a few feet away." He propped the canvas against a kitchen cabinet. She sat back, and he took a seat beside her, throwing his arm over the back of the couch. "I painted it after spending a week in the Florida panhandle a few years ago."

In the painting several tall, elegant greyhounds stood next to their handlers. A dirt racetrack was visible behind them, and the dogs were adorned with colorful racing silks. "A lot of people are against greyhound racing," Jeff said, "but you have to agree, they are beautiful dogs."

"They are." Laurie nodded. "I've heard they make good pets, too, if you have a place for them to run." She studied the painting a few moments. "This will be a great painting to auction at the show, and not just because the subject is dogs. There's so much color in it, it would look good just about anywhere. I wish I had it over the couch in my apartment."

"You'll just have to buy some raffle tickets," Jeff said, turning to her with a smile. They stared at one another for a moment. "*You* make a couch look nice," he said.

Oh, God, Laurie thought. *What a lame compliment.* She was about to laugh, but looking into his face she was spellbound. She followed the movement of his blue eyes as they roved over her hair, her face, her neck. His arm slid down around her shoulders. He leaned close, drawing her toward him, kissing her lightly on the lips.

Laurie sank deeper into the back of the couch. Placing a hand on his shoulder, she grabbed a fistful of his shirt, kissing him eagerly. His body felt warm as he wrapped his arms more tightly around her. His lips grazed her earlobe and then her neck, making her nerves vibrate.

All she could think was that it felt good, and she wanted more. He kissed and caressed her, running his hands through her hair and over her back. She pulled at his shirt, and ran her hand over his arm. He tugged at her blouse, unbuttoning the top button, and kissed her throat. Her pulse raced. She breathed raggedly, clenching and unclenching her fists.

Laurie's eyes flew open as light poured through one of the French doors and into the carriage house. She tried to focus, and realized the light came from the main house across the yard. "I think someone's coming," she said.

Jeff continued to brush his lips over her shoulder, but Laurie struggled to sit up, her eyes straining through the window. "Someone's coming!"

Jeff groaned, sitting up. His face was flushed, and his clothes were askew. "It's Mother," he said, a pained look on his face as he glanced outside. "Don't go away." He looked at her partially exposed breast, and gave her a brief, hard kiss on the mouth. Then he straightened himself and went outside.

Laurie held her blouse closed with one hand and tiptoed to the French door that faced the back of the main house. She watched Jeff walk his mother back to her kitchen door, their voices fading as they entered the house.

It took a moment for Laurie's breathing to slow. She waited, looking across the yard, and noticed the dampness in the air. At first she just heard distant road noise, but then the sound of raised voices came from the main house. Her gaze shifted to her own reflection as she leaned against the door frame, her hand still clutching her blouse.

She stared at her face in the window, and strained to hear what Jeff was saying. She caught "well, if you hadn't been in such a damned hurry" and "you knew I was flying out in the morning." The rest of the words were indistinct, but the tone was all too familiar. It reminded her of DB. She turned, quickly buttoned her blouse, and ran her fingers through her tangled hair. Snatching her purse from the end table she glanced once more at the painting. Finally she left the studio, and drove away without looking back.

Chapter 24.

That night Laurie regretted the iced coffee and tea she'd had earlier in the evening. The late dose of caffeine left her awake in bed, tossing and turning until the wee hours.

Saturday morning she dragged around her apartment in her pajamas, rehashing events of the previous night. She knew she'd blown her chance to find out what Jeff was really going to New York for. And where had he suddenly come up with money to open a gallery? Maybe he wasn't in debt up to his eyeballs, as she'd been led to believe. Or maybe it was something to do with the sale of his mother's house. Maybe Bea had had a change of heart, and decided to divide the money between her two children.

But if that were the case, what had they been arguing about?

Laurie wasn't in love with Jeff, but she missed being intimate with a man. She knew where things were headed on that couch in the studio if Bea hadn't shone a light on the situation, so to speak. Had Laurie gotten out of there just in time? She thought of his heavenly blue eyes, and his arms, strong and warm. He was the future owner of his own studio and art gallery. Even Laurie's best friend thought Jeff was the right guy for her.

But her friend had never even met Jeff.

Not only that, this time Laurie was calling the shots. This time it had to be the *right* man, the one Laurie chose. And there would be no doubts, and no secrets.

She threw some clothes on, schlepped her laptop to the library, and spent the afternoon reading and writing.

By Sunday morning she felt back to normal. Mary had texted to say she was staying home with the baby. Laurie trotted up the stairs to the choir loft, and sat in the second row by herself. She chatted with Tracy, one of the sopranos, as they flipped through their hymnals marking the day's selections with ribbons. She turned to greet the guys as Chase arrived with Rob and Alan, and saw Chase set his guitar case on a chair at the back of the loft.

She had no time to ask him about it, though. Steve the organist led the choir in vocal warm-ups and a run-through of the hymns. Laurie sang through clenched jaws, trying not to spit out the cough drop she had just put into her mouth.

Then Steve handed out some sheet music, and asked Chase to come stand next to the organ console. "Chase is leading our offertory today," he said. "The choir will join in on the chorus. I think this will be familiar to most of you. Chase, why don't you play through it so they can practice their part?"

Laurie scanned the lyrics as Chase played and sang a song about the Good Shepherd, full of images of green pastures, still waters, and feeling revived. The rest of the choir seemed familiar with the tune, although it was new to her.

Laurie hadn't heard Chase do a solo since that night at the Coffee Pot. She loved hearing his clear, mellow voice again.

"He is really good, isn't he," Tracy whispered. Laurie nodded.

The choir sang the chorus a couple of times through as Chase played, and then it was time to robe up. "I thought we were doing one of the spirituals we practiced," Laurie said to Tracy as she wiggled into her cassock.

"I guess Steve wanted a little variety," Tracy said. "He invites whoever is available to play or sing with us, especially if they're any good. Remember we had that trumpet player at Easter?"

Laurie pulled her surplice over her head and lined up in the narthex with the rest of the choir. She looked at her watch and saw it was almost 10:00. Not that St. Mark's was the most punctual church in town. Sometimes between the beginning and the end of the opening hymn it seemed like a whole new congregation had appeared in the pews.

The first half of the service went quickly, and soon Chase picked up his guitar. As he started strumming, people down in the pews turned and looked up to see who was playing. Laurie saw them nodding along as the choir sang the chorus. After the service some of the choir members thanked him.

"I enjoyed that, Chase," Laurie told him. "I mean, I love the hymns and anthems Steve picks, but that was a little easier for me than some. I guess it fit my vocal range better."

"Right. Well, you are an alto. We should do a duet sometime," he suggested, smiling.

"Oh, no." Laurie backed away as he hung his robe. "I'm just here because Mary made me join the choir."

"You have a nice voice, though. You should sing more. Too bad you never had music lessons."

"Oh, my parents tried with piano lessons, but things kept happening. Every time I got started, someone died, and my parents had old fashioned ideas about observing periods of mourning, and not having any music in the house."

"Let me get this straight," Chase said, alarmed. "Whenever you play the piano people die?"

"No!" she said laughing. "What I meant was, I started taking lessons and then my grandpa died. When I started back up again later, my great aunt died. After that I just never started again. My brother and sister had sports and things going on. By then I was working on the school newspaper. My parents were busy, and I just never pushed it."

"Hmmm," Chase said, still smiling at her. "Well, it's never too late." He picked up his guitar case and walked with her towards the door.

"Are you staying for coffee hour? What's left of it?" Laurie asked.

"I've been invited to a cookout by one of the guys at work," he said shrugging, not looking too enthused. He paused, as if waiting for Laurie to comment. She didn't know what to say. She was hoping somehow they could get together, but wasn't quick enough to offer a suggestion.

"Well, have fun then," she said reluctantly. She went to the parish hall and found a group of Treasure Chest volunteers discussing work schedules and summer vacations. Laurie wasn't going to travel anywhere during the summer, so she offered to sub for anyone who had plans for the week leading up to the Independence Day holiday. Between that and the art show coming up in just a few weeks, she knew she'd have plenty to keep her occupied.

* * *

The next afternoon Laurie met with the committee to run through their plans for the Dog Days summer art show at St. Mark's. Members of the vestry were excited about the show, and had set the date for two weeks after the holiday. But Laurie had to keep reminding them that it was a benefit for the animal shelter, and not a fundraiser for St. Mark's.

There would be prizes for the three best works in two categories: two-dimensional artworks, like paintings and drawings, and three-dimensional works like pottery, textile art, and wood carving. Sharon and Jeff from the Chinkapin Arts Center had agreed to be the judges. The only rule was that all the artworks had to involve animals.

All the entrants were required to bring a bag or can of pet food for each artwork entered. People from the animal shelter were already selling raffle tickets for pet-themed items from Top Dog, along with a special raffle: Sharon had agreed to donate her artistic services and paint a portrait of the winner's pet.

An artists' reception would take place on the Friday evening the show opened. The head of the refreshments committee assured them they had their plans in place.

"And here are the flyers which are going to go out all around town, anywhere that will allow us to put one up." Laurie handed copies of the flyer she had made to Glenda, the Top Dog representative, and Mother Barbara. It featured a picture of Jeff's pug painting. Glenda had liked the painting so much she finally purchased it, even though it wasn't a perfect match for her dog Sparky.

"I hope we don't get in trouble for copying that painting without permission," Glenda said, looking at the image of the smiling pug.

"Well, it would serve him right, for making his signature such a complete scribble," Laurie said, "but the artist *has* given us permission. I found out that Jeff Williams painted it." Laurie didn't bother telling her about the night she found that out. "He said he painted it for a high school sweetheart, and hasn't seen it in years. Look here – I've given him credit at the bottom of the flyer."

Glenda looked really pleased. "Now isn't that special! I'm going to make sure everyone who comes into Top Dog takes one of these," she said.

They discussed a few more ideas for publicity, and then split up to get started blanketing the town with flyers. Laurie took a stack to the Chinkapin Arts Center where Sharon was setting up for a class.

"I'm so glad you guys are doing this," Sharon said as she read the flyer. "Anything that boosts the arts is good for us, and for the community."

"Well, I don't think we could do it without your help. Thanks for agreeing to judge and everything."

"No problem. It'll be fun," Sharon said.

She assured Laurie the arts center would loan them some easels and display boards. Then Laurie continued on her way to distribute flyers around town.

Chapter 25.

Laurie was busy the week leading up to the July fourth holiday, but not so busy that she didn't still wonder about the two men on her mind.

The thought of Jeff annoyed her like a mosquito bite that wouldn't stop itching. She wished she knew what he was up to, but certainly wasn't going to call, especially after she had run out on him like that. Plus, she was still prickly about having been accused of interrogating him, especially when he seemed so secretive. She no longer wanted to encourage his interest in her. There was just something a little too smooth, almost fake, about him.

She did hope to hear from Chase, but apparently there was no let-up for him at work. Plus he was helping cover for Mr. Anderson, who was still dividing his time between running his business and visiting his wife at the rehab center.

After working afternoons at the Treasure Chest on Tuesday, Thursday, and Friday, Laurie drove to the shop Saturday morning to work with Anne. It was Independence Day weekend, and usually Treasure Chest vol-

unteers gave themselves holiday weekends off, but nei-
ther Laurie nor Anne had much going on so they decided
to keep the shop open as usual.

Laurie had some differences of opinion with Anne,
but still liked working with her – as long as Evelyn was
not around. It was when the two of them got together
that Anne somehow forgot the shop's mission.

The way Laurie saw it, its primary mission was to
provide reasonably-priced clothing and household goods
for people who otherwise could not afford them, and
once expenses were covered any other proceeds should
go to community charities. Admittedly the shop attracted its share of well-heeled bargain hunters. But the bulk
of their customers were not very well off. It was gratify-
ing to know that the Treasure Chest helped people live
better lives.

Some volunteers thought the Treasure Chest was
there to enrich the church. Laurie had thought Anne
was included among them. But recently something had
happened that changed Anne's attitude, and Laurie
hoped to find out what it was.

"I hear you had a big day last Friday. The shop made
over three hundred dollars," Laurie began. "Didn't you
and Evelyn work that day?"

"Yes, we both worked all day Friday. There was an estate sale in town, and I think some of the people who went to the sale came here as well."

"Oh, Mary and I went to that sale! There were lots of beautiful furniture and crystal and things there."

"Did you buy anything?"

"I would have liked to, but I don't have anywhere to put anything right now."

It was quiet in the shop. While Laurie fetched some hangers, Anne brought a bin full of clothes into the office. That way they could chat and tag clothes and still keep an eye on the counter.

"Now, what do you think we should charge for this?" Anne asked, holding up a sleeveless dress.

"You're asking the wrong person. I haven't bought a dress in a regular store in I don't know how long," Laurie said. "I did find a cute one here a couple of weeks ago. I think I paid six dollars for it."

"We had one in here last week for *ten dollars*. Now, I just think that's too much. And there was another one, real similar, marked twelve dollars just because it was a size two X." She put a hand on her hip and looked at Laurie. "Are we charging by the *yard*? I mean, just because it's a larger size doesn't mean we should gouge the customers." Shaking her head, she selected a paper tag, wrote the price on it, and stabbed it with the pricing gun.

"Here's what makes me mad," she went on, tossing the dress to Laurie to hang, and taking up the next garment. "Last week Juanita Ivey – you know she's one of our regulars – she came in and picked out several things and asked us to hold them until she got paid. And we hold things for people all the time. But when Evelyn saw the clothes Juanita had set aside, she reckoned weren't asking enough for them, and raised the prices!"

"Are you serious?" Laurie asked.

"I am *not* kidding you. She changed the tags. Now, if you had put something on lay-away, and came back to the store and the prices had been raised, what would you do? I know I'd tell the store to just keep the darn stuff. I mean, that's just not right, to raise the prices like that. And for one of our good customers." Anne stabbed again with the pricing gun.

"I know some brands cost more than others at the store," Laurie said, "but it all comes to us for free. I'd like to see us keep our prices lower. I think we'd sell more, and then we could put out more clothes and clear out that back room."

"That's right," Anne agreed. "People don't want to see the same clothes every time they come in. And we have plenty more in the back." Laurie was delighted that she and Anne were in agreement for a change.

Anne continued to tag and Laurie hung the clothes until the bin was empty. As Anne got up to take the bin to the back of the shop, she glanced out the office window. "Good Lord, is that Christine? She and her husband used to come here together all the time, but he has been so sick. I wonder how he's doing."

The door to the shop jangled, and Christine walked in. Anne met her at the counter.

"I'm surprised to see you. How's your husband doing these days?"

Christine mutely shook her head, her eyes filling with tears. Anne rushed around the counter, arms outstretched. "I am so sorry," she said, patting the woman's back. "Here." She led Christine to the chair opposite the counter and sat her down. Christine wiped her eyes and recovered enough to speak.

"Sammy's at hospice now. I've been with him for the last couple of days. I had to get out of there for an hour and just do something normal, so I came here."

"And, we're glad to see you. Are your children in town?" Anne talked with Christine for several minutes while Laurie went back and forth putting away the tagged clothes.

Finally Christine rose. "I'd better head back. They'll be wondering where I got to." Then she asked "Would you pray for me and Sammy?"

Anne took Christine's hand, and offered her other hand to Laurie. "Laurie, you're better with words than I am."

Laurie was startled, but couldn't refuse. The three women stood in a circle holding hands, and Laurie began. "Lord, you know our needs before we ask..." She prayed for God's mercy and comforting presence, and she didn't know what else, but when the three said "amen" and Laurie opened her eyes, Christine appeared more at peace, and left promising to return soon.

"I feel so sorry for her," Anne said, watching as Christine's car pulled away. Then she looked thoughtfully at Laurie. "I guess it's because we're right next door to the church."

"Yeah. People see us as an extension of St. Mark's." *More than just a place to buy cheap items*, Laurie thought.

Few customers came to the shop after Christine left. The two women spent the rest of the day sorting books, organizing kitchen ware, and tidying the shop until closing time. Then Laurie drove home to see about doing her laundry.

Chapter 26.

Back at her apartment, Laurie shielded her eyes with her hands and peered through the steamy window of the first-floor laundry room. She needed to wash and iron her Hawaiian shirt before Sunday's party at Mary's house. For a change, the laundry room was empty.

She ran up the stairs to her apartment and returned in a moment with her laundry bag and jug of detergent. Choosing two washers, she put in her clothes, careful to separate the light colors from the dark, and started the machines. As she turned to leave, the door swung open and Chase dragged in a bulging laundry basket.

"Am I too late? Are all the machines taken?" he asked.

"You're in luck. These washers here are empty."

He picked one and started stuffing clothes in. "Aren't you going to separate those?" Laurie asked, brow furrowed. She had spotted several pairs of white underwear along with blue jeans and colored T-shirts.

"These are mostly sweaty work clothes. It's not worth the extra money to make sure my jockeys stay dazzling. Not too many people see them anyway."

"Well, I'm glad not *too* many people see them. And I guess the ones who do don't mind." She crooked an eyebrow at him and he laughed.

She lingered while Chase checked the pockets of a pair of jeans before adding them to the washer. "How is Mrs. Anderson? She's still in rehab, isn't she?"

"She'll probably be in rehab until the insurance money runs out. Then she'll be miraculously cured." Chase looked at her with a smile. "But seriously, she's coming along pretty well."

"How's Mr. Anderson holding out? I'm sure he's ready for his wife to be home again."

"That's for sure. He's run just a bit ragged. There's no one at home to help out, since Bo is gone."

"They didn't have any other children, then?" Laurie asked.

"A daughter, but she passed away." Chase had his back to her, putting detergent in the machine.

"That's too bad." Laurie watched idly as he closed the lid and swiped his debit card. "I'm surprised you're off work today. Is it because of the holiday tomorrow?"

"Yep, it's the holiday. Anderson cracks the whip, but we'll all mutiny if we don't get *some* time off."

"Is he still thinking of retiring?" Laurie suddenly remembered that she sometimes asked too many questions, and hoped Chase didn't feel like she was giving him the third degree. He didn't seem to mind, though.

"He talked about it again last week. He and his wife have always wanted to retire to Florida one day. Between the thing with Bo, and Mrs. Anderson's hip, maybe they'll go sooner rather than later." He changed the subject. "So what have you been up to, besides laundry?"

"I just got home from the Treasure Chest. We should have been closed today, for all the customers we had. Lots of folks are out of town, I guess. At least Anne and I got the place tidied up." She paced around the laundry room as she talked, and stopped in front of a flyer advertising a fireworks display at the fairgrounds.

"Going to see the fireworks tonight?" Chase asked.

"I don't know. I was invited to tag along with Mary, but her sister and family are visiting. As it is, I'll be at her house tomorrow afternoon for a pool party. They don't need me hanging around all weekend. Plus I'm not sure I want to fight the crowds." It sounded like a good excuse, although Laurie didn't mind crowds, and really did like fireworks.

"I'm sure it will be crowded. But I know a place where you can get a great view of the fireworks without fighting the crowds," Chase said. "Nice spot for a picnic, too."

Laurie turned to look at him. "Dare I ask?"

"I'd rather show you. Pick you up at 8:00?" There was an appealing look on Chase's face. Through his tee shirt Laurie could see the muscles in his shoulders, and her heartbeat quickened.

"Did you say there was a picnic included?" She cocked her head coyly.

"Absolutely. I promise you won't be disappointed."

Not like last time, she thought, remembering how their evening was cut short. "Can I bring something?"

"Whatever you'd like to drink, keeping in mind I'll be driving."

"See you at 8:00 then." She grabbed her laundry bag and detergent and left for her apartment.

That afternoon Laurie worked some more on her novel. She finally felt inspired to draft the steamy romance section, something she had been putting off. After writing for an hour she took a break, stretched, and went to the laundry room to transfer her wet clothes to the dryer. Returning to her laptop, she clicked on the thrift shop's Facebook page, and posted a status about the summer sale scheduled to start next week.

She scrolled through a few news items, and stopped at one about the Tuesday sketching class at the Chinkapin Arts Center. It featured a photo of Jeff leaning over a student drawing something.

She thought again about what Bea Williams had told her – that Jeff was in New York for an art auction. Laurie did a quick search on "art auctions New York" which resulted in several hits, including some familiar-sounding auction houses. She selected one at random, and read the scrolling headlines. *What to see at Americana Week. Private sales. Auctions & Events. Auction results.* It was obviously a huge business, and one she knew next to nothing about.

She clicked off the page, disappointed and frustrated, although she was not sure what she had expected to find. Anyway, she'd been sitting long enough, and it was getting late. She walked half a block to the convenience store and bought a variety of sodas, feeling a little guilty about letting Chase provide the rest of the picnic.

Walking back to her apartment, she puzzled over her feelings about him. Sometimes in her imagination he was a homeless pauper, but his actions never confirmed that notion. She banished the voice in her head that whispered she wasn't such a great catch herself. And she was glad not to be spending another evening alone.

Laurie fetched her dry clothing from the laundry room, tossed everything in a pile on her bed, and stood a long moment staring into her closet. She hoped her red top and navy capris wouldn't seem too patriotic. She knew she looked good in red, and her favorite top always gave her a boost of confidence.

It was shortly after 8:00 and she had just finished showering and dressing when she heard a knock and opened her door. "You ready?" Chase asked. There was a faint, delicious smell of fried food about him. She grabbed the bag with the sodas, and followed him to his car where he stashed the sodas in a cooler.

"So where are you taking me? You're being awfully mysterious."

He glanced furtively around the parking lot, then leaned toward her and said in a clandestine tone, "If I say it out loud, the place will be overrun. Get in." As they buckled their seatbelts he continued "You know Eastman, the school across the interstate?"

"I've heard of it," she said.

"We did a big HVAC job there not long ago – actually one of the first jobs I worked on with Anderson. The school athletic fields back up to the interstate, overlooking the fairgrounds. I know a service road that takes you to a spot directly opposite where they'll be shooting off the fireworks."

"Sounds perfect. Probably a good thing I've put a bottle of insect repellant in my purse."

"I brought some along too, so we should be covered."

"No pun intended," Laurie said. She gave Chase a sidelong glance and saw he was grinning.

She checked him out as he drove. He was dressed in khaki shorts and a sage green polo shirt that looked good with his tan. "How do you manage to stay tanned when you work in attics and crawl spaces most of the time?" she asked.

"I went fishing in Anderson's bass boat with him and some of the guys about a month ago. When I get a summer tan it usually stays with me. And you're looking patriotic today," he observed, glancing at her outfit. "Red and blue. I'm guessing your underwear is white?"

Her jaw dropped. In fact, it was. "That's for me to know and you to wonder, Mr. X-ray Vision!" *Or,* she thought, *as we used to say, for me to know and you to find out.*

They crossed the interstate and drove south along the old state route. Just past the school Chase pulled off the road. Laurie could barely make out a dirt track that paralleled the campus. They bumped along, finally pulling in behind a baseball diamond. She was surprised to see an aluminum picnic table behind the back-stop, and a port-a-john nearby.

"Behold," Chase said. Across the interstate Laurie saw the lights of the fairgrounds and a long line of cars snaking into the entrance. He popped open the car's trunk, pulled out a red-checkered table cloth and spread it on the picnic table.

"Wow! You thought of everything," Laurie said.

"Yeah. I got this from a thrift shop I visit every now and again – Treasure something-or-other." In the trunk Laurie also saw the blanket he'd purchased.

She grabbed two sodas from the cooler as Chase set out the contents of a large white paper bag. "I've been dying to see what you brought," she said. "Whatever it is smells delicious."

"You don't recognize the aroma?" he asked. She gave him a blank look. "Chicken tenders. I picked up all this" he waved his hand over the banquet on the checkered cloth "from the Tasty Chick across from St. Mark's. It's a good thing they don't open until 1:00 on Sunday, or we'd have to move the coffee hour across the street."

Laurie reached for a chicken tender, took a bite, and let out a soft moan. She didn't often eat fried food, but that was because of the calories, not because she didn't like it. "Umm. So good," she said. "These *are* the best chicken tenders this side of Eatonton, and I don't even know where Eatonton is!"

"I knew you'd like them. After all, the mouse liked them."

Laurie doubled over laughing.

Hidden Treasure

They sat side by side facing the fairgrounds and dug in to their feast, polishing off a box of chicken, small containers of mashed potatoes and gravy, coleslaw, and peach cobbler, washed down with cold soda.

Watching the blinking lights and all the cars weaving their way into the parking lot across the freeway, Laurie didn't realized how dark it was getting. Chase handed her a flashlight so she could visit the port-a-john. He stowed the picnic items in the trunk, and spread the blanket on the ground where the grass gently sloped toward the road.

"Want some more insect repellant, or another soda?" he asked when she returned.

She shook her head, so he closed the trunk and sat on the blanket. Moving carefully in the dim twilight she sat down beside him, hugging her knees. They heard crackling, and watched a few bottle rockets and firecrackers across the interstate where the crowd waited for the big display.

A small plane buzzed overhead. Laurie watched it glide past, and then leaned back on her elbows to see the stars twinkling dimly. The cotton blanket beneath her was surprisingly soft. She was keenly aware of Chase's body near her in the darkness, and the faint smell of laundry soap and fried chicken on the warm, humid air.

Chase lay back on the blanket, but then turned on his side, leaning on one elbow. "I never asked you what your middle name is." His voice was low.

"It's May. Laura May Lanton," she answered.

He chuckled. "A good name for a southern belle. I'm going to start calling you Laura May. Good evenin', Laura May," he drawled.

She poked him in the ribs and he squirmed. "So what's your middle name? 'Sanborn,' like the coffee, 'Chase & Sanborn?'"

"Oh, like I never heard that one before!" he exclaimed.

"No, wait. Someone called you Chuck, so maybe it's 'Clown,' as in 'Chuckles the Clown'."

He looked at her again with a sad smile. "You cut me deep, Laura May. It's Wesley. Charles Wesley Harris."

"A good name for a musician. I think I've heard some of your songs, Charles Wesley." She liked the sound of his name. *Charles Wesley Harris*, she repeated to herself.

A few more fizzes, whistles, and pops erupted from the fairgrounds, and in a moment they both sat up as the big show started in earnest. Large sky rockets launched in quick succession and blossomed into dazzling circles of color. Laurie uttered oohs of delight at her favorites, the ones that crackled and burst into bright flowers which sent streamers whistling toward the ground. "The view is perfect here! You did great, Chase," she said, looking at him in the glow.

"Didn't I tell you?" The next rocket ignited with a thump and sailed into the air. It burst in a shimmer of red, white, and blue, and Laurie thought of her white underwear.

With heightened senses she took in everything around her – the cars whizzing by on the interstate, the sound of the fireworks, the smells on the night air, Chase beside her, and her heart beating rapidly. He leaned back on one hand, his shoulder against hers as they sat side by side.

Suddenly he turned toward her. His other hand was in her hair, and his lips were on hers, eager and persuasive. She pressed into him, pulling him closer, and together they sank back onto the blanket kissing deeply as fireworks whistled and crackled overhead.

She felt his warm, strong hands gently sliding under her red shirt and caressing her skin. When he sat up to pull off his shirt she opened her eyes to see his shoulders outlined in a brilliant shower of sparks.

They kissed and embraced, arms and legs encircling one another as Laurie's desire overcame her shyness. Chase's hands stroked her softly. His fingers slid down her waist, tugging playfully at her capris. She pushed him away long enough to shrug them off. Then she reached for him again.

Laurie couldn't get enough of his skin. She pulled him close and held him tight, wrapping her legs around him. His body felt so good, and it had been so long. Her hands slid down his back as they moved together. He raised himself on his arms and looked into her eyes. Then he buried his face in her hair and pressed deeply into her. Fireworks launched in quick succession, matching her throbbing heartbeat, until all sound receded into the background.

Gradually Laurie became aware of normal night sounds again – buzzing cicadas, the traffic on the interstate, and somewhere a mockingbird singing on a streetlamp. She lifted her head and pushed aside the edge of the blanket which Chase had pulled over both of them to keep the mosquitoes off. Sitting up, she saw faint orange lights circling as policemen directed traffic through the fairground exits across the road.

She leaned on her elbow looking at Chase in the dim light. He drew her back down and stroked her hair as she nestled against his chest. "Choir practice is going to come mighty early tomorrow morning," she said without making an effort to move.

"I suppose we'd better get going." He lay another long moment cradling her body against his. Then he groped for the flashlight, switched it on, and lay it on the blanket.

They scrambled about, grabbing the clothes they had flung off haphazardly in their eagerness. "I was right. They are white," Chase said, tossing her panties with a grin.

Laughing and fumbling, they dressed, glancing shyly at each other. Laurie stood to zip her pants, and Chase took her in his arms. She leaned into him and raised her lips to his.

They rode back to town in peaceful silence. Laurie pointed at fireworks out the window as the celebration continued nearby, and Chase took her hand and pressed it to his lips. She felt her heart swell as another rocket climbed into the sky and burst in a shower of glittering sparks.

Chase walked Laurie to her apartment and they embraced again. Then she turned the key in the lock, and with a final "good night" she closed the door.

Chapter 27.

Laurie lay in bed a long time thinking about Chase. She relived the conversation, the kisses, the touch of his hands, his body pressed against hers beneath the bursting fireworks. She hugged a pillow to her chest, wishing he were there.

She wondered if she should have invited him to stay the night. Everything had been so perfect. But there was so much she didn't know about him. Still, the more she learned, the more she liked. Finally she drifted into sleep.

* * *

Her alarm buzzed, and Laurie stretched out a hand to hit the snooze button. On mornings like this she questioned whether being in the church choir was worth it. Having to arrive early to practice before the service wasn't easy after a late night.

She bolted up in bed, remembering what had kept her up late. Falling back against the pillows, she replayed the events of the previous night. Her body tingled as she recalled Chase lying with her on the cotton blanket.

"Charles Wesley Harris," she said aloud. She shot out of bed and into the shower. Then she put on a cotton dress purchased at the Treasure Chest a few weeks before, and rushed out the door.

Laurie arrived at church, and found Chase already in the choir loft. The boy who normally set up Mother Barbara's microphone was on vacation, and Chase sat tweaking controls on the sound system on the far side of the organ. He looked her way, smiled, and rose to join the rest of the choir as she walked by. The other singers gradually took their places in the loft, marking pages in their hymnals and sorting through music.

Mary was back in church for the first time since giving birth. She sat beside Laurie as usual, and greeted her excitedly. "You should have come to the fairgrounds with us. The fireworks were really good, and the grand finale was amazing!"

Laurie glanced behind her where Chase had just taken his seat, and saw him smile into his hymnal. He looked up and raised his eyebrows suggestively.

Laurie tried not to blush. "What are you smiling about? What did you do yesterday?" Mary sounded suspicious, but hadn't seen the look Laurie and Chase exchanged.

"Worked at the Treasure Chest with Anne, did laundry, worked on my novel, went to the store – stuff like that. Where's Roly this morning?" Laurie was curious, and also anxious to change the subject.

"Shelley is looking after him. Everyone *should* have come to church with me this morning, but I couldn't drag them out of bed and get them all washed and dressed early enough."

"Do you have everything ready for your luau this afternoon?"

"Mostly. We just have to do a little last-minute food prep." The organist was trying to get the choir's attention. "Come over around 2:00?" Mary asked in a lower voice.

"Sure. I'll be there."

Laurie had trouble concentrating on the service. Several times she caught herself glancing back at Chase. When choir members passed the peace, Chase gave her a chaste hug, but Laurie felt her pulse quicken and her face turn red. She fanned herself, commenting about the heat in the loft, and her heavy choir robes.

There was the usual chatter and commotion after the service. Chase lingered with her in the robing room as she hung her cassock and surplice. "What have you got going today?" he asked.

"Going to the luau at Mary's. Her sister Shelley and her family are visiting."

"Oh, yeah. I think you told me."

"How about you?" she asked. Chase reached out and smoothed a lock of her hair that had been twitched out of place when she pulled the surplice over her head. She wanted to touch him, to kiss him, but someone might enter the robing room at any moment.

"Oh, I don't know. I may check on Mr. Anderson – see if he needs anything."

She nodded, looking into his eyes. Just then Mary burst into the room. "I'm not staying for coffee hour. I'll see you later." She looked from Laurie to Chase, and back at Laurie.

"Bye. See you." Laurie waved. *It had to be Mary*, she thought. No one else would think anything about two choir members chatting together in the robing room. Laurie gave Chase a gentle push out the door. "Guess we better head to the parish hall."

Chase helped himself to the snacks laid out on the kitchen counter while Laurie filled a cup with coffee. Carol stopped her to ask how things had gone at the Treasure Chest Saturday, and the two talked about things that needed to be done around the shop.

Finally Laurie wandered into the parish hall and stood near Mother Barbara. The priest was telling a couple of visitors about the Wednesday night service. Laurie wasn't listening to her, however. She focused on the conversation between several men at a nearby table. One of them, Paul, was reminiscing about troubles he'd had with an ex-wife years ago. "I don't know what she did with all the child support money, but anytime the kids visited the first thing we had to do was run out and buy them clothes."

Another man, Phil, chimed in. "Mine was always harping about the cost of living. I don't know what she had to complain about. She got the house. I was the one paying rent for an apartment!"

"How about you, Chase?" Paul asked. "Any horror stories?" Laurie listened with interest, hoping to hear something about the wife Chase had left behind.

Chase shrugged evasively. "No, nothing like that. I was never divorced."

"I guess you're one of the few these days, then," Paul said. "Maybe you're just too young." The others laughed.

The men's conversation continued, but Laurie didn't hear it. There was a buzzing in her ears. Never divorced! But didn't Mother Barbara tell her Chase had lost his wife because of drugs? So was the wife still around somewhere, planning to come back when Chase got his act together? Laurie had meant to get to the bottom of Chase's past. Instead she had been so worried about leaving him his "dignity" that she'd never even asked him about it. And now where was she?

Laurie walked blindly to her car without stopping to say goodbye to anyone. Something stung her hand, and she looked down to see she was still clutching her cup. Her hand was shaking, and coffee had spilled onto her dress. She poured the coffee out in the parking lot, and steadied her hands enough to dig for her keys.

What have I gotten myself into? Laurie thought. Always before, she'd been the one asking too many questions, interrogating people when she should be making conversation. Now she realized she hadn't asked enough questions.

Laurie dreaded facing Mary that afternoon. *Mary never hesitates to quiz me about my life. She's not afraid to ask questions*, Laurie thought. She would have made some excuse and skipped the luau, said she wasn't feeling well or something, except that Mary had already seen her at church that morning.

Laurie went reluctantly, avoiding her friend as much as possible. She spent time with Shelley and Mark, and chased their kids, Bonnie and Tyler, around the yard with a squirt gun.

Finally Laurie went into the kitchen to cool off and refresh her glass of iced tea, and Mary cornered her. "I'm so glad the weather is cooperating," Mary said. "I was afraid it might be too hot to be outdoors much. I've really been feeling the heat this summer, especially when I nurse little Ricky. I had to come in here to the air conditioning."

Mary unbuttoned the bottom of her blouse, and sat on a kitchen chair with the baby across her lap as he nursed. "Come sit with me while I feed him," she said.

Laurie wanted to escape. She felt obligated to keep Mary company, but she suspected Mary did not just want to talk about the weather. Laurie leaned against the counter, and sipped her drink without comment.

Mary began again. "I forgot to tell you, I ran into Bea Williams at the market yesterday. She's leaving Chinkapin tomorrow. But she said when Jeff gets back he's going to get a place downtown where he can open his own art gallery. Isn't that great?"

"I heard that too," Laurie said. "I just wonder where he's getting the money for it. He gave me the impression he was drowning in college debt."

"Do you suppose he's getting cash from his mom? I imagine the house sold for a good price, but I don't know what she was going to do with the proceeds."

"I thought Bea wasn't planning to give *anything* to Jeff." Laurie hadn't told Mary about her and Jeff's make-out session in the studio, and she wasn't about to. The sound of him arguing with his mother echoed in her ears.

"Bea told me at the estate sale she would use some of the money to buy a new place in Knoxville. It sounded like the rest would go to Bea's daughter, to help pay for private school for that one grandchild."

Mary shrugged. "Well, he's got money from somewhere." She paused. "He sounds like such an interesting guy. Maybe you should give him another chance. You always used to like creative types. I know you two didn't hit it off that night, but..."

"Please! I don't really like painting, and – I don't know. Something about Jeff reminds me of DB."

"Well, it's going to be hard to avoid him if he and Sharon will be judging your art show next week."

Laurie groaned. She had forgotten all about the show! After doing the publicity and setting the event in motion, she had been able to step aside and let others at St. Mark's take over. There were volunteers to accept the artworks as they were brought in and to set everything up before opening night. Another group was handling refreshments for the meet-the-artists reception. Jeff and Sharon were supposed to come to the church just before the opening to do the judging so Laurie could announce the winners at the reception. She didn't see how she could avoid spending time with Jeff.

Mary's voice recalled Laurie to more pressing troubles. "I think there's someone else you *do* like. You sure were looking all cow-eyed with Chase in the robing room today."

"Cow-eyed? What's that supposed to mean?"

"You know, cow-eyes? Calf-eyes? Goo-goo eyes? Same thing. You two were looking awfully cozy. My father-in-law used to talk about people playing 'grab-ass' in the office supply closet when they were supposed to be working. There wasn't any grabbing going on in the robing room, was there?" Mary sat with a devilish grin on her face, jiggling the baby in her lap.

"There was no *grabbing* in the robing room." Laurie couldn't help smiling at her friend's colorful expressions, and her keen powers of observation. "Since you won't let me alone until I tell you, I went to see the fireworks with Chase last night."

"Well! Can't say I'm completely surprised. You're not going to listen to my warnings about him, are you. If you'd just spend a little less time on that writing hobby, and get out and meet some decent people..."

Now the smile left Laurie's face. *Writing hobby?* Now Mary sounded just like DB. Laurie was fed up with Mary passing judgement and telling her what to do. She could be such a know-it-all! Life was too short to live the way someone else wanted her to. Laurie had ambitions and dreams, and a mind of her own. It was time she trusted her own instincts, and called her own shots.

Then she remembered the comment she had over-heard in the parish hall that morning, and felt a chill that was more than the air conditioning and the icy glass of tea in her hand. Was Mary right about Chase? Was Laurie making a huge mistake? She was confused, and her head started to ache. She didn't want another heart-ache, on top of the barely-healed wounds DB's betrayal had caused.

Suddenly Laurie set her drink on the counter with such force that if it hadn't been a plastic tumbler it would have shattered. "What makes you think you know everything? So I went to the fireworks with Chase. I'm entitled to a little fun once in a while. It's easy for you to be critical. You've got your perfect husband. You've got your beautiful house, and your baby. What have I got? A part-time nothing job, a stinking apartment, and no one."

Her words came out more forcefully than she'd in-tended. She turned away from the shocked look on Mary's face and stared out the kitchen window, holding back tears. In the yard, the others were laughing, prac-ticing for the limbo contest.

"Look, Mary. I shouldn't have snapped at you," Laurie began.

"My life isn't perfect, God knows. And it's really out of control since little Ricky came along. I'm just trying to look out for you. I hate to see you waste your time getting involved with someone who has nothing to show for himself."

And what does that say about me? Laurie thought, feeling more miserable by the minute. Finally she said "Whatever. I had a late night, and I'm not in a festive mood. I think I'll just go home."

Mary looked hurt. She was murmuring an apology, but Laurie refused to meet her eyes. She grabbed her purse and went out the front door, leaving Mary to make her excuses to her family.

Laurie gripped the steering wheel hard. On the drive back to her apartment she thought about what she'd said, about being entitled to a little fun. Was that all it was? She thought about that night at Ranchers – the cowboy and his satin doll, who Laurie had taken for a hooker. If they were out for a little fun, at least they knew what they were getting into from the start.

She could have had a little fun with Jeff, that night in his studio. It had been so tempting, and would have been so easy. But she was glad that she hadn't. Maybe she should go back to "plan A," the plan to stay away from men for a while, which she'd made when she first moved south.

Was she just using Chase? And the most important question, at least in Laurie's mind – was he single or wasn't he?

She pulled into her parking lot. Chase's car was nowhere in sight. Laurie turned off the ignition, and sat thinking. *I'm entitled to a little fun once in a while.* Maybe so, but she had always thought of herself as a "'til death do us part" type – until the divorce. Now she wasn't sure what type she was, but *a little fun* did not feel right, especially if the man was married.

What had felt right was lying in Chase's arms in the warm night air, fireworks blazing. That had felt right. She needed to find out if there was any chance of a future with him.

The temperature in her car rose rapidly. Sweating, Laurie climbed the stairs to her apartment. Once inside, she fired up her laptop and searched the internet, looking for public records in the state of Georgia. She input Chase's name and was overwhelmed at the number of divorce records listed for "Charles Harris." It didn't help that she wasn't exactly sure of Chase's age. She eliminated the ones who were obviously too young or old, but still wasn't sure whether what she saw was proof that Chase was single.

She snapped her laptop shut and walked over to her couch, threw herself face down on it, and sobbed.

Chapter 28.

After the argument with Mary at the luau, Laurie decided to let things cool off for a couple of days. Mary's comment about Laurie's "writing hobby" had stung, probably because that's how DB had always dismissed her dream of being a published author. In spite of it, or maybe because of it, she redoubled her efforts at writing, and also kept herself busy at work.

Still, Laurie missed spending time with her friend. No matter how much Mary got on her nerves, Laurie knew she meant well. And she really hadn't spent much time with her since Roly was born.

Finally, after work on Wednesday, Laurie called Mary to see how things were going and to try to smooth things over between them.

"Is everything ready for the baptism this Sunday?" Laurie asked.

"Yep. I didn't get a chance to tell you that my sister brought the baptismal gown that our dad wore when he was baptized, so that's what Ricky will wear Sunday."

"Oh, cool!" Laurie said.

"Of course I'll change him out of it as soon as I get him home!" Mary sounded exasperated. "I just have visions of my life for the next eighteen years – one long struggle to keep that boy clean! Anyway, Shelley has the luncheon all planned. I won't have to do a thing. I'm so thankful for that!"

"Have you been enjoying her visit?" Laurie asked, more out of politeness than real interest.

"Yep. It's been a bit much, though, having so many people in the house. I mean, I'm still getting used to taking care of Ricky, not to mention my body's still not back to normal. I sent them all off to play miniature golf and ride the go-carts the other day, which the older kids enjoyed. And tomorrow or the day after, Pete and my brother-in-law will take the kids to that new Marvel movie while Shelley and I watch a chick flick or something at home. Maybe you can come over?"

The invitation sounded non-committal. Laurie answered, "Maybe. Give me a call, and let me know when." She could hear voices in the background.

"Hey, I'm going to have to let you go," Mary said. "We're starting to get lunch ready. The kids have been swimming this morning, and we want to get them out of the sun for a while."

"Sure. Okay. I'll talk to you later. Or if I don't hear from you, I'll see you Sunday morning."

Hidden Treasure

Laurie didn't count on hearing from Mary. She had plenty to keep her occupied anyway, including her work every morning at the *Journal*, work Thursday afternoon at the Treasure Chest, and a final planning session Friday for the art show.

She stopped to pick up some lunch and a drink at the Coffee Pot at noon Friday before the meeting. She hadn't been sleeping well, and thought an iced coffee or a frappe with a double shot of espresso might perk her up.

After she placed her order, she picked up a few art show flyers leftover from the stack she had dropped off a week ago, and carried them to the bulletin board in the back of the café near the stage. She was just tacking one up when she heard the door open, and saw Chase standing by the cash register, looking up at the menu posted on the wall overhead.

Laurie felt a familiar flutter in her chest, and held her breath. Chase paid for his order, and leaned against the counter as he waited. He looked just as good as he had the night Laurie first heard him play at open mic.

Suddenly he turned his head, and recognized her with a start. He straightened and walked toward her.

He was about to say something, but before he could get the words out she asked "Have you heard about the Dog Days summer art show being held at St. Marks?"

She didn't wait for an answer. "All proceeds benefit the animal shelter. Here. Have a flyer. Take two." She thrust a couple of flyers at him. Confusion crossed his face as he looked from her to the flyers and back again.

"Um... Thanks. I've already given some of these to the people at work, but... Hey, I'm sorry I haven't been able to see you, or anything. We've been slammed since the holiday, but I really wanted..."

Laurie cut him off. "No worries. I've been pretty busy too, with work and this art show and all. It'll be here before we know it." She looked him up and down. Obviously Chase was on a lunch break from work. He was wearing a stained pair of khaki pants and a very sweaty tee shirt. Laurie focused on his clothes, not wanting to look into his eyes.

"Look, Laurie," he began again. "Are you busy tonight? I was hoping..."

"I really need to spend some time at my computer. I'm trying to finish something to submit for the writing group next week. Plus there's a writing contest I wanted to enter." Her throat felt tight. She walked over to the counter where her food was ready for take-out, and took a drink of her coffee.

The barista had been trying to get Chase's attention. Finally she slid his iced coffee toward him on the counter. He caught it just before it fell, turning back to see Laurie pick up her things and head to the door.

"Laurie! Wait. Can't you sit for just a minute? Sit down, and let's talk."

A pair of women at another table turned their heads to look at them. Laurie paused, embarrassed. She turned and perched on the edge of the nearest chair, nervously twisting the top of her paper bag. "I have to meet some people at church in a few minutes."

Chase pulled a chair out from the table and sat, watching her. He didn't seem to know what to say, or what was wrong.

Laurie finally spoke up. "Look, Chase, I'm just not sure there's a future for us. Maybe we should not have gotten carried away the other night."

"Carried away? Laurie, why are you saying this? Why are you acting like this?"

"I don't know. It's just that..." She lowered her voice. "I haven't been divorced that long. I'm still deciding what I want to do with my life. It's like I have a second chance, and I don't want to..." She stopped, but he knew what she had been about to say.

"Don't want to mess it up? Is that what you were thinking? What's that supposed to mean? Are you saying I'm a waste of your time?"

"I don't know, Chase, I just..." Laurie wasn't sure what she meant, or what she was saying. She wanted Chase, but couldn't shake the feeling that he belonged to someone else. "Maybe I just want more than you can give me."

"Like what? More what? More ... money? Or what?"

Laurie felt herself tongue-tied. She was never this way when she interviewed people for newspaper articles, but where love was concerned... She tried to think of what Mary might say. "Well, look at you!" Laurie exclaimed. "It's not like you have much to offer a woman."

His expression registered shock and hurt. "I'm not good enough for you, is that it?" He gave a derisive snort. "Last time I checked, you lived in the same cheap apartment building I do. And that's not a Mercedes you're driving."

Laurie stuck her nose in the air and crossed her arms. She wasn't happy to be reminded of her status in life. "I'm concentrating on building my career," she shot back.

"Uh-huh. Let's see. There's your part-time job at the paper, and your volunteer gig in a second-hand store, and your little writing hobby." Chase counted them off on his fingers. "Which one is the 'career' part?"

Laurie's mouth flew open and she dropped her arms. *Little writing hobby?* "Well, that's not exactly a three-piece suit you're wearing, 'Mr. All That.'"

He put his hands on his hips, and stuck out his elbows, looking her up and down. "Little church mouse," he said, half under his breath.

Laurie recalled the mouse in the bird cage at the Treasure Chest, and the sound of Chase's warm baritone as he sang that song about the mouse who gnawed the oak tree down. Her heart flip-flopped. She looked into Chase's eyes, and her pulse hammered in her ears.

Her cell phone suddenly rang, making her jump. She yanked it out of her purse and saw that Sharon was calling. She turned away from Chase to answer, and spoke briefly before hanging up with a sigh.

"Well, we're down one judge for the art show," she said. "Our friend Jeff bailed on us. Apparently he's *still* somewhere out of town, or on the road, or wherever. I don't know, and I don't really care. But it would have been nice if he had told us a little sooner." She was exasperated, and took a sip of her drink. "Look, Chase, I'm sorry. I'd love to continue our conversation, but I have to meet some people at the church to make sure this art show is going to get off the ground. I'll be really, *really* glad when the whole thing's over." She sighed again. "I'm just tired, and the coffee's not helping."

"Anything I can do?" he asked, looking concerned.

"No. It's fine. Fine, as long as nothing happens to Sharon! It'll be downhill after the show opens a week from today. I'm a little worried about the opening night reception, but... Anyway, you know where I'll be. And it'll be fine."

She gave him one more, long look. *It'll be fine as long as you're single*, she thought. Then she grabbed her drink and her sandwich and hurried out of the café.

* * *

Finally the day of Roly's baptism arrived. Laurie got up early Sunday to get ready. She put on her cheery floral print dress, and checked herself out in the mirror. She had worn it to church a few times already that summer, but figured it didn't matter. No one would really be looking at her.

She was more worried about whether Mary actually still wanted her as Roly's godmother. Mary had promised her the honor long ago, but Laurie wondered why she hadn't chosen someone else, like maybe her sister.

Laurie hurried to her old Malibu in the apartment parking lot, purposely not looking for Chase's car. She drove to church, and took one of the few spots in the shade. She was glad to see only two cars already there.

One belonged to Steve, the organist, who always came early to warm up on Sunday. The other car was Mother Barbara's – just the person she wanted to talk to. Laurie found the priest in her office reading over her sermon.

"Good morning," Mother Barbara said. "Are you all ready for today's exciting event?"

"I am ready. At least I looked over the service in my prayer book last night. I always like the way we do a baptism. I kind of wonder, though..."

"Wonder what?" Mother Barbara asked.

Laurie thought the priest had a way of looking at her – patient, but relentless. If Mother Barbara knew you needed to talk about something, she waited you out until you spilled your guts.

"Well, it's just – why am I the godmother? I mean, why me, since I'm just a friend, and not someone closer like Mary's sister?"

"Well, let's see," Mother Barbara began. "Shelley is Ricky's aunt, right?"

"Of course," Laurie nodded. *That's obvious*, she thought.

"And she'll be the baby's aunt regardless. She doesn't need any other designation. She'll be a part of his life by default. But with you as the godmother, Ricky has another special person in his life – someone he'll have a lifelong, caring relationship with, besides the members of his family. That's a precious gift for a child. You know, I think the more loving people there are in a child's life, the better it'll be for that child. Not only that, it's a comfort for his parents to know there are others who care about him and have willingly obligated themselves to be there when he needs them."

"I guess," Laurie nodded.

"A lot of people think it's just an honorary title, and it is an honor of course, but it's a responsibility too. And the flip side is that *you* have another person in *your* life – a godson. He'll always be your godson, and that's something special to have as well." Mother Barbara smiled.

"I guess I wasn't seeing all that," Laurie said, feeling better.

A moment later Mary and her family arrived at the church. Laurie was eager to see Roly in his vintage baptismal gown, and found the baby asleep in his carrier. "I got up extra early to feed him," Mary said. "Hopefully he'll stay quiet for a while."

The family, along with Laurie and a friend of Pete's who was to be the godfather, all followed Mother Barbara into the nave to walk through the ceremony before the service started. Then they took seats in the first couple of pews as Steve began playing a prelude on the organ.

The choir assembled in the narthex as usual, and processed around the church singing the opening hymn.

They walked up the center aisle and then split into two columns to take the side aisles. Chase walked by on Laurie's side of the church, and their eyes met as he passed.

His glance distracted her. She had purposely been avoiding him, but was starting to regret it. She fumbled in her prayer book for the page with the opening sentences for a baptism. Finally she caught up with the rest of the congregation.

"There is one Body and one Spirit," Mother Barbara said.

"There is one hope in God's call to us," the congregation replied. Laurie was glad she had reviewed the service.

"One Lord, one Faith, one Baptism," Mother Barbara continued.

"One God and Father of all."

Then came the collect, or prayer for the day, the readings, and the sequence hymn. It was one of the few Sunday's that Laurie sat in a pew downstairs and not in the loft. She rarely got to hear the choir from down in the nave. It sounded like a much larger group than just the handful she sang with every week.

She could clearly hear Chase singing the hymn. Not that he stood out in a bad way or anything. His voice added a richness the choir wouldn't have had without him. Laurie glanced from time to time at the baby, but Roly was now sleeping peacefully in his mother's arms.

After Mother Barbara's sermon, the point in the service arrived for the baby to be presented for baptism. The baptismal party stood and took their places near the altar. Laurie glanced up into the choir loft. Other members of the choir had their eyes on Mary and the baby, but Chase was looking at Laurie. Quickly she dropped her eyes back to her prayer book.

"The candidate for holy baptism will now be presented," Mother Barbara said.

Laurie and Mary exchanged a smile. Laurie had threatened to call the baby Roly, but instead she said with the others "I present Richard Leonard Roster to receive the sacrament of Baptism."

The service continued with the parents' and godparents' vows to raise the child in the faith. Then came the interview of the candidate, a sequence of questions which they answered on the baby's behalf, and the whole congregation joined in a renewal of their baptismal covenant. It was mostly the familiar creed, in question and answer form, with additional questions which Laurie always found meaningful.

"Will you seek and serve Christ in all persons, loving your neighbor as yourself?"

"I will, with God's help," they answered.

"Will you strive for justice and peace among all people, and respect the dignity of every human being?"

"I will, with God's help." Laurie thought of how disrespectfully she had treated Chase at the café, and closed her eyes.

After more prayers, Laurie followed Mary and the rest of the party to the back of the church where they gathered around the baptismal font. "We thank you, Almighty God, for the gift of water," Mother Barbara said.

As the priest poured water into the basin Laurie remembered Chase's quip from months ago: about water being a blessed element because it was needed to make coffee. She smiled, glanced upwards, and caught Chase's eyes again as he stood near the loft railing. This time he was smiling at her. Laurie felt her throat tighten. She either needed to get over Chase, or get to the bottom of his marital status.

With difficulty Laurie brought her attention back to the ceremony. Parishioners craned to watch as Mother Barbara poured water over the baby's head. "Richard, I baptize you in the name of the Father, and of the Son, and of the Holy Spirit." Quickly she wiped his little head with a white cloth. The baby squirmed and whimpered, but miraculously remained asleep, even through the resounding "Amen" voiced by the congregation.

Laurie gazed with fondness at her godson cradled in the priest's arms. She wondered whether she would ever stand with her baby at a baptismal font. She focused on the present again in time to catch the ending of another prayer. ".... Give him an inquiring and discerning heart, the courage to will and to persevere, a spirit to know and to love you, and the gift of joy and wonder in all your works. Amen."

"Ricky, you are sealed by the Holy Spirit in baptism, and marked as Christ's own forever!" It was always so joyful the way Mother Barbara said those words.

"Let us welcome the newly baptized," she said as she walked the baby up and down the aisle so everyone could see the sleeping infant. There were plenty of "oohs" and "ahs," mostly from the women in the crowd. They spoke the welcoming prayer together, and again Laurie felt her heart in her throat, and rapidly blinked away tears.

After the service Mary showed off Ricky in his special gown, and accepted congratulations from her friends. The baby was finally starting to wake up and get active, so the members of the party drove over to Mary and Pete's house for the planned luncheon.

It was mostly a family affair. Laurie, the godfather, and Mother Barbara were among the few guests. Shelley immediately started setting food out on the kitchen counter, which served as a buffet, and Laurie helped her.

There were chicken salad and pulled pork sandwiches, cold salads, munchies, and a cake decorated with blue and white frosting flowers. Everyone loaded up their plates with food, and the guys took the older kids out to the deck where they could be as loud and messy as they wanted.

"I'm starving," Mary said to the women as Ricky began to caterwaul. "And you're starving too, aren't you? Aren't you?" she cooed to her son as she took him to the nursery to change him out of the baptismal gown into a soft, comfortable onesie.

She returned and settled with him at the kitchen table near Mother Barbara. As the baby hungrily nursed, Shelley placed a plate of food where Mary could reach it, and then went to fill a plate for herself.

"Everything was beautiful this morning, Mother Barbara," Shelley said. "That flower guild of yours did a great job. I loved the flowers around the baptismal font, and the little bows at the ends of the pews."

"Yes, they did a lovely job as usual. And I didn't drop the baby, so all is well!"

"I'm amazed he didn't scream when you poured the water over his head," Shelley said.

"My little angel wouldn't scream," Mary said smugly.

"Huh!" Laurie snorted. "Your little angel has been known to scream, throw up, and blow out his diaper at the most inopportune moments!"

"How they talk about you," Mary said to the baby.

"My two sure did. At least the screaming and the diaper blowouts. If you only knew what a cleaning job I had to do on that baptismal gown after Tyler wore it! Yuck! Bonnie was the screamer."

"I think I've seen everything at baptisms. And then there are babies who are fascinated with the water. They get such an amazed look on their faces." Barbara smiled at Ricky as she discarded her paper plate. "Ladies, I hate to eat and run, but unfortunately two of our fellow parishioners are in hospital today. I'm going to pay them a visit. Enjoy the rest of your afternoon."

Shelley offered the priest a piece of cake before she left, but Mother Barbara declined, and Shelley saw her out the front door. She returned to the kitchen for more punch, and glanced out the window to make sure everything was okay with the kids out by the pool. The three men seemed more interested in their conversation on the deck, but luckily Bonnie and Tyler were busy with a Frisbee at the moment.

"And now you're a godmother, Laurie," Shelley commented, turning back to the group in the kitchen.

"Yes. A fairy godmother. But I didn't have my wand with me earlier, so I haven't been able to give the child a fairy gift yet."

"Hmmm. What should it be?" Mary mused.

"Everyone in this neck of the woods would wish for unstoppable football powers."

"Football is so dangerous, though," Mary said wrinkling her nose. "Maybe soccer?"

"Do they even play soccer in Georgia?" Shelley asked. "You might have to settle for baseball."

"I know," Laurie said. "One of the fairies in the Sleeping Beauty cartoon gave Aurora the gift of song. I could give Roly the gift of song, and then we could have him singing in the choir with us."

"That's a good idea," Mary said. "He sure can cry loud enough when he wants to, so I know he's got a good set of lungs! Wasn't it different hearing the choir from downstairs?"

Laurie only nodded. She thought of Chase, watching her from the choir loft, and sighed.

Roly had just finished nursing, and Mary was buttoning her blouse. "Here, I'll take him," Laurie said, tossing a thin receiving blanket over her shoulder. "You haven't been able to eat."

"Yes, finish your food," Shelley nodded. "Then we'll cut this cake and get out the ice cream."

While Mary ate, Laurie hoisted the baby to her shoulder and gently patted his back. "You're going to have to whack him a little harder," Mary said. "It's weird, but he likes it."

Laurie patted a little harder, and Ricky obliged by producing a loud burp that made the women laugh. "He gets that from his father's side," Mary said.

Laurie danced the baby back and forth, swinging her hips and singing "Roly-Poly puddin' and pie, kissed the girls and made them cry. When the boys came out to play Roly-Poly ran away."

"He's so sweet," Shelley said. "He almost makes me want another one. Almost!" She laughed.

"He sure has opened my eyes," Mary said. "If only I could have spent more time with your two when they were infants. I told myself having a baby wouldn't change my life too much. Huh! Boy was I wrong. This little man *runs* my life."

Mary and Shelley fixed dishes of cake and ice cream for everyone as Laurie paced around the room with the baby. Holding him made her want a baby, there was no "almost" about it. She loved the feel of his weight and softness in her arms. She closed her eyes and hummed softly.

Shelley noticed, and commented, "Gee, Laurie you're a natural. We need to get you married off so you can have one of your own."

"And then we can go to the playground together!" Mary said. "But we need to get you a man first."

Laurie huffed. "You tried that, remember? It didn't work out too well."

"DB was a dud," Mary said. "I mean a real man."

"Are there any eligible bachelors in Chinkapin?" Shelley asked.

"Well," Mary began.

Laurie cut her short. "I'm pretty particular about men these days," Laurie said. *First, they have to be single*, she thought. "I think I'll do my own matchmaking. Or maybe I'll just wait for Roly to grow up. What do you think about that, huh, little guy?"

Mary looked at her for a moment, considering, while Shelley called the rest of the group in for cake and ice cream.

Chapter 29.

The next week flew by, and it was Friday almost before Laurie could blink. The opening reception for the art show went more smoothly than she had dared to hope. All her efforts to publicize the event paid off, first in the number of artists who entered their artwork, and then in people who showed up at the church Friday night.

The set-up committee had done a beautiful job arranging the entries. There were paintings of all sizes, pencil sketches, and digital art arrayed on floor easels and table easels around the parish hall. Fiber art hung from the walls or was draped on stands. A table in the middle of the room displayed wood carvings, pottery, a wire sculpture and other three-dimensional art.

The dog shelter was absolutely thrilled with the response. Everyone who brought art to exhibit in the show had also brought pet food, and since it had been publicized as a benefit many of the visitors brought food donations as well. Volunteers from Top Dog loaded the food into their van as it came in, and had already made a couple of trips to the shelter to drop it off.

After welcoming everyone to the reception and announcing the winners of the art show, Laurie retreated to the church kitchen where the refreshments were set up for a glass of wine. Mother Barbara met her there, and pointed to the guest book on the counter. "Look at all the people who have signed our guest book just today, and the show will run until Sunday!" she said. "I don't recognize most of these names, which is good! It means that many more people know where we are."

"And we didn't have to put 'across from the Tasty Chick' on the flyers," Carol pointed out, coming to join them after she snagged some cheese and crackers. Laurie smiled, thinking of Mary.

Mary was not at the show opening. Pete was away on business again, though he was due to arrive home later that night. And new mother that she was, Mary was still reluctant to entrust her infant to baby sitters for an evening. She had texted Laurie with an apology, and said she'd see the show on Sunday after church.

Laurie had hoped that Chase would wander in, but so far she hadn't seen him. She picked up a paper plate and half-heartedly loaded it with what she supposed would be her supper.

Mother Barbara sat with her in an out-of-the-way corner while Laurie ate. "You look about worn to a frazzle. I hope you're planning to treat yourself to some well-deserved rest after this show is over."

"Oh, yeah. Well, no. Actually, just work as usual. I'm trying to come up with more feature ideas for the newspaper. That last big article I wrote was such a hit. I really want to focus, and move my career forward. I feel like coming to Chinkapin has given me an opportunity to start over, and I want to take advantage of it."

Laurie remembered what Chase and Mary had both said about her "writing hobby," and took another sip from her wine glass.

"Just don't focus entirely on work and ignore the other areas of your life," Mother Barbara cautioned, choosing a cookie from her plate.

"Well, I haven't been having as much success in other facets of my life."

"Sometimes you just have to let things unfold in their own good time," the priest said. Laurie looked at her, wondering if she knew more about Laurie's feelings than she was letting on. Then she added "I'm going to mingle some more," and wandered off to chat with the visitors.

Laurie sat and brooded for a moment. Then she polished off the food on her plate, and refreshed her lipstick. She needed to get into the parish hall and mingle too. She wanted to get some feedback from the guests, and snap a few pictures to submit to the newspaper.

Yep. When your personal life is going to hell, fall back on your career, Laurie mused. Working on her career was fine, but relationships had always been important to her too. Actually more important.

What was it Chase had called her? A little church mouse? She smiled. *And what's so bad about that*, she thought, and returned to the reception.

* * *

More visitors trickled into the art show throughout the day on Saturday, and several members of the church, including Laurie, were available to answer questions while the parish hall was open. In place of the refreshments in the kitchen, the counter displayed flyers for the Chinkapin Arts Center, the animal shelter, Top Dog thrift shop, and St. Mark's Treasure Chest. Laurie made sure she told everyone to visit the Treasure Chest before they left.

She was thrilled when Joan and Evelyn stopped in the parish hall after the Treasure Chest closed that afternoon. "We made two hundred and eighty dollars today!" Joan told her.

"That's way above average for a Saturday, especially in the summer," Evelyn said.

"And we had lots of new customers who say they'll come back. I don't know whose idea this art show was, but we should do it again next summer." Joan flashed a thumbs up sign, and strolled over to say hello to a couple of visitors.

"How much money have you brought in over here?" Evelyn asked.

"We'll keep selling raffle tickets through Sunday," Laurie explained, "so we haven't totaled it up yet. Of course it's all going to the animal shelter."

"What?" Apparently that was news to Evelyn. "I thought it would go to the church! We need to replenish our maintenance fund." She looked irritated.

"Well, the show was always only intended to raise the church's profile in the community, and help animals," Laurie explained patiently. She was sure she'd said all this before. "Mother Barbara told me last night that one family inquired about our church and said they would come for services Sunday. And you've had newcomers to the shop who will probably be back, so that's an extra benefit."

Evelyn rolled her eyes, turned her back on Laurie, and flounced off.

Laurie heard the outer door open, and Chase walked through the kitchen and into the parish hall. He looked completely different from the day she'd had the argument with him at the Coffee Pot. He wore a clean pair of jeans, a short-sleeved shirt in a retro print, and clean shoes. He'd obviously been to a salon, because his hair was more stylishly cut than usual, softening the angularity of his face.

Laurie noted how fashionable he looked, and regretted how shallow she had been, so critical of Chase's appearance and his occupation. She knew he had been out working a hot and dirty job. And an important one! After all, who in Georgia wants their air conditioning to go out in July?

"Hey, Laurie." He stood with his hands in his pockets. "Have you had a lot of visitors today?"

"People have been trickling in pretty steadily. We've still got a couple more hours. The good thing is a lot of visitors went from here over to the Treasure Chest. Joan said they had a great day over there."

"Glad to hear it." He wandered off to look at the artwork.

Laurie watched him as he strolled around, studying everything. She wondered how much he actually knew about art. She remembered he'd studied music in school, but maybe studio art was a part of his liberal arts education as well. She thought idly about that, and also about why she hadn't seen him all week. Then she remembered how discouraging she'd been.

Chase returned and stood beside her, his arms folded. "There are sure some talented people in Chinkapin," he said.

Laurie nodded agreement. "Are you an artist, Chase?"

"No," he said quickly, and shook his head. "When I was a kid I tried to copy the pictures in some of my comic books. But once I really got going with music I quit drawing."

The two idly watched the visitors strolling through the parish hall. Then Chase said "I didn't see anything by what's-his-name, your buddy Jeff. Didn't he submit some artwork?" His eyes were on Laurie with a guarded, appraising look.

The color rose to her cheeks as Laurie thought about the night in Jeff's studio. "Actually he was supposed to donate a painting to be auctioned off, but that fell through at the last minute." She blushed a little deeper now. "I guess because he went out of town." She started fanning herself, then realized she was using a Chinkapin Arts Center flyer, and put it down. "And he's not my friend."

"Did you get your writing done last week?" Chase asked.

Startled, Laurie remembered she'd told him she would be busy writing something for her writers group. "Um ... yeah. I did," she said. It wasn't much, but she had submitted a short, short story. "I also wrote up an article about this show and the meet-the-artist reception last night, and sent it off to my editor. I hope it'll be in the newspaper this week. I'm sure the winners will be interested in seeing their names in the paper." At least that part wasn't a fib.

"So what did *you* do last night?" she asked, to turn the conversation away from herself. "I thought maybe I'd see you here."

"Open mic," he answered tersely. "Besides playing, I set up and put away the sound system."

"Oh," Laurie said. "Right. Was it crowded?"

"Less so than usual. Some of our regular crowd was probably here." He smiled at her. "You know – Chinkapin on a Friday night. There's usually not so much going on."

Laurie looked down, remembering what she'd said to Jeff when she went to his last Friday night art class.

She desperately wanted to ask Chase about his comment at church two weeks ago, and find out whether he was still married, but she didn't know how to begin. Before she could think of what to say, Joan walked over and started asking Chase questions about air conditioners. She was afraid hers was going out, and considered beating it to the punch by replacing it before it actually died on her.

Suddenly all three were startled by a loud crash. They turned in the direction of the noise, and saw a large painting on the floor.

"I'm so sorry! I must have bumped it by accident. I didn't really hit it that hard! And it just fell." A woman stood wide-eyed, with both hands on her cheeks. She looked from Laurie to the painting, not sure whether to pick it up, or leave it alone for fear of making things worse.

Laurie hurried over to inspect the damage. "I'm really sorry," the woman said again. "I'll... I'll pay for the picture." Her voice trailed away uncertainly.

"Well, fortunately it looks like the painting's not damaged, just the frame." Laurie lifted the heavy canvas and tried to prop it back on the easel, but the frame kept coming apart at one corner, and the painting wouldn't stay put.

"Lay it back down for a second," Chase said. He had appeared by her side, and helped her ease the painting to the floor. "I've got some duct tape out in the car. I think we can mend it from the back, or at least stabilize it so it'll stay on the easel."

Laurie examined the canvas more carefully and was relieved to see that her initial assessment was right. The painting didn't have a scratch on it. It must have hit the floor right on the corner of the frame. She looked up, waiting for Chase. The woman who had bumped the painting had disappeared.

"Lord, I hope that frame wasn't too expensive," Joan said, shaking her head at the damage. "Sometimes they're worth more than the painting. And I think this big easel is a little rickety. Maybe we can swap it with another one." She looked around the room, and found a smaller painting on a somewhat sturdier easel.

Chase returned with a roll of duct tape and his pocketknife. Carefully he turned the painting over, squared it in the frame, and ran long strips of tape along the back, reinforcing the frame at the corner. Finally he lifted it and placed it on the new, sturdier easel.

"There," he said. "If no one bumps it, it'll be all right." He smiled at Laurie.

"You almost can't see that it's broken," Laurie said. "Thanks, Chase."

"No worries." He strolled around the parish hall again, nudging a few easels to make sure there were no more disasters in the making. "So, how much longer is the show open this afternoon?" he asked when he had completed his rounds.

"Until five," Laurie answered. "Then I just have to lock everything up." She wondered why he had asked. Maybe he would ask her out. But then something else occurred to her. "You look nice today, Chase. Are you dressed up for something special?"

"Actually I'm playing a sort of a happy-hour gig at Salty Dog. It's a new seafood place over by the freeway."

"That sounds cool. How did they find you?"

"My friends at the Coffee Pot are in the chamber of commerce with the restaurant owner. They mentioned my name when they heard the restaurant was looking to have some music on weekends." He still held the roll of duct tape in his hand, and picked idly at the sticky edge.

"You don't seem thrilled with the gig. Does it pay much?"

"It pays enough. I just don't think I want to tie myself up with a regular gig. I've been there before, and it takes up a lot of time, gets in the way of other things."

Laurie was wondering just what other things he meant. They stood in awkward silence a moment before she asked "Can anyone come and hear you play?" She smiled a little uncertainly.

Chase glanced up quickly, trying to read her expression. Laurie guessed he was thinking of their last encounter at the Coffee Pot. She was glad when he didn't bring it up. "Would you like to meet me there? We could have something to eat afterward. I only signed up to play from four until six."

She considered for a moment, and then nodded. "Tell me where it is again, exactly."

Chapter 30.

Salty Dog was an interesting place to say the least. Mermaids, pirates, parrots, whales, even pink flamingos were liberally scattered throughout the place, which smelled like fresh paint and fried seafood. Laurie wondered if the *Journal* should start running restaurant reviews, and what she would write about this place if they did.

She followed the sound of a guitar to a roomy lounge. Quite a few tables were occupied. Apparently word had gotten out about it already. People were always eager to check out a new place in town.

Chase sat on a stool on a small raised platform near the end of the bar. He finished playing a slow, swaying tune with an end-of-summer feel to it, before announcing he was taking a break. Then he joined Laurie at her table where the two drank sodas and chatted until he had to go back on stage.

When his gig was over they shared a seafood platter. Laurie was famished, and the food was better than she expected, considering they were so far from the ocean. They ate side by side on the leatherette bench in the booth, careful to leave a little space between them, and kept their conversation casual.

Chase was easy to be with. They discussed neutral topics like the art show, and music, and things happening around town, and Laurie was mostly relaxed. Still, she could feel the electricity between them. She knew she would have enjoyed another passionate encounter. But she couldn't bring herself to broach the crucial subject of his marital status, so she gently brushed aside his flirtatious advances.

She thought about it later that night, alone in her apartment. She knew she would just have to ask. She wanted to ask, and wondered why Chase said so little about the woman he was (and maybe *was still*) married to.

Then again, Laurie hadn't said anything at all about her life with DB. She thought how odd it was that someone she had been married to for years now meant so little to her. She imagined maybe that was how Chase felt too.

Sunday morning Laurie was in the choir loft for the church service as usual, and then went immediately back to the parish hall. Mary had to rush straight home, but others who had not yet seen the art show lingered through coffee hour to take it all in, and to buy a few last raffle tickets.

All that was left was to pick the raffle winners. Mother Barbara did the honors, and gave the winners' information to Glenda so she could arrange to distribute the prizes. Everyone else left the church long before the show was officially over.

Laurie wanted to make sure nothing else happened to anyone's creations, after Saturday's near-disaster. She and Glenda remained until the last artist had picked up their work. Glenda offered to pay the painter for the broken frame, but the artist declined to be reimbursed for the damage. Returning the borrowed easels could wait. Laurie was glad when she finally switched off the lights and went home.

* * *

The *Journal's* office was quiet, as always on a Monday morning, and Laurie was grateful for that. She dragged herself in barely on time, not that anyone watched the clock that closely. Work occupied her mind for a couple of hours. Still, since she was tired, she found it hard to concentrate.

Her thoughts kept drifting back to Saturday evening and the time she spent with Chase. Any other time she would have talked it over with Mary, but for a change she decided to keep her own counsel.

She went to chat with Scott, the editor, about restaurant reviews and other ideas for feature articles. The summer was winding down, and news in Chinkapin was slow. There were no school sports to report on, and it was too soon to be running articles about the fair, so Scott was glad to entertain any ideas she came up with. Finally, with little going on, he let her leave early.

She drove home for her laptop, and then up the old state route to the Redding library. She wanted to get away from Chinkapin for a while. She headed to the periodical section first, settled into one of the leather chairs, and browsed the Sunday edition of the *Journal-Constitution*.

When she finally returned it to its place, a copy of the New York *Post* fell out of the rack. She stooped to replace it and froze, staring at a photograph over the headline "Homer painting fetches $1.7 million at art auction." The picture looked just like the watercolor from the Treasure Chest!

Laurie sank onto the edge of the leather chair gripping the newspaper. Lips parted in disbelief, she read the caption under the photo, and then scanned the article taking in the key details. An auction of late 19th and early 20th century American art had taken place at one of the big houses in New York "netting $163 million, with the night's top price obtained for a watercolor painting by Winslow Homer that went for $1.7 million. Just four out of 56 pieces failed to sell amid lively bidding in the saleroom. It was the final sale of the week marked by major auctions at Christie's, Sotheby's, and Phillips, one that testified to a resilient market despite recent economic downturns."

The article went on about various lots for sale, featured artists, and what the pieces were valued at. Laurie scanned further, hoping to read more about the Homer painting, and found this paragraph.

"The top scorer, Winslow Homer's *Afternoon at Homosassa,* was painted sometime in the early 1900's, and had been estimated to sell for at least $1.5 million. New York dealer Jose Schwartz beat out other bidders to take the painting home for $1.7 million. Only recently rediscovered, the painting was held for decades in a private collection in Georgia. Between 1884 and 1905 Homer made several trips to the tropics, visiting Bermuda, Florida, Cuba, and the Bahamas. He was an avid fisherman, especially preferring the waters of the Gulf of Mexico. He painted a series of watercolors around Homosassa between 1903 and 1905. His Florida watercolors are marked by spontaneity and freshness, and often depict the jungle just beyond the waters where he fished. This painting features a tropical seaside landscape including palm trees and other foliage."

Laurie looked again at the photo in the newspaper, and then sat back in shock. The painting had been in a private collection in Georgia. Jeff Williams had been in New York during the time when it was sold. It was the same painting, all right.

Growling under her breath, she pulled out her phone and snapped a picture of the article. Then she searched the internet, and downloaded a copy from the newspaper's website.

Laurie's dislike for Jeff had been simmering for a while, but was quickly coming to a boil. She didn't know how much of the $1.7 million was the auction house's cut, but certainly Jeff was a whole lot richer than he had been before the Treasure Chest gave him the painting.

Correction, she thought. *Before the Treasure Chest gave the Chinkapin Arts Center the painting.* What if Jeff was selling the painting on their behalf, with no intention of keeping the money for himself? Laurie decided she'd better hold off on condemning the man or saying anything to her friends at the thrift shop until she found out the rest of the story.

There was one person she was going to tell, though.

The two hadn't spoken for a week, other than a quick greeting on Sunday. As soon as Mary heard Laurie's voice on the phone she started to apologize. "Laurie, I'm sorry for always telling you what to do and what not to do, or who to hang out with. I know it hasn't been easy, being completely uprooted and coming to Georgia. I feel bad because I'm the one who asked you to move down here. I promise to quit sticking my nose in where it doesn't belong."

"Never mind about that," Laurie said. She was glad to hear Mary apologize, but had other things on her mind. "You're not going to believe this. Remember Bea Williams told us Jeff went to New York to auction a painting? And remember I said I bet it's *our* painting, the one the Treasure Chest gave him? Well, guess what's on the cover of the Sunday edition of the New York *Post*? And it just sold at auction for $1.7 million." Laurie paused. "Mary, are you there?"

"I'm here. I had to sit down. Did you say $1.7 *million*?"

"That's what I said." Laurie told Mary how she had stumbled on the newspaper article at the Redding library.

"Wow. Well, that might explain where he suddenly got the money to open an art gallery. So what are you going to do?" Mary asked.

"I need to make sure of the details. I don't want to rush into anything." She thought a minute. "Jeff is supposed to come home tomorrow to lead that sketching class at the Chinkapin library. I think you and I should go."

"I think it's high time I met this guy. After all, I've been shipping you two ever since I heard about him, and I haven't even laid eyes on him." She was silent a moment. Laurie could hear baby noises in the background. "I know Pete's not going anywhere this week, so I'm sure he'll watch Ricky for a couple of hours. I'm game to go, if you'll drive. I'll be ready when you get here," Mary said.

"Uh-huh. I know you better than that." Laurie smiled.

* * *

Tuesday after work Laurie grabbed lunch and drove to the Treasure Chest. She hoped keeping occupied would make the day go by faster. She was sorry to find Evelyn working at the counter. Anne was tagging clothes in the back room. "How's it going today?" Laurie asked.

"Slow. I guess a lot of people are still on summer vacations. We've had a few customers in, but most people just seem to want to visit."

Laurie was not in a mood to visit. She just wanted to stay busy. "Anything in particular we need to work on today?" she asked as Evelyn rearranged items in the jewelry case. A customer came in and started browsing the women's clothing.

"Watch the counter a minute while I make a phone call." Evelyn went into the office for her cell.

A moment later Laurie heard her arguing with someone on the phone. "Why am I even discussing it with you? Let me talk to Mr. Anderson." Laurie's ears pricked up at the name. "Well, you just call him, and tell him who I am. I *know* he'll put a rush on this job."

Evelyn jabbed at her phone and came out of the office with arms folded across her chest. "Why should I be arguing with Chase, Mr. Nobody from Nowhere, about getting my air conditioning fixed?" She obviously didn't expect an answer, so after a moment Laurie went to the staff kitchen and put some music on the old CD player.

As she was adjusting the volume, she heard the bells on the shop door jangle. A minute later Virginia stuck her head in the kitchen doorway. "Hey, Laurie," she said.

"Virginia! Hi. I thought you were out of town."

"Are you kidding? My husband never takes me anywhere."

"Are you staying to work then?"

"No. I just brought in some tomatoes and bell peppers. Take what you want before the others get them."

"Thanks!" Fresh tomatoes, and the thought of sharing them with Chase, put a smile on Laurie's face. Then her worries returned. She still hadn't asked whether he was married or not.

The bell on the door jangled again and one of their customers, Coreen, walked in carrying something in her arms. It wasn't unusual for people to bring in donated items, or a bagful of plastic grocery sacks for the shop to re-use. Laurie held her hands out and was surprised to have a cat dumped in her arms.

"Oh my gosh!" She looked from Coreen to the cat. "This can't be Raindrop, can it? That itty-bitty kitten? Oh, he's beautiful." Though still young, Raindrop was growing into a beautifully marked tiger-striped cat. "And friendly!" Laurie laughed at how loudly the cat purred.

"Yep. He's our baby. And he really loves my husband. They're together all day. Rainy lies on his stomach when Tom watches TV."

"How is your husband these days?" Anne asked. She had walked up, and was stroking the cat.

"Oh, he's a whole lot better. He's gone back to work part time, and I think he'll be able to start full time pretty soon." Coreen watched the cat walk back and forth across the counter sniffing things.

"Well, we're glad to hear that."

"Do you all have any umbrellas or ponchos or anything? You know, it's supposed to rain later in the week, and the kids lost my umbrella somewhere."

"We can't keep umbrellas around here, they're so popular, but we do have a couple of ponchos. I'll show you." Anne led Coreen through the store to find them.

At 4:00 Laurie walked through the shop switching off lights as Evelyn and Anne counted money from the cash drawer. "How did we do today?" she asked.

"Not bad," Anne said. "A hundred and seventy dollars, but most of that was in the last two hours."

"At least we got the shop cleaned up this morning," Evelyn added, punching keys on the calculator. Laurie wondered what needed cleaning, since she and Anne had tidied the shop recently. "We can finish this if you'll take out that bag of trash."

"Sure thing. See you." Laurie set her purse and the tomatoes in her car, and carried the trash bag to the dumpster at the back of the parking lot. She lifted the lid, and heaved the bag over the edge. It hit with a dull reverberation.

Holding her breath, Laurie peered into the dumpster. Besides the trash bag there were a few broken toys, a dented frying pan, and an old guitar with a broken soundboard. Slowly she lowered the lid on the dumpster.

Laurie drove home with her fresh tomatoes, and scanned the parking lot for Chase's car. She was disappointed when it was nowhere to be seen, but reminded herself it was still early for him to be off work. She hesitated a moment, and then sent him a text: *I have something you might want. Call me later.* Of course she meant the fresh tomatoes, but if he thought she meant something else, well... That would be okay too. Provided she got the answer to her question that she was hoping for.

Chapter 31.

Just after 6:30 Laurie drove over to Mary's house. She rang the doorbell and waited in the front hallway as Mary gave a raft of instructions to Pete concerning taking care of Ricky. As the two women walked out the door Laurie asked, "Does Pete ever get tired of you telling him what to do?"

Mary tossed her head. "He knows when to ignore me," she said.

"Dang! I never knew that was an option!"

"Are you going to drive, or are you going to talk?" Mary said, giving Laurie a cold stare. Laurie laughed, and the two drove to the Chinkapin library for the sketching class. A small group was already gathered at tables in the meeting room, some with their own sketch books and pencils. A still-life arrangement of children's toys lay on a table in the middle of the room. Jeff was greeting students as they arrived.

"Good evening, ladies," he called to Laurie and Mary. "Welcome. Grab a sketchbook and a pencil if you need them, and find a seat." He extended a hand to Mary. "I don't think we've met. I'm Jeff Williams."

"Mary Roster. Nice to meet you." She and Laurie chose sketchbooks and pencils from the table near the door. Laurie noticed a large fishbowl labeled "donations," which held a few dollar bills. She fumbled a couple of dollars out of her wallet and dropped them into the bowl. Then they took seats near the front of the room.

Mary's eyes were on Jeff as he greeted more students. "Nice looking, in a cold, calculating kind of way," she commented.

"Yeah, he grows on you. Like an icicle. Look, I need you to get as much info as you can. If I ask too many questions he'll think I'm interrogating him again."

Jeff clapped his hands once and rubbed them together as he walked into the middle of the room. "Okay, friends, let's get started. Some of you have been asking for a still life, and I didn't have time to arrange for a live model, so let's see what you can do with the grouping in front of you. I'll be sketching along with you, but I'm here to answer any questions you have. Feel free to move your seats to get a different perspective, and remember, you don't have to draw the whole grouping. You can select one or more items and concentrate on them."

"Now what do we do?" Laurie whispered to Mary, clenching her pencil.

"Just draw, I guess. I don't think there's much instruction to this. It is a free session, after all."

Laurie looked around the room at the other students. Most were busy drawing, but a few had gotten up from their seats and strolled about, eyeing the still life from different angles. Gradually they all got to work, some chatting quietly together as they sketched.

Jeff busied himself with something in one corner of the room, and suddenly soothing, new-age music flowed from a small stereo. Then he walked among the students, occasionally making comments.

Laurie eyed the still life nervously. It included a rubber duck, alphabet blocks, a spinning top, and some other old-fashioned toys. She thought she'd be safe starting with the blocks, and drew some lines on her sketch pad as Jeff walked in her direction.

"Did you get rid of your old painted-up jeans? I kind of miss all the pretty colors," Laurie said, noting the new-looking clothes he wore.

"Oh, not hardly," he said. "I would have changed into my painting jeans, but I just had time to drive down from Atlanta and stop by the arts center for supplies."

"How was Atlanta?" Laurie asked. She figured he'd just come from the airport, but was hoping he would volunteer some information about his trip.

"Rush hour on I-75 – what can I say? Crowded, as usual." He walked on.

Laurie looked at Mary's paper. She was drawing the bouncy ball. "Ask him something next time he comes around."

Jeff sketched for a while until a student hailed him with a question. Then Jeff adjusted the volume on the stereo and started his rounds again. This time Mary took her chance.

"We met your mother at her estate sale, Jeff," she said, smiling.

"You did. Well, how about that."

"She had some lovely antiques. I was hoping to buy an armoire, but someone beat me too it."

"I heard a good crowd turned out," he said.

"And it was amazing how fast the house sold! I mean, it was barely on the market." Mary fished for more info, smiling sweetly while Laurie jabbed at her paper with her pencil.

"Yes, we were a bit surprised. But Mother had put the word out among her church friends, and one of them knew someone who was looking for just such an old place. So now she's off to Knoxville." Jeff moved on around the room.

"You'd think he'd seem a little happier about getting his mother's affairs settled," Laurie whispered to her friend.

"I was thinking the same thing."

They sketched in silence a while. Laurie was getting frustrated, and found herself erasing as much as drawing.

"You're supposed to use the pointy end of the pencil, not the rubbery end," Mary said.

"I know, but it's not coming out the way I want. What am I doing wrong?"

"Don't press so hard on the paper, for one thing," Mary advised. "And try using short, quick strokes, like the way you put on eye liner. If you try to draw all around your eye it goes crooked, so you do, like, little dashed lines." She demonstrated on her paper, drawing an outline of the rubber duck. "That way if you make a mistake it's easier to fix."

Jeff walked over and looked at Mary's drawing. "That's very good," he said. "I have a feeling you've done this before."

"I just doodle, that's all."

"How are you doing, Laurie?" He turned his attention to her paper.

"Oh, getting frustrated."

"Try to relax. It's supposed to be fun." He put his hands on her shoulders and started kneading them, gently pressing his thumbs into the muscles at the back of her neck. Instead of relaxing, Laurie tensed uncomfortably.

Mary tipped her sketchbook toward him and asked a question about shading. Jeff took a chair on the other side her and shaded a section of her drawing. "Oh, I like how you do that. You make it look so easy. Are you going to be staying in Chinkapin, now that your mom has moved?"

Laurie stopped scribbling and listened.

"Yes, I think I will. I didn't realize how much I've missed my old home town. I plan to open an art gallery, and keep teaching at the arts center. Maybe you'll come and take lessons." He flashed his charming smile.

"We'll see," Mary answered. The music stopped, and Jeff went to change the CD.

Laurie frowned at her picture. It looked more like a pile of wire coat hangers than a still-life of toys. She got up, stretched, and strolled around the room, glancing at other people's art work. She checked her watch, hoping the hour was almost over. She wanted more information, but didn't think she should grill Jeff in front of the others.

She took her seat again and scribbled on her paper as Mary shaded her drawing. "I'm ready to get out of here. Are you almost done?" she asked quietly.

Mary looked up in surprise. "Sure, almost. We haven't found out very much, though."

"I know." Laurie sighed.

Around the room people started gathering their things to leave. Laurie tore her paper out of the sketch book, and returned the book and pencil. "Finished already?" Jeff asked.

"I think so. Time to call it a day, anyway."

Mary handed in her supplies. "Well, this was fun. Hope to see you again soon." Laurie flashed her a dirty look, which she ignored.

"Here's a schedule of events." He handed Mary an arts center brochure. "Come and try painting one of these days. Laurie can tell you about our Art Night Out."

"Are you going to be at the arts center the rest of the week?" Laurie asked.

Jeff nodded. Another student approached him, and the two women left.

"Well, that was a bust," Laurie said, dropping her sketch into the trash bin outside the library.

"I don't know, I kind of like my picture." Mary admired her drawing as they walked to Laurie's car. "Maybe I'll add some color, and hang it in the nursery."

"I meant as far as information goes. I guess I'm going to have to ask him outright. Maybe I'll just call him tomorrow."

"Well, let me know if you learn anything. If Jeff is suddenly a millionaire because we gave him a painting, I think the least he could do is share the money with the Treasure Chest and St. Mark's."

Chapter 32.

Laurie dropped Mary off and drove home, plotting how she would approach Jeff the next day. She was determined to learn the truth about the auction and whether he intended to keep the money.

As she went through her bedtime routine, she thought about just dropping by the arts center Wednesday to see what she could find out. If Jeff wasn't there, she could always ask Sharon a few questions, and possibly save herself the embarrassment of accusing Jeff of something he wasn't guilty of. She had just put on her pajamas when she heard a knock on her door, and remembered the text she had sent Chase. She threw on a light robe and, without looking through the peep hole, flung open the door.

"Jeff! What are you doing here?"

"Is that how you welcome a friend? I was hoping you'd invite me in." He sauntered through the door before Laurie could get over her surprise.

"I asked you, what are you doing here?"

"Well," he began with a sheepish look on his face, "you know, I *was* staying at my mother's house, out in the studio. Long story short, her realtor has padlocked it, and I can't reach anyone in their office. Everything I own is in there except what's in my suitcase, and I don't have anywhere to spend the night. I was hoping you had room for me." He moved in closer, and with a playful smile caressed the silky sleeve of her robe. He lifted his hand to stroke her cheek.

She brushed it away, taking a step back. "Oh, no! No way, Jose. You need to *leave*." She pointed toward the door.

"Aw, c'mon, Laurie. I know you're attracted to me. Wouldn't you like to do a little research, get some new material for the sexy romance scene in one of your novels? I don't know about you, but I'm feeling inspired."

Laurie was distinctly uninspired. "There are plenty of motel rooms along the interstate," she growled. "Or what's the matter? Hasn't your check cleared yet? The fat check from the auction house? Your mother said you were going to New York, Jeff. Want to tell me about it?" Her voice was getting louder.

His eyebrows rose. Then he turned from her and shrugged. "Okay, I was in New York. What has that got to do with anything?"

"Why were you in New York, Jeff? Why?"

"Business. But I didn't come here to talk business with you. Besides, I don't know why that's any concern of yours."

"I'll tell you why. Because you were selling the painting we gave you for the arts center. A Winslow Homer. Quite a find, wasn't it?"

"Well, what do you know about that? I didn't realize you followed the art market that closely."

Laurie ignored him, not wanting to admit she stumbled on the information. "You got a tidy sum for it too, didn't you? What are you going to do with the money?"

"Ah, now we get to the heart of the matter." He turned back to her with a smile. "What am I going to do with the money?" Laurie remained at the door, hands balled into fists, as Jeff ambled farther into her apartment, looking around. "Maybe I was planning to set you up somewhere with a little more style. I was surprised when you showed up for the sketching session. I had a feeling it wasn't for the love of art. I was hoping it was because you wanted to see me." He sat on her sofa and patted the seat next to him.

"Get out," she snarled, stamping her foot.

He laughed, but remained seated and shook his head. "Laurie, Laurie. How am I going to make a living in art if I can't use my education to my benefit? I went to school, and learned a few things. I recognized the painting for what it was – a painting both you and the previous owners had given away for nothing. And now you're upset about it. If it had been up to your friends at the Treasure Chest it probably would have ended up in the dumpster. Now it's saved for posterity."

Laurie blushed, knowing what he said was true. Silently, she extended one arm, pointing the way out the door.

"I think you're just jealous because I'm *doing* something with my life. Poor thing, with your little writing hobby," he continued. Laurie stiffened, seething.

Jeff got up, walked slowly by her, and paused with his hand on the door jamb. "Bye, Love. When I set up my new gallery I'll have you over for some private art lessons."

With both hands she shoved him out into the hall. Just as she slammed the door, she caught a glimpse of a male figure retreating down the stairway.

Laurie paced around her apartment, fuming. *Little writing hobby*, she thought. What a jerk! What nerve! And what was she going to do about it? If only she'd got a receipt from the arts center when she'd given Jeff the painting. Maybe she could go to the people who donated it, the Marshall's. And say what? That they'd both given away something worth a lot of money?

She sat on her bed, suddenly exhausted. Then with a groan she remembered the figure she'd seen on the stairs as she shoved Jeff out the door. She *knew* it was Chase. She checked the clock on the night stand, surprised to see how late it was, and decided against calling him. She lay on her bed and willed herself to fall asleep.

A storm blew up during the night. Thunder rumbled and rain lashed against the window, waking Laurie several times. At one point her eyes flew open and she clutched at the blankets, sure that the ceiling was coming down. Later she dreamed of drawing a tropical storm scene, but when she tried to tear the picture out of the sketch pad, it wouldn't budge.

* * *

Wednesday morning Laurie woke feeling groggy, and with a vague unease at the back of her mind. She dodged puddles in the parking lot and drove to work. At least the weather was cooler after the night's rain.

Once at her desk she made a few fruitless phone calls. Then she slouched in her chair and swiveled from side to side, scanning *The Register*, the *Journal*'s sister newspaper from the next county. It seemed to be mostly ads: a furniture store, a few restaurants, a real estate company, two HVAC installers, including Anderson's.

An ad for a clothing shop caught her eye, and she stopped swiveling. Island Time boutique was running a sale on swimwear. Their ad featured a photo of bathing suits artfully arrayed in front of a background image of a seaside resort.

Laurie turned to her computer, pulled up the Treasure Chest Facebook page, and scrolled back a couple of months to her post about the half-off sale on bathing suits. There in the background of the photo was the watercolor painting Jeff had just sold.

And now what? she thought. This info and five dollars would buy her favorite beverage at the Coffee Pot, that's what. Laurie called Mary. "I have news," she said. "Do you and Roly want to meet me at the café?"

"I need to get out and buy some diapers, so – sure we can stop by."

A short while later Mary walked into the Coffee Pot lugging the baby carrier. Laurie was already sitting at a table with her latte, and watched over Ricky while Mary ordered a chai tea. Just as she placed her order, Carol walked in to the café, on a break from her job near the courthouse.

"Well, look who it is!" Carol leaned over to look at the baby. "He's just as sweet as ever."

"Get your coffee and come join us," Laurie said. "There's something you might be interested in hearing."

A moment later Mary and Carol had their drinks and sat at the table with Laurie. "So, what have you found out?" Mary asked, eager to hear the latest.

"What's this all about?" Carol asked.

"I need to get you up to speed," Laurie said, pulling her smart phone out of her purse. She tapped the screen, scrolled for a few seconds, and handed it over. "Remember when we had that sale on swimsuits at the Treasure Chest?" she asked.

Mary glanced over her shoulder as Carol looked at the old Facebook post. In the picture were a few bathing suits, a turquoise cover-up, and some flip-flops. "Yes, I remember. I was there when you posted this. And there's the painting my boss brought in. I think we gave that to Jeff What's-his-name at the arts center." Carol handed the phone back to Laurie. "Why are you showing me this?"

Laurie tapped and scrolled again. This time she showed Carol the article in the New York *Post*.

"Oh, my word!" Carol read the headline aloud. "'*Homer painting fetches $1.7 million at art auction.*' Well, this is the same painting, isn't it? I mean, it sure looks like it."

"The very same. Homer, as in Winslow Homer, famous American artist."

Carol zoomed in on the photo and then read a little of the article. "One point seven million dollars. Well, what's he going to do with the money?"

"That's the one point seven million dollar question," Mary said.

"Mary and I went to his sketching class last night hoping to find out, and I've talked to him since then," Laurie said. She didn't mention that Jeff had come to her apartment and tried to weasel his way into spending the night. "As far as I can tell, he has every intention of keeping the money all for himself."

Carol furrowed her brow. "Uh-uh! Now, that's not right. We gave that painting to the arts center, not to Jeff. He shouldn't be keeping the money."

"How can we prove that, though?" Mary asked. "Did anyone else at the arts center see the painting? Sharon or anyone?"

"Sharon wasn't there the Friday I went to Art Night Out," Laurie reminded her. "I had to help Jeff with the set-up and everything."

"I wish we had tried to find out something about that painting," Carol said. "We normally check into the value of *some* things that are donated to us, like jewelry and old china and such. At least Evelyn does."

"Like DB's pocket watch," Laurie said.

"Right." Carol sighed, shaking her head. "I guess since my boss just gave us the painting, I assumed it wasn't worth much."

Laurie remembered how she had found the painting shoved into a cupboard at the Treasure Chest. She also remembered how she had been in a hurry to give the painting away, back when she was trying to get Jeff to notice her. She wished she had never met him. "Would it do any good to talk to a lawyer about this?"

Carol shrugged. "It wouldn't do any good talking to the lawyers where I work. All they handle is real estate and wills and such." She sipped her coffee and added, "Plus, it's not like he stole the painting from us. So maybe it's just 'finders keepers losers weepers.'"

"Maybe." Laurie sighed. "Jeff recognized the painting for what it was, or at least was curious enough to look into it. I don't think you can take someone to court for being a dirtbag. Just goes to show, the guy I left behind up north isn't the only dirtbag around."

Carol looked at her watch. "I need to get back to work. There are a few things I have *got* to finish today. Do you think we should tell the others about the painting?"

"Not yet," Laurie said. "Maybe somehow I can get him to share the money. But that man has a scarcity mentality. Not to mention he's selfish." She paused. "I need to think about it some more. There's something I'd like to try."

"Well, I hope you have some super powers we don't know about. It would be nice to have a little of that money for St. Mark's."

Maybe not a super power, Laurie thought. *But I do have a little writing hobby.*

Chapter 33.

The women parted and Laurie went back to the *Journal* office to discuss an idea with Scott. She was interested in writing a series of articles profiling Chinkapin's small businesses. There were antiques shops, clothing boutiques, a jewelry shop, a book store, two florists, a bakery, her favorite coffee shop, a ceramics shop, and others. "Who owns them, and how did they get started?" Laurie asked. She was certain there were interesting stories behind each of them.

"I bet articles like that would be good for circulation too," Scott said. "I mean, anytime you mention a place in the paper and print pictures, they're going to want extra copies to give their friends and relatives, and to post where people can see it."

Scott gave his tentative approval for the series, requesting a sample the following week.

Laurie spent that afternoon browsing Chinkapin's shops, chatting with merchants, learning, and taking notes. She would have enjoyed it all immensely if her mind hadn't kept jumping to thoughts of the painting, and of Chase. Plus there was another thing bothering her – and this time maybe she was the dirtbag.

After walking from one end of downtown to the other, Laurie returned home late that afternoon, tired and footsore. She retrieved a small bag from her car and was fumbling with her apartment key when the strumming of a guitar caught her attention.

Her apartment complex offered little in the way of amenities, but on the pawn-shop side of the parking lot, on a narrow strip of grass, there was an old park-style charcoal grill, and next to it, a wooden picnic table. A Chinkapin oak had struggled up through the packed sandy soil to throw a bit of shade over the table. There was Chase, sitting on the table top with his feet on the bench, picking out a tune. He nodded in her direction, not taking his hands off the guitar.

Laurie sat on the bench near him and closed her eyes, listening to the mellow, melancholy song he played. It was still cool after the previous night's rain. A faint breeze ruffled the leaves overhead. She reached both hands up to lift her hair away from the back of her neck.

"You were playing that song the other night at Salty Dog, weren't you? What is it?"

"Something I wrote," he said with a shrug. "You like it?"

She stared at him a moment, making sure he wasn't pulling her leg. "I do," she admitted. "A lot."

"I got your text yesterday, but we were out pretty late on a job," Chase said. "I was going to stop in and see you, but I think you had a friend over."

Laurie groaned, and then scowled, looking up at him. "Is that what you call it when someone barges in uninvited and then won't leave?"

"Ah!" he said, eyebrows raised as he strummed a few chords.

"And *friend* is not the word I would use either. I've told you that already." She picked angrily at a splinter of wood on the end of the picnic table. "No, I have a few other names for that guy. 'Slime ball' maybe. Or 'thief'."

"Wow," Chase said. His chords took on a menacing sound.

"Listen to this. Maybe you'll have some ideas." Laurie told him about Jeff and the painting, leaving out her initial attraction to the artist.

She finished her tale. "So the weasel walks off with $1.7 million, or whatever it is after the auction house takes its cut, and we don't think we can do anything about it. And the worst part is, I'm the one who gave away the painting!"

She tore at the splinter again. "He's a dirtbag. And I'm a dirtbag." She glowered at Chase. "Maybe even you."

With a discordant twang, he stopped strumming. "Me? What did I do?"

Laurie's heart was racing. "I heard you tell someone in the parish hall a few Sundays ago that you've never been divorced. Chase, are you still married?" she demanded.

He stared at her a moment. "So you're afraid there might be a wife somewhere waiting to spring out at you?"

Laurie folded her arms across her chest, tucked her chin, and looked at him sideways through narrowed eyes. "I just know what I heard. You were acting pretty single that night under the fireworks." She hugged her arms closer to her chest.

Chase looked down at his guitar and strummed slow, alternating chords which reminded Laurie of a funeral march. "I'm a widower," he said, and laid the guitar down on the table.

Laurie raised her head and stared. Why had that possibility never occurred to her? Was she that dim? Or maybe she just wasn't used to young people dying. Her shoulders and arms relaxed. "I'm sorry," she murmured.

Chase looked across the parking lot at the traffic out on the street. "Jenny and I met in college, and got married right after graduation. She was really smart in finance and economics, and got a job at an investment firm, which allowed me to follow my dream chasing the music scene. She supported my career bigtime, following me to nightclubs, and working her job in the day.

"But, there were some crazy people in those clubs. Real partiers. Someone turned her on to drugs – meth, you know. I used to wonder how she could keep up with my schedule and then go to work in the morning." He laughed bitterly. "I didn't figure it out until she lost her job."

Chase took a deep breath, and then went on. "So I got her into treatment, which took all the money we had, but eventually she was off drugs. Except I guess some people never really get off them. When she came home so we could start over, one of her old pals found her and gave her some shit." He spat the words out, frowning. "About 3:00 one Sunday morning I came home from a gig and found Jenny dead in our apartment."

Laurie's mouth widened in a silent "O" as comprehension dawned at last. *He lost his wife because of a problem with drugs*, she thought. *Her problem, not his.* She felt a strange combination of pity and elation. She didn't know what to say, and shook her head.

Chase shrugged. "I felt like it was my fault. I couldn't touch my guitar for a while, and couldn't go back to the clubs. I didn't know what to do. After the treatment and the funeral and everything, I was really broke. God knows my family did what they could. But I just bummed around a while, and couch surfed. Lucky for me, my in-laws reached out to me and offered me a job, so I came down here."

Laurie cocked her head. Then her eyes widened. "Andersons are your in-laws?" she asked.

Chase nodded. "So now you know – I *am* single, to answer your question in a round-about way. I should have told you sooner."

She leaned her head against his knee closing her eyes. He stroked her hair. "So am I off the dirtbag list?" he asked.

"Yes, you're definitely off the list." They sat in silence, listening to the traffic and the breeze whispering in the leaves.

"So what did you get at the store today?" Chase asked, eying the bag she had brought from her car.

"Something," she said evasively. "All right, underwear, if you must know."

A smile spread over Chase's face. "Should I guess? Are they white?"

Laurie was smiling too now. "That's for me to know and you to wonder." She let him peep in the bag.

"Ooh, zebra stripes! And red with black lace! Sweet!" Then he furrowed his brow. "So why are *you* on the dirtbag list? Or maybe I don't want to know."

"It's another long story, and it all started with a guitar, oddly enough."

Chase picked up his instrument again and strummed softly. Laurie stood and paced a moment, and then sat next to him on top of the picnic table, elbows on her knees. "You know, people donate anything and everything to the Treasure Chest. We've seen it all. Several weeks ago somebody donated a guitar with a broken soundboard; the front was cracked, and pushed in. I'm surprised you didn't see it." She gently elbowed Chase as he strummed beside her. "We never know what people will buy. We didn't even know if this guitar could be fixed. But someone priced it at fifteen dollars.

"Well, one day a couple of scruffy-looking guys came in. I'd never seen them before. One of them brought the guitar up to the counter. He pointed out the break in the soundboard, but obviously he wanted the guitar. He picked it up and put it back down a few times, and kept looking at it. Finally I told him he could have it for five dollars. He said he didn't have five dollars, but he offered to trade his pocket knife for it. He had a plain little pocket knife that he showed me. But I told him no, a man needs his pocket knife."

She paused a moment, and then resumed. "Anyway, at the time we'd just had one of those Treasure Chest committee meetings where some of the volunteers talked about how the income from the thrift shop kept the church going, and how much we needed the money. They forget they started the Treasure Chest as a *ministry*, to provide things cheaply to people who need them. They forget that everything comes to us for free. But I got sucked into that mindset of needing to make money; it's all about the money."

Laurie paused to watch an ambulance drive by. "Like I said, I told him a man needs his pocket knife. But what do I know what a man needs? Maybe he needed that guitar, to fiddle around with. By that time his friend was at the counter buying a tee shirt. I hoped *he* would have the five dollars. But my guy put the guitar down, and the two of them left.

"Well, as soon as they left... You know, I frequently suffer from 'delayed intelligence'. As soon as they left I thought, it's a broken guitar, for cripe's sake! I was willing to let it go for five dollars. I should have swapped it for his pocket knife, if that's what the man wanted to do. Or I should have just *given* it to him. But by the time I picked up the guitar and ran to the door, the guys were nowhere to be seen.

"I've felt bad about it ever since. Maybe the guy could have fixed the guitar, or used it for parts. Maybe he just needed something to tinker with. I keep thinking how we're supposed to give to the poor, and if you have two cloaks give one to the person who has none. All the stuff I nod my head about in church on Sunday morning, and then forget as soon as I walk out the door!

"So the coda to this musical tale is that Tuesday afternoon I was at the Treasure Chest, and Evelyn and Anne had been 'cleaning' again. Well, I carried a bag of trash out, and there in the dumpster was the guitar." She looked at Chase, who had set his own guitar down again and was regarding her. He put his arms around her and she leaned her head on his shoulder. "So I'm a dirtbag," she said.

"You're not a dirtbag. We all suffer from delayed intelligence sometimes." Laurie nuzzled Chase's neck, and wrapped her arms around him. She felt drained, but at least the man she was in love with was single, and not a dirtbag.

One other thing still nagged at her. "Remember when you said we'd better take a look at the roof at the thrift shop?" she asked, pulling away. "Every time it rains lately there are puddles on the floor back by the linens room.

I'm worried about how much rain came in during that storm last night. If I had a key to the place I'd drive over right now and check things out."

"Wasn't anyone there today?" Chase asked.

"Nope. We're closed Wednesdays, remember?" He nodded. "We need a new roof. We have no money to spare, and we just gave away a painting worth $1.7 million. There has *got* to be something we can do."

"I'll listen while you puzzle it out, in exchange for a home-grown tomato," he said. "Do you still have one? I have a package of bacon in my fridge. I bet we could make some killer BLT's."

Laurie put both arms around his neck and kissed him. "Hold the mayo on mine, and you're on. I'll be over in a few minutes." She gathered her things and dashed across the parking lot.

Chapter 34.

Laurie sat on the couch in Chase's apartment and put her tired feet up. She was glad to let him do the little cooking required to fix their sandwiches. He certainly had mastered the art of frying bacon flat and crispy. Whether it was that, or the hearty bread, or the thick slices of home-grown tomato, Laurie couldn't remember when she had tasted such a delicious sandwich.

The two ate together side by side on the couch. Afterwards Chase grabbed his guitar and played a song he was working on – a romantic little pop tune – smiling at Laurie as he sang the catchy refrain. Leaning back on the armrest, she dug her feet under his legs as she listened.

Then she sat up and swung around, angling to lean her head on his shoulder. "Hey! Hold your horses," he said, lifting his guitar out of the way and setting it on the floor.

He put his arm around her shoulders, pulling her close, and brushed her hair away from her face. She snuggled against him, looked into his eyes, and raised her lips to meet his.

* * *

Laurie closed her eyes against the morning sun, trying to recall the dream she was having. She felt disoriented. Had she slept on the bed upside down? Didn't the morning sun shine in on the other side of the room? And why was the window so high on the wall?

The smell of coffee instantly roused her as Chase walked into the bedroom carrying a mug.

"Here you go, with milk and sugar. Sorry it's not a latte. Maybe someone will donate a fancy espresso machine to the Treasure Chest one of these days." He handed her the cup and sat on the edge of his bed, kissing her on the forehead.

"Wait a minute. Don't spill!" Laurie said. She set the coffee on the nightstand and pulled him down on the bed next to her. She took a deep breath, teasing out the scents of coffee, fresh linens, and men's deodorant. "Did we just spend the night together?"

"Yes we did, Laura May," Chase replied. "I hope it's the first of many nights."

She snuggled deeper into the creaky bed and hugged him closer, remembering the pleasures of the evening before. "Mmmm," she sighed. "Delicious. Now where's that coffee?" Chase rose and handed it to Laurie again as she sat up.

"Sorry to mess up your morning, but it is a work day, and I have to get moving." He turned away and stripped off pajama bottoms. She sipped coffee and smiled as she watched him dress. Finally he picked up his shoes and sat at the end of the bed. "Are you enjoying yourself? You can stay as long as you like, you know."

"I *am* enjoying myself. But I have to get to the office and start on those articles I talked about. One way or another, Chinkapin is going to know about that painting."

"Good luck." Chase kissed her again. "I'll call you when I get off work."

Laurie waited until he left, and then threw off the covers and scooped her clothes off the floor. As she stood, she caught sight of her reflection in the mirror. "What are you looking so happy about?" she asked, and laughed.

* * *

When she arrived at her office, she went straight to her computer and started writing. She worked steadily until her cell phone buzzed. She hoped it was a text from

Chase. Her mouth fell open, and she read it a second time.

Treasure Chest closed due to roof leak. Meeting in parish hall 1:00 tomorrow

Immediately she called Carol. "What happened?"

"Oh Laurie, you would not believe the hot mess they found this morning. It rained Tuesday night, and today there was a mushy pile of ceiling tiles and gunk on the floor outside the linens room. You can see daylight through the roof."

"Oh, no," Laurie groaned.

"Oh, yes," Carol said. "It's mostly in the hallway, there by the utility closet, but the flooring is ruined, since the water sat so long. Don and Fred have been helping to shovel the stuff out. They've already filled up the dumpster."

"And the roof?"

"Don is calling contractors right now. It might be a while before we can get anyone to come out and fix it, though."

"How's the rest of the shop?" Laurie asked.

"Some other spots were messed up, too. You know, the usual where we always have to put buckets down when it rains." Carol sighed. "It's not like we didn't know we needed a new roof. Now we need the ceilings repaired, and maybe a new floor too. I just hope we can get a loan from the diocese, or refinance the building, or something. Mother Barbara is working that end of things. Who knows how long the shop will have to be closed. And obviously we won't be able to accept donations for a while either. I hate to think what this will mean to the church."

Laurie was silent for a moment. "I guess I should post something about it on our Facebook page," she offered.

"That would be good. Please do. If you want, you can post some pictures of the disaster scene. I took a bunch, for insurance purposes, that I can send you. I'm sure a lot of people will be curious to see what happened."

"Sure. Send me a few. Look, I'm kind of in the middle of something. If you don't see me later, let me know how everything's going."

"I'll let everyone know what's happening."

Laurie stared at her computer screen with unseeing eyes for a few moments. Then she opened a new document, and started typing again. She spent another hour working at her desk, and then called Jeff's number, hoping he wasn't teaching a class. Luckily he answered on the second ring. "Jeff! How are you?"

"Finer than split frog hair," he replied. "To what do I owe the pleasure?" Over the phone he sounded cooler than usual. Laurie imagined ice in his sparkling blue eyes.

"We parted badly the other night. I was hoping you'd let me buy you a drink over at the Coffee Pot."

"Hmmm." He paused. "I'm not sure. I have to meet a lawyer about some real estate later this afternoon."

"I won't take much of your time. Also, I've been working on a series of feature articles profiling local businesses. I wanted to discuss the possibility of an article, when you get your gallery and frame shop up and running. What do you think about a nice write-up in the *Journal*?" She crossed her fingers.

"Well then, why not?" he said.

Laurie smiled to herself. "Meet me in twenty minutes?"

"See you there."

Laurie hung up before he could change his mind. She pulled a few pages off the printer, shoved them and her tablet into her purse, tucked a copy of the *Journal* under her arm, and walked to the Coffee Pot. While she waited for Jeff, she ordered her favorite latte and sat with her back to the wall so she could watch the door, looking over the articles she'd drafted.

A few minutes later Jeff strolled into the café and Laurie thrust the pages back into her bag. He ordered black coffee as usual. "I was surprised when you called this morning. I guess you've decided I'm not such a bad guy after all?"

"Time will tell," she said. "Come sit here so we can talk." Jeff took a seat next to her on the bench, a little too close, but Laurie willed herself not to scoot over.

"So, things are going well with your plans for opening a gallery?" she asked.

"Yes. Everything's moving along quickly. The people at the bank have been very helpful, and the realtor found me an excellent property on Commerce Street. It's got big display windows, a serviceable counter, and there's a roomy workshop in the back." Jeff sipped his coffee looking pleased with himself.

"Sounds perfect," she said. "And expensive."

"Oh, that won't be a problem." His smug smile galled Laurie. She hid her face in her mug, not tasting the drink.

"And how's your writing career coming along?" Jeff asked. His tone was mocking, until he noted the copy of the *Journal* beside her. "You said you were working on articles about local businesses. It *would* be nice to have a piece in the paper about my new gallery."

"That's what I was thinking. I drafted a couple of samples, from different angles. Take a look at this." He watched as Laurie dug the sheets of paper out of her purse. She handed one to Jeff, and held her breath.

A headline was scrawled in pencil across the top:

Local man defrauds arts center of $1.7M painting

She watched his expression darken.

It's not clear whether local artist and gallery owner Jeff Williams knew just how valuable the painting was when he covertly removed it from the Chinkapin Arts Center, but it's certain he intends to keep all the proceeds for himself.

Williams, a temporary employee of the Arts Center, fraudulently took possession of the painting and later sold it at auction in New York, pocketing $1.7 million. Williams' plans for the money include investing in real estate.

The long-lost watercolor by famed American painter Winslow Homer was donated to the Chinkapin Arts Center by the Treasure Chest, a charity thrift shop operated as an outreach ministry of St. Mark's Church. The thrift shop had no knowledge of the painting's value.

Treasure Chest personnel vow to prosecute Williams to recover at least a portion of the funds. According to Treasure Chest spokesperson Laurie Lanton, "The money should be divided between the Treasure Chest, the Chinkapin Arts Center, and Mr. Williams. We think that's the fairest way to handle things. And we intend to persevere in this effort until we are satisfied with the distribution of funds."

Jeff crumpled the paper and slid away from Laurie. "This will never hold up in court."

"Maybe not in a court of law," Laurie admitted. "But the court of public opinion can be pretty tough. You have no right to keep that money and you know it."

"You can't prove that painting was ever in your shop," he challenged.

"Au contraire, mon frère," she said. Sliding her tablet out of her purse, she showed him the Facebook posting with the painting in the background. "It's pretty obvious where this picture was taken. I'm sure Mr. Marshall, who donated the painting, will remember too, since he remarked about this photo of it at the time."

"So what? You told me no one wanted it. What's wrong with me finding something no one wanted and recognizing it as valuable?"

"That would be okay if you were just anyone. But you work for the Chinkapin Arts Center, and you accepted the painting on the center's behalf. Sure, you have a right to make a living with your art education, but what you're doing is wrong. You know it is, and I'm going to make sure everyone knows about it. Unless you divide the money some way or other, your name will be mud. No one will come to your classes or your gallery."

"You're crazy. And you're a little too late. Look, that money is as good as spent. And you're little two-bit newspaper is not going to stick its neck out for you. I'll sue them for libel."

"A suit you'll lose, Jeff." She was pretty sure he was right, but continued bluffing. "But guess what. They don't need to print this article for me. I can take out an ad in the paper, or write a letter to the editor. I can use social media to get the truth out." *You dirtbag*, she thought. *You'll find out what I can do with my little writing hobby.*

He stared at Laurie, convulsively crushing the paper in his fist. Then he jumped up from the bench knocking over his half-empty coffee cup, and stomped out the door. Laurie watched through the window as he disappeared down the street. *I didn't get to show him the other article I drafted*, she thought, as a server with a cloth hurried over to wipe the table.

Laurie was hungry after the latte, and anxious to learn what was happening at the thrift shop. She drove over to the Tasty Chick, bought a large order of tenders, and took her food across the street to St. Mark's.

Carol was in the parish hall with Mother Barbara. Laurie sat down with her lunch, and Mary and Evelyn soon joined them.

"I guess you heard about the mess they found at the Treasure Chest this morning," Mother Barbara said. "I was just asking Carol to sharpen her pencil and figure out if we have the money in our budget for a new roof."

Carol shook her head. "We had plenty until we replaced the HVAC system. Now, we might could dip into the church's building fund, and put the plans for the new church doors on hold, but that wouldn't be near enough."

Evelyn pouted. "Those doors are the first thing anyone sees at St. Mark's, and they are *worn out*. They are in *horrible* shape." She had been lobbying the vestry to replace them.

"Ladies, I'm hoping the church is about to get a big windfall," Laurie said, munching on a piece of chicken. She filled the others in about the painting, and her confrontation with Jeff.

"I can't believe how selfish he turned out to be." Mary shook her head.

"Well, maybe your threat to expose him will put the fear of God in him," Mother Barbara said. "Even if he splits the money three or four ways, he'll be left with several hundred thousand."

"I don't care how he splits the money," Laurie said, "as long as he doesn't keep it all. I mean, the Marshall's did give the painting to us, and we did give it to the arts center. The arts center should get the lion's share."

Laurie finished the last of her chicken tenders. She crushed the cardboard to-go box and wiped her fingers on a paper napkin just as her phone rang. As soon as she saw who the call was from her eyebrows flew up. She answered, making waving motions to the others. They stared, listening to her side of the conversation. It was mostly mono-syllables, but when she ended the call she whooped and pumped her fist in the air. "He's splitting the money three ways, giving us and the arts center each a third!"

"There's our new roof, Mother Barbara," Carol said.

"And then some! New roof, new front doors for the church, and a whole lot of money for outreach!"

Chapter 35.

Later that afternoon Laurie sat at the kitchen table of her little apartment and tapped the keys on her laptop. She clicked a few times with the mouse and then stared at the screen. For a change she wasn't working on her writing. She was playing with a free monogram generator on a wedding planner website, trying to decide whether she liked the design it had just created with the letters LMH. *Laura May Harris*, she thought. *I like the sound of that.*

It was after six that evening when Chase finally called as promised. "I have great news," Laurie told him. "My idea worked! Jeff is sharing the money. The Treasure Chest and the arts center are each getting a third!"

"Leaving poor Jeff with just five hundred thousand or so," Chase said. "Oh, well. Guess he'll have to start scouring thrift shops for more paintings."

"Let's celebrate," Laurie said. "But not the Tasty Chick. That's what I had for lunch."

"Come to my apartment in twenty minutes. That'll give me time to shower, and we'll go from there."

Laurie fluttered around her apartment for a quarter of an hour before dancing down the stairs to Chase's place. She had barely knocked when he flung the door open, holding a bottle of champagne.

"Wow! You *are* ready to celebrate," she said.

He threw his free arm around her waist and kissed her lips warmly. He leaned his head back to look at her, but she drew him close and their lips met for another long moment. "Maybe we should close the door," he said finally.

"So, do you know how to open that thing?" She pointed at the bottle. "And do you always keep champagne in your fridge, for special occasions?"

"Well, before I heard your good news, I got some good news of my own. At least, I think it's good. We'll see what you think." As he talked he twisted the wire bale from the top of the bottle. Laurie reached in his cupboard and brought out a pair of juice glasses, the closest thing he had to champagne flutes.

"Here's the deal. You remember Mrs. Anderson had that broken hip, and then there was that whole situation with Bo. All that helped old man Anderson make his decision. He's retiring, they're moving to Florida, and he's offered the business to yours truly to manage." Chase bowed, still holding the champagne bottle. "He'll remain a silent partner until I earn enough to buy him out. After that, it's mine, all mine. I'll be the new owner of Anderson HVAC." He set the bottle down, and took her hands. "It's not glamorous, but it's a good business, and a good living."

"Oh, Chase, that's fantastic! Pour me some champagne, and promise you'll let me write an article about you and your new business for the *Journal*."

"I promise."

* * *

Laurie swiveled in her chair at work Monday admiring her by-line on the front page of the *Journal*. The headline said *"Homer painting fetches $1.7M for local artist."* She read the lead she'd started days ago when she first approached Jeff with the two proposed articles.

Local artist Jeff Williams had a hunch there was something special about an old watercolor painting donated to the Chinkapin Arts Center. That hunch has paid off, netting $1.7 million Williams is sharing with the arts center and the painting's donor, the Treasure Chest thrift shop in Chinkapin.

"As soon as I saw it I suspected it was by Winslow Homer, an American painter who did a series of similar watercolors early in the 20th century," Williams told the Journal.

The unsigned painting was given by Homer over one hundred years ago to a relative of local lawyer Greg Marshall, who donated it to the Treasure Chest. Marshall was delighted about the sale of the painting. "I'm just glad we donated it," he said. "Otherwise it was going out with the trash. Jeff did a fantastic job in recognizing it for what it was. Now the painting is saved for posterity, and a couple of organizations we admire will benefit from the proceeds."

Laurie's phone rang. She answered and stopped swiveling, surprised to hear Jeff's voice.

"I called to thank you for the article you wrote. It was probably better than I deserved." He sounded contrite over the phone.

"I had most of it drafted last week. You ran out of the Coffee Pot before I could show you."

"Are we friends again?"

"Don't push it," she said. "I *will* still write an article about your new gallery though, after you open."

"That would be great. And you'll have even more to write about. Remember the painting I showed you of the racing greyhounds? I shared it with a few buyers when I was up in New York. The upshot of it is, I've been commissioned to deliver forty new paintings to a racetrack/casino chain in Florida. I'm going to be pretty busy for a while."

"Wow! That's awesome!" Laurie said sincerely.

"By the way, I got *two* commissions here in Chinkapin to do pet portraits, all because of your art show flyer with the painting of Lemon the pug on it. So I really didn't need all the money from selling the Homer painting."

"Oh, is that right? So you deciding to split the money had nothing to do with me planning to smear your reputation?"

"Hey, I know you have fun banging out stories, but you're little writing hobby had nothing to do with my decision."

You conceited dirtbag, she seethed. She wanted to choke him through the phone.

"So how are things at the Treasure Chest?" he asked.

"The new roof will be finished by the end of the week. Then they'll repair the ceiling and the floors, we'll tidy things up, and the shop should re-open weekend after next. Which reminds me, I need to post that on Facebook. G'bye, Jeff."

* * *

Laurie dashed up the stairs to the choir loft seconds ahead of Chase, and slid into her chair next to Mary just as Steve finished leading the choir through their vocal warm-ups. Laurie was surprised when Mary made no comment about her and Chase arriving together. She was sure Mary had noticed.

"Where's little Roly?" Laurie asked.

"Down in the nursery. Hopefully he can do without me for an hour. But I told the nursery attendant exactly what to do if he gets fussy."

"I'm sure you did!" Laurie said, burying her smile in her hymnal.

Mary glanced back at Chase and leaned in closer to Laurie. "And how are things going with you two?" Her attitude toward Chase had changed since Laurie explained a little about his past, and told her about his future as owner of the largest HVAC business in the county.

Another smile curved Laurie's lips, but she didn't have a chance to answer. At that moment Steve called for everyone to turn to hymn number 657. He was surprised by the choir's joyful enthusiasm as they started singing.

Love divine, all loves excelling
Joy of heaven, to earth come down.

THE END

If you enjoyed *Hidden Treasure*, Look for these other titles in the Chinkapin series:

Finders Keepers
Second Home

And here are more ways you can support your favorite authors:

- Buy their books from your favorite retailer or online store.
- Ask your bookstore or library to carry their books.
- Write a review on social media, or wherever you share info about books.
- Recommend books you enjoy to your friends or your book club. A word-of-mouth recommendation is still the number one reason people buy books.

ABOUT THE AUTHOR

Margaret Rodeheaver writes short fiction and novels for children and adults. She enjoys music, reading, and travel, and loves discovering quirky coffee shops. She lives with her husband near Macon, Georgia.

For information on the latest books by Margaret Rodeheaver (and also the occasional freebie) sign up for email updates at www.MargaretRodeheaver.com